FREEING
Emily

A SECOND CHANCE DARK IRISH MAFIA
ROMANCE

CONTENTS

17. Liam
18. Emily
19. Liam
20. Emily
21. Emily
22. Liam
23. Emily
24. Liam
25. Emily
26. Emily
27. Emily
28. Liam
29. Emily
30. Liam
31. Emily
32. Liam
33. Emily
34. Liam
35. Liam
36. Emily
37. Liam
38. Emily
39. Liam
40. Emily
41. Liam
42. Emily
43. Liam
44. Emily
45. Liam
46. Emily

AUTHOR NOTE

While you don't necessarily need to read **Saving Paige** before this book, it is recommended to fully understand the story.

Freeing Emily is a Dark Irish Mafia Romance that is not suitable for readers under the age of 18. While this book is not as dark as Saving Paige, it still contains content that may be triggering to some readers.

Content that is labeled *graphic* is graphic so please take special consideration before proceeding.

If you have no triggers and/or wish to go in blind, please continue to the prologue.

Remember, this is a work of fiction and for entertainment purposes only.

If you have any questions or concerns, or if any triggers were missed, please email me at kaitemauthor@gmail.com

Content in this book includes but is not limited to:

graphic rape, murder, grief, loss of parent, arranged marriage, psychological torture, abduction, physical torture, isolation, hallucinations, depression, anxiety, panic attacks, suicidal ideation, drug addiction/abuse, eating disorder, nightmares, therapy sessions, disassociation, human trafficking, gun violence, physical violence, breeding kink, praise kink, degradation, self-harm, visual impairment, trauma, knife play, explicit language, detailed sex scenes, and arms dealing.

Remember, your mental health matters.

PLAYLIST

Bryce Savage – Inside Her Head

Survive My Own Head – Ashley Kutcher

Always Been You – Jessie Murph

I Think I'm OKAY – MGK Ft. YUNGBLUD

At My Best – MGK Ft. Hailee Steinfeld

Gasoline – Halsey

Colors – Halsey

Ghost – Halsey

More – Halsey

Sobriety – Jessie Murph

Pray – Jessie Murph

Helium – Sia

Voices In My Head – Falling In Reverse

Indestructible – Solence

I Miss You – Clean Bandit Ft. Julia Micheals

Girl In The Mirror – Ashley Kutcher

I Should Just Go To Bed – ROSIE

At My Worst – Pink Sweat$ ft. Kehlani

Never Be The Same – Camila Cabello

Voices – Jana Kramer

Chemical – Post Malone

I'm A Mess – Bebe Rexha

Consequences – Camila Cabello

Drunk In My Mind – Benson Boone

Intrusive Thoughts – Natalie Jane

One Life – Dermot Kennedy

Save Me – Jelly Roll Ft. Lainey Wilson

I'm Here – Sia

Tell Me It's Okay – Fells Ft. Kimmie Devereux

Emotionless – Ashley Kutcher

To the girls who find themselves lost to the voices in their heads.

Don't let them win.

PROLOGUE
Emily

"How are you feeling today, Emily?" Dr. Morrison sits in the brown seat across from me. Her gray-streaked brown hair is twisted into a low bun at the base of her neck, and her glasses sit on the bridge of her nose. My file sits open on her lap, and a recorder sits on the coffee table between us. Her demeanor is calm, and her body language is warm and welcoming. And yet... All I feel is the suffocating weight of anxiety. My legs bounce uncontrollably, and I twitch like I'm strung out on drugs. My skin prickles and I feel itchy. The need to scratch and pick at the sensation engulfs me and I struggle to keep my hands from moving to relieve it.

"Good. Really good." My voice is far too cheerful, and she catches my lie with ease.

"Let's try that again, shall we?" she gives me a pointed look with her head slightly tipped in my direction. Her eyes bore into mine.

"I'm not really sure how I feel," I say honestly.

"Have you been doing the breathing exercises we discussed at your last session?"

I nod and fidget in my seat. Coming to see Dr. Morrison makes me uncomfortable. I know it's supposed to help me with my trauma, but I just don't want to talk about what happened to me. I don't want to have my demons revealed. I've been through so much in such a short amount of time that I haven't processed everything just yet. Every day is a new mountain that I need to climb and sometimes I feel like I'm climbing Mount Everest. Slowly losing air the higher I hike.

"And your sleeping? How is that going?" she asks in a gentle tone.

My eyes bounce between her deep chocolate brown ones, trying to decide if I can manage to lie well enough for her not to push on the subject. Her expression remains impassive but from the look in her eyes, I know she can see the wheels turning in my head.

"I'm struggling." I concede with a defeated sigh.

She nods and jots something down in my file.

"During your last session, we talked about the possibility of some medication to help with that. Have you thought about if that's the route you'd like to take?"

"I don't want anything that will sedate me." Panic slips through my voice.

She nods and glances down at my leg which hasn't stopped moving since I sat down.

"We can try something that can treat any anxiety symptoms you might be having but can also help with sleep without being sedative," she suggests, lifting her gaze back to mine.

My fingers twist the fabric of my gray cardigan and I gaze out of the window of her office as I mull over her offer. Sleep is a luxury I've barely been able to afford in my life now. I'm lucky if I can manage an hour of it. The lights need to be on. The room can't be noisy but also can't be too quiet. I can't have the blanket wrapped around me too tightly either. It's infuriating that my entire existence has been altered in such a significant way because of the monsters who kept me.

I know I need the sleep. Declan has started to notice the dark circles around my eyes despite the concealer I use to hide them. He already has so much going on with Paige and her own trauma and running the empire my father built. I can't be another burden for him to bear.

Reluctantly, I agree with her suggestion.

"We'll trial a medication called buspirone and see how you respond."

"Okay, thank you, Dr. Morrison."

She smiles softly at me, "You'll be okay, Emily. I know it."

I nod despite not believing a word that comes out of her mouth.

Part One

CHAPTER 1
Emily
MEXICO

The deadbolt unlocking echoes through the room, and we all cower as best as we can with the limited room available. I try wrapping the material of the ripped dress over my knees but it's too ragged to hide any skin.

Igor's gigantic frame fills the doorway like a villain in a slasher movie. Dark and foreboding. Every fiber of my being screams to run and seek shelter.

Scanning the room, he searches for his next victim. Every day one of us is taken to be used as the guards see fit.

Some never return.

I've been taken three times since being placed in this room. Each time, I was raped until I bled from every hole due to the violence in their thrusts. My body has been persistently littered with bruises of handprints and fingerprints from being slapped or squeezed.

I've been treated for STIs and STDs several times since my kidnapping, but the men here apparently are not because I keep getting reinfected.

Igor sets his sights on a thin Hispanic woman chained in the center of the room. When she notices that she's been chosen, she begins pulling on the chain in an attempt to pull it from its bolt in the ground.

I lower my head to avoid watching him take her. Her Spanish pleas echo in the quiet space, and it pierces my heart. My bottom lip quivers as I continue to avoid watching another one of us being taken.

Her cries are silenced with the slam of the large metal door. The bang echoes in my ears like a bass drum until whimpers, cries, and prayers replace it.

Praying under my breath, I begin scratching at the skin on my thigh - a new habit I've formed since being kidnapped. Pain is the only way I can escape from the misery in my mind. The only way the voices stop echoing in my subconscious. Scars now litter my body from where I have either scratched, picked, or cut myself but I can't stop. The agonizing need to silence the noise is unbearable.

"Hey," a whisper causes me to nearly jump out of my skin.

I turn my head to a beautiful woman close to my age with light green eyes, olive skin, and long dark waves. She holds her hands up.

"Do you know where we are?" she asks softly with a natural rasp in her voice.

"We're at an auction... in Mexico," I mumble nearly inaudibly.

Her face pales and she searches my hollow eyes. I'm not sure what she's looking for. There's nothing there anymore. My once bright blue eyes have now become as gloomy as the Black Sea.

"My name is Paige Henley," the smile she gives me is sad, but I struggle to feel any emotion at the sight of it.

"I'm Emily," I try to offer her a smile in return but I'm sure it looks more like a grimace.

Her lips part slightly, and her eyes fill with panic that I don't understand.

"E... Emily?" her voice cracks as her eyes become glossy.

"Emily Moore," I confirm. She doesn't look familiar at all but then again, I've met an astronomical number of people in my lifetime.

A shaky hand raises to her lips as she continues to stare at me. Recognition and sadness begin to cover her features. My brows knit in confusion and the uneasy feeling that I'm not going to like what I hear spreads through my body.

"Oh my God... you're Declan's sister, aren't you?" her question comes out in a pained whisper.

My body fills with adrenaline at the sound of my brother's name on her lips. The fact that she knows who I am gives me some small piece of hope that maybe Declan knows she's missing and will come.

"You know Declan?" I say and hunch forward. Each beat of my heart booms in my ears.

"Y-yes... Oh my God... Emily." she sobs into her hand, tears flowing down her cheeks. "How are you here? Declan said you were in Ireland with your mom."

The shame of my stupidity replaces my adrenaline. My stomach churns and I chew on my bottom lip.

I tell her about meeting a guy in Ireland just a few days after arriving and him kidnapping me. I foolishly allowed myself to try and find a distraction to help the emotional pain I was feeling, and it cost me everything.

I'm not sure how my abduction has been hidden from Declan and my ma for as long as it has and it's unclear if I'll ever find out.

When I ask her how she knows my brother, she tells me he's someone very important to her, but she was too afraid of being with him, so she ran and ended up here.

My brother seems to have found the love of his life and she here in purgatory.

Ain't that a bitch?

The back of my eyes burn as tears form. Reaching over, I intertwine my fingers with hers and we sit in silence surrounded by our depressing reality.

CHAPTER 2
Liam
3 YEARS AGO

"Take Liam with you to the docks to check the shipment we are set to receive today." Conor — the Irish mafia boss — gestures to me.

Declan and Rhys nod their heads in acceptance of the order.

"Let's go," Declan says to me and strides out of the study.

Today is my first official day in America. Cormac — Conor's brother — sent me and a few other men from Ireland to work under Conor after he recently had an altercation with the Russians and lost several men. I'm not entirely sure how I feel about being here. I've never been to this country, and I don't know much about Conor aside from him being a ruthless and cruel leader.

Keeping my strides even with the two men before me, I collide with a small body when we pass through the foyer, and they fall to the ground with an "oof".

"Shite, I'm sorry," I exclaim.

I work to help whomever I knocked over when bright, turquoise-blue eyes meet mine. I'm rendered completely immobile and speechless. The sweet scent of berries and wildflowers assaults my senses. Electricity sweeps across every surface of my skin.

"Emily, are you okay?" Declan says, scooping her body from the ground.

Emily shrugs him off and then turns to me. Pink tints her cheeks, and she offers me a small smile. "I'm sorry. I wasn't watching where I was going."

"No, I'm sorry. I was tryin' to keep up with Declan and Rhys."

She pushes a strand of red hair behind her ear and nods.

"Where are you headed?" Her eyes flick to Declan.

"To the docks. We'll be back in a few hours," He replies.

I'm not sure what's come over me. My eyes refuse to stray away from her stunning face. Her slightly upturned nose is littered with freckles that span across her cheeks. Her pouty lips are the perfect shade of rose pink. She's petite with soft curves that demand worship. I'm captivated by her beauty in ways that I can't comprehend.

Declan notices my stare, his jaw ticks and his eyes narrow.

"Liam," Rhys's voice cuts through my daze and I startle.

"Aye?"

"Let's head to the car."

He spins on his heels and makes for the front door. I quickly shoot a glance in Emily's direction then follow Rhys.

"What the fuck was that?" he asks the moment I meet him by the SUV. He crosses his arms over his chest and looks at me in annoyance.

"I haven't the slightest idea what you're takin' 'bout," I say with a raised brow.

He gestures an arm to the mansion. "Do you have a death wish, kid? That's Declan's little sister."

"How was I to know? I've never met her."

Just as he is going to reply, Declan exits the mansion and stalks toward me with a venomous glare. Stopping just inches away from my face, he jabs a finger into my chest.

"Stay away from her," he snarls.

I raise my hands in surrender, "I wasn't aware who she was. I'm sorry."

"Well, now you know and I'm warning you. Stay away from her."

"Yessir."

With one final jab in the chest, he shoulders past me and slides into the SUV.

Movement catches my attention and I swing my gaze to the mansion. Emily is standing at the entrance facing our direction. I feel her gaze on my skin like the heat of the summer sun. Electricity strums once more throughout my body.

Rhys coughs under his breath and I meet his eyes. They flare slightly and he juts his chin toward the car. Spinning on my heels, I climb in.

The crates filled with weapons are arranged meticulously around the warehouse. Grunts fill my ears as the men haul them into the vans and trucks for transport. The smell of gunpowder and metal invade my sinuses.

"Rhys, Finn, and I monitor the shipments, but Finn is now going to be handling outside communications for my da, so we'll have you help monitor them." Declan steps up to my right and I turn my head to meet his eyes.

Slipping my hands into my pockets, I turn back to the men and nod. "Alright, when do you want me to start?"

"Today. Finn is going to be heading out to Arizona with my da to discuss an arrangement with a gang out there."

I nod again.

"I have some business to handle so I'll leave you and Rhys to it. He'll show you what is expected of you." With a pat on my back, Declan leaves the warehouse.

I continue to scan the area. The operation is running like a well-oiled machine.

"Follow me," Rhys says with a flick of his chin for me to follow.

We check the quality of the weapons as well as the ammunition. Rhys talks with some of the men that are overseeing the process. As he discusses everything, I can't stop my thoughts from venturing toward Emily.

She is breathtaking. She doesn't appear to be that much younger than I am either. She's completely off-limits but I know it's going to be difficult to avoid the draw I feel to her. Her allure is hypnotic.

I've never experienced this feeling before. It's as though she's created a space in my soul made specifically for her. It's an absurd thought, especially since I've only just exchanged a handful of words with her.

Regardless, I want to make her mine. Declan's threat seems minuscule compared to the mesmeric need to be with her. To claim her.

"Liam." Rhys's voice breaks my trance and I meet his annoyed glare. "Get your shit together, kid. We have shit to do."

Shelving my thoughts of Emily, I follow Rhys as we make our way further into the warehouse.

Walking into the foyer, I struggle with the want I have to go search for Emily.

"Declan is down in the cellar. Follow me." Rhys pivots and makes his way down a long corridor. He opens a large wood door and steps into an office. He strides in and stops in front of another door that is just behind the desk in the center of the room. Pushing it open, a stairwell is revealed.

We walk silently down the concrete steps to another door at the end of the staircase that opens to a large open room. A metal table sits to the right with a black bag and an assortment of tools set on the surface. Declan stands in a pool of blood and body parts are scattered in the center of the room with his back to us. In the back of my mind, I tell myself to heed his warning. But another part of me says to throw caution to the wind and take what I want.

Peering over his shoulder, he nods a greeting and then steps away from his victim. The body in the seat is nothing but flayed skin and meat. My stomach churns at the sight. I'm no stranger to torture but feck, this person looks like they got into a fight with a meat grinder.

Metal clanks as Declan sets his tools on the table. Blood coats his hands, face, and tattooed chest.

"Everything good?" He asks without lifting his head. His movements are slow and predatory as he scans his tools. He moves as though he's not even human.

"Yeah, shipments are already heading where they need to," Rhys replies as he steps through the blood and strides to Declan.

"Perfect. My da will be gone for a few weeks, so I'll be in charge until then."

"Declan!" Emily's shriek comes from above and we all jerk our heads in the direction of the door before bolting up the stairs. I take each step two at a time with Declan and Rhys at my heels. Jumping over the desk, I pass through the threshold of the office door.

"Where are you?" I shout, scanning from left and right. My heart is pounding in my chest with such force that it's almost painful. Her reply comes from upstairs, and I sprint up the steps.

Declan shoves past me and runs down the hallway before pushing a door open. We enter the space that I assume is Emily's bedroom just by the smell of berries and wildflowers. Declan makes a beeline to the ensuite.

Emily is lying in the center of the shower with a towel wrapped around her. A gash on her leg is bleeding profusely.

"What the hell happened?" When Declan reaches for her, she shrieks.

"You're covered in someone else's blood! Don't touch me!"

Declan looks over his shoulder and gestures for me to help but there is a clear warning in his eyes.

14

Emily's blue eyes meet mine and I'm flooded with nerves. Walking slowly, I crouch next to her. The humidity of the shower causes sweat to slide down my back.

"Hold onto me," I whisper, and she wraps her small arms around my neck. Goosebumps spread over my skin despite the heat of the room. Sliding my arms under her frame, I lift her from the tiled floor. She hisses when her leg touches the fabric of my shirt.

"How did you get hurt?" Declan asks as he scans the room.

"I fell in the shower and hit the edge of the bench."

My shirt is wet from the water sliding down her soft skin and I struggle to keep my body from reacting to her proximity.

"I'll call the doctor to come check her out." Rhys pulls his phone from his pocket and leaves the room to make the call.

"Set her on the bed," Declan orders.

My heart is beating so hard, I'm sure Emily can feel it. I can feel her eyes on my profile but resist the urge to peer down at her. Gently, I place her onto the plush mattress that is littered with pillows.

I scan the room, looking anywhere but Emily. I don't know if I'll be able to hide the bulge in my jeans if I look at her in that towel again.

The door swings open and Rhys steps in with the family physician a few moments later. He quickly walks over to where Emily lies and begins assessing her wound.

Anger, possessiveness, and jealousy flow through my blood at an alarming rate. I feel a growl threatening to escape my chest each time his fingers touch her delicate skin.

What the hell?

Quickly, I spin around and exit the room before I do something I'll surely regret.

CHAPTER 3
Emily
3 YEARS AGO

I watch as Liam flees from my bedroom shortly after Dr. Robbins begins working on my leg.

His face morphed into a weird combination of emotions that I couldn't figure out. He was like a concrete wall when I bumped into him earlier. But the moment I met his gorgeous hazel eyes... Everything disappeared. I knew my da was hiring someone to come replace Finn at the docks, but I didn't anticipate *him*. I'm not sure what it is about him that calls to me, but I want to explore it.

With wavy light-brown hair, broad shoulders, and a towering height, Liam is beautiful. His strong jaw calls for my fingers to caress his stubble. His plush lips demand mine.

His spicy musk scent wrapped around me like a warm blanket when he lifted me into his muscled arms. I wanted to immerse myself in that scent. The feel of his heart beating rapidly caused my stomach to swarm with butterflies.

I affect him just as much as he affects me. It's thrilling and I hope something can come of it.

"You hurt yourself pretty good here, Emily," Dr. Robbins says with a shake of his head.

"It's not like I meant to fall," I reply with an eye roll.

Declan stands behind Dr. Robbins and meets my eyes. "What were you doing?"

"I just lost my footing when I was moving around."

He purses his lips and nods. I know he doesn't believe me. I'm not a very good liar but I'm not going to tell him I was trying to shave every inch of my body. He doesn't need to know that or the *why* I decided to do it.

It's not like Liam would be interested in anything with me anyway. I'm sure he's experienced, and I'm anything but. I don't even need to mention the fact that he works for my father.

I hiss from the sharp sting caused by the antiseptic Dr. Robbins is using to clean my wound.

"Sorry, I'll need to numb you for this next part," Dr. Robbins mumbles and preps the supplies.

Another sharp sting followed by a burn causes my face to twist in pain before the numbness sets in.

"This will need a few stitches," Dr. Robbins begins working on mending my wound and Declan watches his actions closely.

Declan is an overbearing brute when it comes to me. I'm the kid-sister. Unfortunately, I'm also a mafia princess. That means I'm at a much higher risk of danger than Declan. Where he is mountainous in height and build, I'm petite, like my mother. Declan is a force to be reckoned with. He has a thirst for blood and thrives in hectic situations.

Me? I'm too soft. Too gentle. I can't even muster the courage to kill a damned spider.

I can't help but glance repeatedly at the doorway in hopes of seeing Liam standing there.

The way my body responded to his was surprising. I wasn't sure what to think of it. I've been surrounded by men my entire life but not someone so close to my age outside of Rhys and Declan.

Rhys has been best friends with Declan for as long as I can remember but he's as much of a brother to me as Declan is. Nothing romantic will ever be happening there.

But Liam? The attraction was instant and unavoidable.

Despite being eighteen, I've never had a chance to explore any relationships because of my status with the mafia. I'm meant to be pure for any plans for an arranged marriage.

But maybe I can convince my da to let me at least try something with Liam. It's a huge stretch that he would be willing to let it happen, but I want to at least try.

"There you are." Dr. Robbins packs up his supplies and then rises from the bed.

"Thank you, Doc." I offer him a small smile that he returns before exiting the room.

"Were you able to finish showering or do you need help?"

"You're not helping me." I can't hide the repulsion in my voice.

Rhys snorts when Declan's face twists with disgust.

"I was going to have Ingrid help you," he grunts.

"I think I can manage. Just won't use the rain showerhead." I shrug.

"Alright, be careful."

Declan strides over and places a gentle kiss on the top of my head then makes his way to the door. Rhys shoots me a wink then follows him out.

A few days later, I walk slowly down the steps to avoid too much irritation to my stitches as I make my way over to the front door. I spot Liam walking in the same direction from the hallway.

"Liam!" I call out before I have a chance to talk myself out of it.

His head whips around to the sound of my voice and I watch as his gaze travels down my body. His Adam's apple bobs up and down when he swallows tightly.

I lightly bite my bottom lip as I absorb his attention.

When he meets my eyes, I turn into a blushing fool. There is a clear heat there and I can feel it burning into my body like a hot Arizona summer.

Shoving his hands into his pockets, he clears his throat.

"Anythin', you need?" His Irish accent is thick and unconsciously seductive.

"I... Uh." I rack my brain for a reason for calling his name as I make my way closer to him.

His head quirks slightly and he raises a brow.

"I wanted to see how you were doing. You ran out of my room pretty fast the other day." I lower my chin slightly to hide the embarrassing blush that threatens to spread over my face.

He straightens and rolls his shoulders back.

"Yeah, everythin' is good." He nods and gives me a tight smile.

"Oh. Good. That's good."

This whole exchange is painfully awkward now that he has hidden the heat from his eyes.

"Listen, I've gotta get goin'." He gestures his thumb over his shoulder.

"Right. I guess I'll see you later then?" I can't help the hope that leaks in my tone.

"Er... Yeah."

When I smile at him, I swear I see longing in his eyes before he steels his features and leaves.

The tips of my fingers lightly brush along the vibrant flower petals as I walk through the garden. My da had this specifically made for my ma before she decided to stay in Ireland to take care of my grandma. Now, it's mine.

The garden is my favorite place on the property. The honeybees, hummingbirds, and butterflies moving from flower to flower fill me with so much contentment. I love sitting among the foliage and watching them. It brings me a sort of peace despite the crazy lifestyle I lead.

Finding a soft patch of grass, I lay out the throw blanket I brought with me and lie down. My bright red hair fans out and I watch as clouds move slowly across the blue sky.

It's silent aside from the soothing sounds of the tree leaves rustling with the gentle wind. My eyes flutter closed, and I listen to the peaceful noises around me. A soft smile spreads over my face when I hear the songbirds' melodies.

As time passes, I feel myself begin to drift off to sleep.

"You look like a Disney Princess."

I shoot up to the sound of Liam's voice. My head spins and I set my hand down to steady myself.

"What?" I ask as soon as I've regained my bearings.

"I said, you look like a Disney Princess." His eyes are filled with humor and a small smirk plays on his lips. The white tee he wears stretches over his broad frame and emphasizes his muscular build. The black cargo pants he has on wrap around his firm thighs. Combined with his black boots? This man is a walking wet dream.

"What makes you say that?" My heart is pounding wildly against my chest, I worry he'll hear it.

He shrugs and walks toward me, his eyes studying me when he stops just a few feet away.

"A beautiful woman in a sundress lyin' in the middle of a garden, surrounded by flowers and birds. You just need to start singin'."

I can only focus on the fact that he called me beautiful. I feel the warmth spread over my neck and up to my cheeks and I dip my head shyly.

"What are you doing out here?" I whisper and look up into his mesmerizing gaze.

"Yer da sent me to search for you."

"Do you know what for?"

He shakes his head but stares at me through swirls of green and amber. I feel exposed in the best way.

Clearing my throat, I stand and start folding my throw blanket.

"Here, let me help you." He reaches out and his arm brushes against mine causing us both to suck in sharp breaths.

"Sorry," he mutters. I don't miss the slight flush of his cheeks when he turns away from me.

My stomach is an explosion of nerves. I feel like a little girl experiencing her first crush.

After folding up the blanket, we make our way through the path that leads to the mansion.

"Your ma will be arriving from Ireland in just a few hours. She's expected to stay with us for a few months this time."

My cheeks burn from the stretch of my wide smile. I haven't seen my mom in months and I'm so excited to see her and share this newfound crush I've developed. She's my best friend and I share just about everything with her. I know she'll support me in trying to convince my dad to allow some sort of relationship to form.

"This weekend, we'll be having a party to celebrate her arrival."

Declan and I nod from where we stand on the opposite side of my father's desk in his study.

"Is there anything we need to do to prepare for the party?" I ask.

My dad's eyes soften when he glances at me.

"No, *mo stór*. You don't need to worry about anything."

"Okay, Da. I'm going to see what I have to wear for the party then."

He nods and then turns to Declan.

"I need you to stay here so we can discuss some important security measures for the party."

When I exit the room, Finn is standing outside waiting to step inside. I smile as I step past him.

"The Russians are becoming more aggressive in their methods..." My father's voice is cut off with the click of the door shutting behind Finn.

Worry gnaws at me at what that could mean for this weekend.

It's no secret that our family and the Solkolovs have bad blood since my dad refuses to align with Vladimir's flesh trading. It's disgusting the sheer amount of people that promote and indulge in purchasing women like they're nothing but a slab of meat. Nothing has gotten too out of hand but only time will tell if that changes.

Pushing my emotions aside, I make my way back up to my bedroom.

CHAPTER 4
Emily
MEXICO

Scorching pain burns my throat when I swallow. Dehydration set in not long after I was thrown into my prison. It's a new kind of agony.

Leaning against the stone wall, I struggle with silencing the demons that taunt me. They laugh incessantly at the torment I'm forced to endure.

Paige and I have been separated more times than we've been together. I'm not sure how long I'm expected to be isolated, but Nikolai demanded it despite still being in Russia.

His reasoning? I belong to him.

When I first arrived here, he claimed me and has been my tormentor ever since. He's the head of the snake that coils around me, sucking the life out of me with each tightening of his grip.

It's been a slight reprieve that he was ordered to go to Russia. He isn't here to humiliate me any chance he can. He isn't here to record my rapes and broadcast them to the guards for their sick pleasure or strap me down to a chair and force me to listen to the screams of past women and children.

I've always known the world was cruel. I've been aware of the mistreatment of women long before I was brought to this place, I just never realized how long the suffering extends. It's like an eternal Hell that burns a fire so blistering hot that it scorches everything in its wake.

My fingernails sting and threaten to lift due to the repeated stress I've placed on them from my scratching. I can't stop the need to cause myself pain. It has become a necessity at this point.

I've begun to hallucinate. I see Declan. My ma. My da – who has long been dead – and I see Liam. Each of them either gives me words of comfort or spews vile insults and promises in complete disgust.

The latter happens far too often.

I wince when I try to lick my cracked lips. The skin splits on contact and the taste of copper coats my tongue.

"Despicable."

I turn my head slightly and see Liam sitting across from me. His eyes are filled with disappointment and hatred.

"Why are you still fighting to stay alive?" his tone is laced with displeasure.

"I don't want to die here," I croak. My voice sounds as though I've spent my twenty-two years of life smoking two packs a day.

Liam chuckles darkly with a slow shake of his head and then he disappears.

Clanking echoes down from the grate above me followed by grunting. The metal scraps along the concrete as it's pulled away and tossed aside.

"Time for some fun," Igor's deep voice sends fear racing through my veins.

He reaches and hauls me roughly from the hole in the ground and I wince from the stiffness in my muscles. My knees buckle when he sets me down and I fall to the concrete. He scoffs in annoyance as if I'm a total inconvenience for him. A kick in the ribs causes me to cry out in pain. I try to curl into myself to protect my stomach, but he kicks me again.

"Get up," he grunts.

With shaky arms, I try with all my might to push myself up to my feet. I whimper as my joints scream in protest. Despite my withering frame, I feel like I'm lifting hundreds of pounds.

I'm not sure how long I was left down there but it was long enough for my limbs to refuse to function.

Once I'm standing, Igor pushes me forward. I stumble but remain upright as he walks me toward my next personal Hell.

Igor pushes the black-steel door open, and I see the metal chair in the center of the windowless room that I've become far too familiar with.

"Sit."

I sway on my feet as I make my way over and fall into the seat. There is no point in trying to resist any orders. It will only end badly for me.

Men that I wasn't aware were in the room with us begin strapping me down with the leather belts on the arms of the chair. My head is pushed back, and another belt is pressed against my forehead, immobilizing me completely.

Loud cries and screams boom through hidden speakers in the room. I slam my eyes shut and try to focus on anything other than their painful wails that cut through my ears like hot knives.

I gasp as ice-cold water is doused onto my body. The men laugh loudly when I begin to shiver and my teeth chatter violently.

"There's your nice drink of water," Igor sneers then turns around and leaves the room.

One of the other men grips my jaw tightly and I whimper from the rough handling. He twists my face, forcing me to meet his black eyes and dread overtakes me.

"I'll be seeing you after this is all done," he purrs and shoots me a wink before he slams his lips against mine.

I curl in my lips as best as I can and choke down the bile that threatens to spill. He brutally squeezes my cheeks causing my mouth to part and shoves his tongue down my throat. The rancid taste of stale cigarettes invades my mouth and I gag.

Tears stain my face when he finally releases his hold. His palm connects with my cheek when he pats it in condescension.

His boots thud against the floor when he retreats. The slam of the door shutting ricochets off the walls, and I'm clouded in darkness with nothing but the sounds of those experiencing unbearable torture to keep me company.

The screams have long since faded into the background. My eyes have adjusted to the darkness enough that I can make out the outline of the door in front of me. I feel defeated. Hopeless. I'm left isolated for days at a time with little to no human interaction. It's agonizing.

Each day of isolation becomes harder and harder to survive. It's becoming more challenging to decipher what thoughts are truly mine and what are those that the demons feed me.

"You'll find a way back home, *mo stór*. Just hold on." My da's gentle voice drifts around me like a caress and my lips quiver.

"I don't know how much longer I can hold on *daid*." My voice cracks. "I'm just so tired."

"Fight, Emily. You need to fight." His voice is firm.

"I'm not strong enough," I whisper.

"You're my daughter. You're strong beyond words."

A sob breaks from my lips. "I'm scared."

I swear I can feel the ghost of his hand stroking my hair. It's as painful as it is comforting.

"It's okay to be afraid, *mo stór*. Just don't give up hope."

He'd be disappointed if he knew that hope disappeared from me a long time ago. How can anyone maintain any semblance of hope in a place like this?

"I'll try." I lie.

After spending two days strapped to the chair, covered in my urine, I was hauled out and tossed into the communal showers with the other women. I saw Paige, who looks as decayed as I feel.

We weren't able to provide each other with any sort of comfort. Not after the days we've spent away from each other. We've essentially become mute. Hiding in the recesses of our minds; only I'm not alone in mine.

Paige's skin is becoming more and more damaged as time passes. Her already small frame has become skeletal, and it makes me fear how much longer she has before succumbing to the inevitable death that awaits us.

My dad's spirit pushes me to remain hopeful. To keep holding on. But there is a thin line between being optimistic and utterly pathetic. I've toed that line for far too long and I'm beginning to step over it.

CHAPTER 5
Liam
3 YEARS AGO

The metallic scent of copper invades my nose as soon as I push the door to Declan's cellar open. Grunts and curses accompany the sounds of instruments clinking on the metal table. The energy in the air causes the hairs on the back of my neck to stand erect. Declan comes into view and he stands shirtless above his victim. Every surface of his skin is coated in blood. His shoulders rise and fall in sync with the deep pants he releases.

He's a scary motherfucker and I don't ever want to find myself on his bad side.

Then stay away from Emily.

Each stolen glance in her direction takes my breath away. She's beautiful beyond words. She carries herself with such unconscious grace. She is always offering sweet smiles to the staff that work tirelessly throughout the mansion.

When she speaks, her soft and sweet voice flows to my ears like a gentle melody that I wish I could record and replay over and over.

Declan rolls his neck, eliciting loud popping sounds. Looking over his shoulder, he nods in greeting when he sees me enter the room.

"Everything good with the warehouses?" he asks, stepping away from the bloodied body in the seat.

My stomach twists when my gaze falls on the hollowed-out skull. The stories I heard about Declan when I was in Ireland don't compare to the reality of him.

"Aye. Everythin' has been shipped to the buyers." I nod, putting my hands in my pockets.

"Good. My da has an assignment for you. There have been some issues with the Russians recently and we need someone to keep an eye on Emily during my ma's party." His eyes narrow. He scans my face for any expression changes and feck is it hard not to show my excitement.

"I don't know why he chose you but..." he takes slow steps in my direction and anxiousness thrums in my veins. His eyes flare. He stands inches from my face in an intimidating stance. I'm tall – standing at six feet –but Declan towers over me as if I'm nothing more than a pebble he can kick away with the toe of his expensive leather shoe.

"Don't do anything but monitor her. Don't get close to her any more than necessary. Don't be fucking friendly. *Nothing.*"

I discreetly swallow the lump in my throat.

"Yessir." I say with a dip of my chin.

I watch as Emily poses in front of the camera next to a black horse. We're standing in the forest that surrounds the estate. She's wearing a beautiful emerald-green gown. The fabric flows softly in the light breeze. Her hair is braided intricately, making her appear like a regal queen from the Middle Ages. She's truly breathtaking.

Every so often, she will glance at me, and her cheeks will flush. It sends a thrill through me that I've never experienced. We've barely exchanged more than a handful of words at a time and yet I can't control how my thoughts focus solely on her.

Seeing her walk around the mansion, walk the grounds, or simply sit in her little garden with a tranquil face makes me want to give everything I have to her. She has such kindness to her despite the violence that surrounds her life that I hope never leaves.

She tips her head up slightly and gazes distantly. I take the time to study the slender curve of her neck and profile. Freckles scatter her skin like constellations in the night sky and I wish so deeply to trace them. It's so hard to stay distant from her when all I want to do is pull her close and submerse myself in the depths of her ocean eyes and swim in her scent of berries and wildflowers.

I don't know how to handle all these emotions she conjures in me. I'm completely bewitched by this woman, and I barely know her.

When she dips her chin, her eyes meet mine and time stops. She sends me a small smile which showcases the small dimple on her left cheek.

I'm in so much trouble.

It's become more difficult to remain professional with her. I know I should heed Declan's warnings. I'd be fecking stupid not to. After all, the man is an absolute maniac and would relish in torturing and dismembering me. But I can't shake this pining. This aching *need* to just leap with Emily and free fall.

We turn to the sound of tires driving up the gravel words to the estate. Through a gap in the trees, we see a convoy of SUVs announcing the arrival of Caetlin – Emily's ma – and Emily immediately beams in happiness as bright as the sun.

Taking the reins of the horse, Emily mounts it and takes off on a gallop in the direction of her ma. A small chuckle passes my lips at just how much she wanted to reach her ma that she completely disregarded the photoshoot she was doing.

Placing my hands in my pockets, I begin my trek through the forest and head toward Emily.

Emily is clutching her ma tightly when I meet them. Caetlin sees me over Emily's shoulder and curiosity fills her eyes. I've seen her once or twice in the past but only from a distance. Standing in front of her now, Emily looks nearly identical. Both have beautiful red hair that cascades down their small frames. Both have those mesmerizing eyes and scattered freckles. It's astonishing. The only difference they seem to have is their age. Caetlin has lines that reveal the years she's spent smiling and laughing.

When they pull away, Emily meets my eyes before whispering something in her ma's ear. Caetlin's eyes once again flick to me, and she studies me with a look I can't decipher.

"You must be Liam," she says and offers me a hand which I take.

"Aye. It's a pleasure to officially meet you," I say with a nod and a gentle shake of her hand.

She smiles with a twinkle in her eye before glancing at Emily and shooting her a wink.

"*Dia duit, mam,*" Declan says, descending the front steps.

"*Dia duit, mo pháiste.*" Caetlin pulls Declan into an embrace. When she pulls away, she cups his face.

"How are you, *mo stór?*" She asks in an affectionate voice.

"Good ma. How was your flight?"

He places his hand on her back and leads her to the door.

When we step inside, Conor walks down the foyer with open arms and a huge smile plastered over his face. Caetlin spots him and her face lights up just as Emily's did when she first arrived.

"*Mo shuul!*" *My life,* he bellows, pulling her into his chest. He exhales against her hair as though releasing the tension he has been carrying. A small smile surfaces on my face, and it draws Emily's attention.

My eyes veer in her direction. Her head tips slightly as she studies me curiously. I quickly break eye contact with her to avoid attracting Declan's notice. My skin pebbles in awareness as she continues to stare at me.

"Liam, meet with Finn at the warehouse in Manhattan." Conor's order comes in a tone filled with contentment.

I meet his eyes and dip my chin. "Aye, sir."

Shoving my desire to look at Emily, I spin on my heels and head out the door.

CHAPTER 6
Emily
MEXICO

The pain and tenderness in my ankle from the shackle dull the voices in my head. They dull my yearning to scratch at my skin just enough that my injuries have finally had a chance to heal. The damage I've made to my thighs from my incessant scraping is deep and will forever be marked on my skin. It will be a reminder of the destruction I've sustained to my soul. Of the devastating reality that I'm no longer... me.

I absentmindedly graze the raised scar I have along my inner thigh from when I first arrived here. The lumpiness of the discolored skin is thick and the sensation of my finger touching the area is slightly clouded from the nerve damage I've created.

Time seems to pass in a depressing blur while also standing still. In the time I've been placed back into the room where Paige is held with the other women, many have been taken. Few have returned.

Part of me hopes they died. It's the far lesser evil than being sold to sadistic monsters.

The deadbolt on the steel door brings me back to reality. Paige and I huddle into each other, shielding ourselves as best as we can. We've been a part of the small number of women that haven't been taken. I'm not sure if that's a good thing. The unknown is terrifying. What could possibly come from us not being used and abused for an extended period?

"Everybody up." Two men grunt and we slowly rise to our feet with wobbly legs.

The door is pushed open further and Vladimir steps in with a smug sneer plastered on his atrocious face. I feel rage when I see him. He has been a thorn in my family's side for as long as I can remember and now, I'm a pawn in his plot for revenge on my family.

"Hello, ladies," the satisfaction in his voice makes my inside contort.

We stand silently, waiting for whatever plans he has for us. This is the first time he's come pay us a visit and it's unsettling.

"My name is Vladimir Solkolov, Pakhan of the Russian Bratva. Prepare yourselves, as we will be leaving for your next home." He wraps his fingers around the collar of the suit jacket and examines each of us with such intensity that I want to throw up.

His eyes land on Paige and my stomach falls. His gaze doesn't stray when he whispers into the ear of the man next to him. Suddenly, a small army of men step into the room and begin hauling us out. Some resist and are dragged by their hair. Others don't engage in any struggle for a chance to escape. They've accepted that this will be their lives moving forward.

I'm not entirely sure which group I fall in. A part of me wants to fight. The other part of me isn't sure if it's even worth it at this point.

As the room empties, my terror rises, and I shiver. Paige and I intertwine our fingers and clutch each other's hands as firmly as our skeletal bodies allow.

Only one man moves to remove my shackle but not Paige's. When he doesn't attempt to release her from her chains, fear unlike anything I've felt overpowers my system. We grapple to cling to each other as I'm dragged away and hold on until the very last second when I'm forced to release her.

Paige's eyes are wide with terror. A broken sob escapes me when we pass the threshold of the door and she's no longer in view.

Russia. We've been moved to Russia. Even if we managed to break out of here, we'd be captured almost immediately. Vladimir's family controls nearly the entire country. We're fucked.

I haven't laid eyes on Paige since we arrived, and it's been five days. Dread consumes me. Is she alive? What is happening to her? Will I ever see her again?

When we first arrived, everyone was separated and placed into different *cells*. Some in groups. Some alone. I've been unfortunately subjected to isolation once again. My senses are continually obstructed when I'm locked in dark rooms. My eyes are tired from the strain I place on them to see anything. I'm forced to use my smell and hearing often. The unpleasant sounds and odors overwhelm me each time.

I sit with my back pressed along the concrete wall in a windowless room so dark that I can't make out anything inches in front of me. Not that it would matter anyway, I know the space is empty. I'm alone. As time passes, I'm beginning to enjoy the solitude. I'm beginning to enjoy the visits from the demons that mock my entire existence.

"Féileacán." Liam's voice calling me *butterfly* causes my throat to tighten. I can't see him, but I feel the ghost of his hands softly stroking my cheek. My eyes close and I try to manifest his presence into reality.

Sorrow and grief surge so quickly that I feel like I'm drowning. I've lost a love I never even had a chance to have.

Liam has been a part of my life for years and just when I began to have a taste of the love we could have had, it came crashing down. My father told me he agreed for me to have an arranged marriage to some bigshot billionaire. The marriage would have allowed my father to move his money through his banks without drawing the attention of the feds.

So, Liam started pushing me away.

The memories I created with him haunt me as much as they console me. I never had the chance to tell him I love him and when he pushed me away, I knew that he didn't feel the same. He didn't fight for me when I begged him to. He didn't ask me to say no to the marriage. He did nothing.

"Féileacán," he says again, only this time it sounds further away.

"What do you want?" I croak. My throat burns from thirst. It's been several hours since I've been given any water.

I receive no response and I no longer sense him. Once again, I'm left alone with my thoughts.

I resent Liam for the time we lost. For the love, I was forced to shove down into the recesses of my heart. I've tried to understand his reasoning for abandoning me but have come up empty. How could he forfeit what we had? Was I not good enough? Was I really just a warm body to sink into for the time being?

I've asked myself these questions again and again. My ma says that the love I deserve is coming but when? When will it be my chance for a happy ending?

Obviously, that's not something that will ever happen, seeing as I'm Vladimir's prisoner and Nikolai's toy.

Closing my eyes, I will my ears to block out the agonizing screams of the women outside my cell and fall asleep.

CHAPTER 7
Emily
3 YEARS AGO

"So, tell me about this Liam boy." My ma strokes my hair from where my head lies on her lap. Her fingers gently massage my scalp in a soothing motion.

I shrug. "There isn't much to tell, ma. I just met him a couple of weeks ago. But I don't know how to explain this feeling. I just want to be near him. All. The. Time."

She chuckles softly. "I know how that is, *mo stór*. And do you know how he feels?"

I give a small shake of my head. "No, but it's almost as if he gets tongue-tied around me." I turn over to look up at her. Her blue eyes, which are nearly identical to mine and Declan's, soften. "He gets all stiff and struggles to make eye contact with me sometimes."

"Have you spent any time alone with him?"

"Just in passing. But…" I smile. "Whenever we glance at each other from across any room. My breath stalls, Ma."

Her smile widens, and her head tilts slightly.

"My skin gets tingly as soon as he walks into a room. It's like I sense him before I see him."

She chuckles and I blush.

"You probably think it's silly," I say with a sigh and then turn back to my side.

"No, my love. In fact, I know exactly how that feels."

I stare at the intricate swirls of the blanket at the end of my bed.

"Do you think... Do you think you can talk with daid about me possibly exploring something with Liam?" I whisper as if I'm afraid my father is on the other side of my bedroom door.

Her hands pause and move to my shoulder. I turn my head and meet her eyes.

"Of course, Emily. I'm sure he will understand once I explain to him how you're feeling."

"Thank you, ma. I really think there is something there."

She gently caresses my cheek with the back of her forefinger as she stares down at me.

"When you know, you know."

As I'm walking down the steps of the mansion, I spot Liam walking in my direction. His head is down, looking at his phone, but his steps falter and his head whips up. When he sees me looking at him, his eyes widen slightly. Pocketing his phone, he licks his lips, and then slowly walks up to me.

"Hi," I whisper.

He clears his throat and offers me a small smile. "Hi, Emily."

The way he says my name sends chills down my spine. I subtly bite my lower lip before returning his smile.

"What are you doing today?" he asks, shifting on his feet.

"I was actually headed toward the garden. Do you want to come with me?"

He dips his chin and rubs a hand on the back of his neck. "I'm here to get my next orders from your *daid,* Em."

"But he did say you need to watch me, right?"

His brow rises. "At your ma's party."

"Semantics," I say, flicking my hand in dismissal. Each beat of my heart pounds in my ears as I try to mask my nerves. This will be my chance to spend some alone time with him.

"Uh..." he glances toward the mansion and then back at me.

"Here." I hand my blanket and journal to him. "You can say you helped carry my things for me."

He chuckles under his breath and then a smirk tilts his mouth.

"Alright, let's go."

I sit next to Liam on my throw blanket surrounded by wildflowers. He only just started to relax, and we've been out here for about twenty minutes. We've been watching the clouds flow by and the energy between us is tense with longing.

Our conversations are not nearly as awkward as that day in the foyer, but I can't seem to form coherent sentences around him.

And you said he gets tongue-tied.

I snort.

"What?" Liam says.

"Huh?" I ask.

"You just snorted, what's so funny?" the smile he gives me makes my stomach flutter.

I shake my head and roll my eyes. "It's nothing."

He nudges me with his shoulder. "Come on, you can tell me."

I stare into his hazel eyes which soften as he waits for my reply. Mustering up my courage, I release a deep breath.

"You make it hard for me to come up with sentences that make sense."

A slight breeze causes a strand of my hair to fall from the clip it's in. Liam swallows tightly and then reaches out. There is a slight tremble in his hand when he pushes the strand behind my ear.

"The feelin' is mutual," he says quietly.

My heart somersaults. I feel the skin on my cheeks and neck heat.

"I got you something." He whispers.

Surprise flashes across my face. "What?"

He stuffs his hand into his pocket and pulls out a slender rectangle-shaped box.

"I had heard you lost your butterfly necklace and so..." his sentence trails off as he opens the lid of the box.

A beautiful silver butterfly pendant sparkles on an equally exquisite silver chain. There are several small stones encrusted in the pendant and the light reflects off it like a dream.

"This one has a small tracker in it that will help us find you if anything goes wrong."

When I knit my brows and look up at him, he chuckles.

"You know the lives we live, Emily."

I smirk because he's right. We live dangerous lives whether we want to or not and it means safety needs to be at the highest priority.

"May I?" Liam asks, gesturing to the necklace.

I smile widely. Turning my back toward Liam, I scoop my hair over my shoulder.

His arms reach over, and he places the necklace on my neck. Every brush of his fingers on my skin sends electricity down my spine and my heart racing.

"There." He whispers before clearing his throat.

My hair falls to my back when I return my gaze to Liam.

His eyes quickly glance at my lips before rising back to mine. My body warms as desire begins to heat my blood.

When I lick my lips, Liam's eyes track the movement, and I watch as his pupils dilate. My chest rises and falls rapidly as my breaths begin to shallow.

Liam's hand rises and he cups the side of my face — his hand rests at the hollow of my neck. His callused thumb caresses my skin softly and my eyes flutter.

"This is a bad idea," he says, though I'm not sure if he meant it for me or him.

He leans in, his lips stopping inches from mine. The swirls of green and amber are nearly hidden from how blown his pupils have gotten.

He closes his eyes tightly and breathes in deeply before releasing it.

"Fuck it," he says and his lips crash against mine.

My heart soars at the feel of him. His lips are soft, yet firm. His movements are gentle, yet hungry. It's everything.

Our tongues meet, stroke for stroke, and I'm completely lost in this kiss, lost in Liam. His fingers slide up from my cheek, and he removes my clip.

My core tightens when he grips my strands in his fist and deepens the kiss. I moan into his mouth and a satisfied groan escapes him.

Just as I make the decision to climb onto his lap, his phone pings, breaking our trance.

Liam pulls his mouth away from mine so fast as if he lost himself in me as much as I did him. He's panting so hard, and I can see his heartbeat from the vein in his neck.

He shakes his head as though clearing his mind and then pulls his phone from his pocket.

His face hardens when he stares down at the screen.

"I gotta go."

My heart falls and I can't stop my shoulders from sagging.

He pockets his phone and then studies my face. His eyes soften and he strokes my cheek with the back of his fingers.

"I'll see you later, okay?" he says softly.

I nod and chew on the inside of my cheek.

His forefinger and thumb grasp my chin and tip my head up, so I have to look into his eyes. He smiles at me and then presses a soft kiss to my lips. When he pulls away, he shoots me a wink and then rises from the blanket, and toward the mansion.

There's definitely something there.

CHAPTER 8
Emily
3 YEARS AGO

Standing in front of a full-length mirror, I admire my reflection. The material of the dress is soft against my skin. My hair is in an updo to accentuate my slender neck. The neckline shows just enough cleavage to be seductive yet elegant. My make-up is simple and natural. The necklace Liam gifted me sits against my chest. I thumb the pendant and a small smile spreads over my lips.

I've always had a love for butterflies. Despite being small, they're hardy. Some migrate for miles upon miles through windy climates and over the Great Lakes to make it to their homes in Mexico. They're also beautiful beyond words and gentle.

It feels like we are one in the same.

My bedroom door opens, and my ma slips inside. She wears a stunning floor-length navy-blue gown. The A-line cut highlights her beautiful figure. My ma is absolutely exquisite.

"Wow, ma. You look beautiful." I walk over to her, and she pulls me into her arms.

"And you, *a leanbh* look remarkable." Her Irish accent is thick due to her continued residency there.

She pushes a loose strand of my hair behind my ear. Her eyes are tender with love.

"Have you spoken to that Liam boy?" she asks softly, and I blush.

"Da and Declan have him running around with different jobs."

She hums. "I spoke with your father about him."

My heart skips a beat but then plummets when she gives me an apologetic look.

"I'm sorry, Emily. He refused to listen to me when I mentioned a relationship with him."

I swallow the lump in my throat. "Did he say why?"

She shakes her head slowly. My shoulders slump as sadness begins to seep into my veins.

My ma hugs me tightly. "Your love will come, Emily. Let's head down to the party and focus on the good."

She wraps her hand around mine and we walk out of my room.

Soft music, the clinking of glasses, and the voices of conversation fill my ears when I step into the ballroom. People from all over the underground have come to celebrate my ma coming to the US. She's beloved by many, which is heartwarming. My ma has been a part of this world her entire life and she's no feeble wife. She's a force all her own.

In Ireland, she helps run a small section of the mafia that was left to her by my father. She commands her circle with such ferocity and passion. It fills me with pride to know I have such strong parents.

I only wish that strength was something I had. No matter what I do, I can't find it in myself to be violent. I'm a caged bird in a world surrounded by some of the world's most dangerous men and women.

As I'm scanning the room, I feel the thrum of electricity travel down my spine causing the hairs on the back of my neck to stand straight. I know it's Liam before I turn around. I always feel him everywhere before I see him.

I force myself to avoid looking for him. Not in a room where my secret attraction will be noticed, and assumptions will be made.

My mother and I meander through the throng of powerful people. Some of the men eye me like I'm a slab of meat and it makes me feel queasy.

"Emily, come here. I have someone I want you to meet." My father holds his hand out. I spare a glance at my ma and while she smiles at me, her eyes are filled with apology. My brows furrow and she shakes her head the slightest bit.

Placing my hand in my father's, I'm pulled to his side. Two men stand in front of us. One is older, about my da's age with a thick head of peppered black hair. His assessing gray eyes are framed with black eyelashes. He's tall with a slender but muscular build. I would say he's attractive, but he makes me uncomfortable with how his eyes travel over me.

The man to his left is a near-carbon copy of him, just closer to my age. He also watches me with interest that I don't quite like.

"Emily, this is Mr. Monroe and his son Ryan."

"Hello." I greet, timidly.

Ryan smiles at me and holds out his hand. "It's a pleasure to officially meet you, Emily."

"Officially?" I ask with a glance at my father while shaking Ryan's hand.

"Why don't you two go dance?" My father suggests, ignoring my question.

My brow raises but I allow Ryan to pull me toward the dance floor. He places his hand on the small of his back. His frame towers over mine despite the heels I'm wearing.

I can feel the blistering heat of Liam's eyes on me, but I resist the urge to search for him.

My dad has encouraged me to spend time with Ryan throughout the entire night. It's very odd considering he's never encouraged this before.

Does this mean Ryan will be who he decides to marry me off to?

Sure, Ryan is handsome and nice, but there is no spark. No desire to be close to him like I have with Liam. But I guess now is the time for me to do my mafia princess duty and help form an alliance with whomever my father wants.

Ryan tells me that he's twenty-five and is the CEO of his father's banking empire. He gloats about all of his materialistic possessions which is a major turn-off.

Do women really find that attractive?

They must if he thinks that's a way to woo me.

I internally eye roll when he goes on and on about all the money he makes and how successful he is.

I get it, dude. If you weren't, my dad wouldn't want us to interact.

"Emily." My ma's voice chimes, and I internally throw a fist into the air at being rescued.

Turning to her, she gestures for me to follow, and I do.

We walk down the long hallway toward my bedroom, and the entire time, she sends me mischievous smirks over her shoulder.

"What are you up to?" I ask playfully.

"You'll see."

She stops in front of my door and shoots me a wink before swinging the door open.

Liam is standing in the center of my bedroom. My eyes quickly shoot to my ma's, and she nods her head in Liam's direction.

"Go." She whispers.

"But what about the party?"

She scoffs, "I'll handle your father. Go *mo stór.*"

I step in and the door closes with a soft click.

My heart beats against my chest like it's trying to burst out of it. My palms are sweaty, and I feel my stomach coil from the anxiety that is coursing through me.

"You look phenomenal," Liam whispers, his eyes sliding down my body. Every inch of my skin begins to heat.

"Thank you," I say with a small dip of my chin to hide the redness spreading over my cheeks.

"What are you doing in here?"

He offers me a smile and then chuckles quietly. "Your ma saw me huffin' and puffin' in the hallway outside of the ballroom."

"And why were you doing that?" I ask in a soft voice.

My breath catches when he steps toward me. He stops just inches in front of me and I have to crane my neck to meet his eyes.

"Seeing that snobby banker put his hands on you made me want to rip his arms off and feed them to him."

I search his stare, trying to spot any evidence of a lie, but there is none. I can't hold back the shiver that surges through me. My core clenches – searching for something to hold onto – and I swallow tightly to suppress the moan that threatens to escape.

I lick my lips and Liam's eyes follow the movement.

"Liam..." I whisper.

He groans and closes his eyes, "don't say my name like that."

"Like what?" I close the small gap between us and place my palm against his chest. His heart is beating as rapidly as my own and I love it.

When he meets my eyes, his are hooded and filled with so much heat, I can feel it burning me.

"Like you want me to throw you on the bed and fuck you into oblivion."

"Maybe I do."

CHAPTER 9
Liam
3 YEARS AGO

I slam my lips against hers and she instantly melts into me. Wrapping my arms around her, I cup her perky ass in my palm and squeeze which causes her to moan. Her fingers dig into the fabric of my shirt as she searches for perch.

Our tongues clash against each other and we kiss as though this is our last day on this earth. My hands travel over every soft curve and dip of her body, memorizing the feeling of them.

I can't find it in myself to give a fuck about what Declan or Conor would do to me if they found out about this. I *need* to have Emily. She's like a beautifully dangerous siren who sings her song solely for me until she becomes my demise. And Emily surely will be.

My hands grip behind her thighs, and I hoist her up. She wraps her legs around my waist, and I spin around toward the bed. She bounces on the mattress when I throw her onto it and crawl over her body.

I pull the strap of her dress down, exposing her perfect breast. Her dusty-rose nipple is hard and demands attention. Dipping my head, I wrap my lips around it and suck. Her back arches into me, her hands slide into my hair, and she lets out a whimper.

"Liam. Please."

My lip tips up into a satisfied smirk at her begging.

"What, *Féileacán?*"

I kiss her collarbone, then her neck, and finally her lips. She moans into my mouth, and I feel it deep in my bones. We begin tearing at each other's clothes until we're both completely bare.

I sit on my heels and look down at her stunning body. It's even more beautiful than I imagined. She's picturesque with her bright blue eyes staring up at me with adoration.

I pump my cock slowly and I bite down on my bottom lip as I watch her, watch me. Her eyes flare slightly, and I see a hint of fear in them. My hand stops and I tip my head in question.

"Are you okay?" I ask.

Her throat bobs when she swallows. Her eyes don't stray from my erection.

"Emily."

Her eyes flick to mine and the obvious hesitation in them causes my mind to race.

"Are... Are you a virgin?"

She doesn't answer my question, but the silence is confirmation enough.

I climb off her and stand at the end of the bed.

"Why didn' you say anythin'?" I ask.

She sits up and wraps her arms around her knees. "I didn't want you to stop."

"Emily, I can' just fuck you. I'll hurt you."

Tears brim her eyes when she looks up at me and it slices through my heart.

"Please don't cry." I lean forward and cup her face when I see the first tear fall. I hold her firmly when she tries to pull away.

Her eyes bounce between mine and I physically hurt at the pain I see in them. Setting my forehead on hers, I breathe in her delicate scent. She sniffles and lifts her hands to wipe her tears.

"Please, Liam." She pleads in a broken voice. My eyes flutter closed, and my resolve disappears. I unravel the bun she has her hair in, and the strands fall over her shoulders.

"Lie back on the pillow," I say softly, and she complies. Her chest rises and falls with each labored breath she takes.

Climbing onto the bed, my hands move slowly over the porcelain skin of her calves and up her thighs. Goosebumps rise and I smirk. When my touch nears the apex of her thighs, she sucks in a breath. I pause and flick my gaze up to her.

She watches me for a moment before spreading her legs and exposing herself to me. Her pussy glistens with her arousal and my cock twitches.

"I'm goin' to prepare you to take me, okay?" I meet her eyes again and she nods.

Settling my face between her legs, I set them over my shoulders, and breathe her in deeply.

"Feck, Emily." I groan. "You're mouthwaterin'."

She bites down on her lip as her face turns a deep red. I watch her pussy clench and she squirms.

Keeping my eyes on hers, I lower my mouth to her pussy. The first swipe of my tongue causes her hips to buck, and a whimper escapes her lips. The taste of her causes my cock to become so painfully hard that I grind myself into the mattress.

"Oh my God." She moans and her back arches off the bed when I lick her from bottom to clit in one long and slow swipe.

Her sounds cause me to become ravenous and I eat her like my life depends on it. I use one hand to press down on her pelvis while using the other to probe her entrance with my middle finger.

Her pussy clenches around my finger like a vice when I press into her, and she releases an animalistic moan. Adding another digit, I curl my fingers and fuck her with my hand. She claws at the bed, pulling the sheets as she begins grinding her hips against my face.

"That's it, baby. Fuck my face."

I don't stop my assault on her pussy until she tenses and her face morphs into a silent scream. The sound that comes out of her mouth when she comes will be engrained into my brain for the rest of my existence.

When she relaxes, I pull my finger from her slick cunt and suck it into my mouth. She watches me in awe.

"You taste better than I imagined, Em."

"Thank you," she says with a shy smile.

I climb off the bed and reach for my pants that are on the floor. Rifling through my pocket, I pull out the condom I have and turn toward her.

"Do you want to do the honors?" I ask, holding the foiled packet out to her.

She nods and moves to crawl to me. I know she doesn't mean for her movements to be seductive but fuck I could combust just at the sight of her on her hands and knees for me.

She gently takes the condom from my hand. I watch with hooded eyes as she places the wrapper between her teeth and pulls. The sound of the foil ripping is the only sound aside from our ragged breaths.

"Can you show me how?" she whispers.

Taking her wrists, I guide her hands to my cock and help her slide the condom around me. I groan at the feel of her small hand.

Once I'm sheathed, I cup the back of Emily's head and pull her into a kiss. She opens for me without hesitation and my blood heats.

I pull the back of her thighs until she falls onto her back again. Her legs fall open and I settle myself between them.

"Are you ready?" I ask, my eyes searching hers.

She nods and I position myself at her entrance.

"Relax as much as you can," I say before gently pushing myself into her. She hisses and slams her eyes shut. Her face is twisted in pain, and I stop. She shakes her head violently.

"I'm okay, don't stop."

I clench my jaw so tightly that I swear I can hear my teeth break.

"Fuck, you're so tight." I grit.

We simultaneously release the breaths we were holding when I'm fully seated inside her. I dip my head and kiss her shoulder and then her neck.

"I'm goin' to move now, okay?"

She nods.

She grimaces when I pull myself out to the tip. Thrusting back into her, I let out a groan. She wraps her legs around my hips as I begin to fuck her leisurely.

"Faster," she moans, digging her nails into my back.

Increasing my thrusts, I begin fucking her as she asked. Her moans are music to my ears. She's gripping my cock so tightly that I have to concentrate on not coming before I'm ready.

I want to live in this moment.

"Your pussy is fucking amazin', Emily. Fuck she's perfect."

The sting of her nails slicing into my skin only heightens my senses. I dig my fingers into her hips when I lean back and pump into her forcefully.

"Oh God, Liam." Her eyes roll into the back of her head.

"Does that feel good, *Féileacán*? Do you like the feel of my cock inside your tight cunt?"

The feeling of her tightening around me gives me the answer when she's not able to. Her moans bounce off the walls and fill me with unimaginable satisfaction that I'm the one who gets to hear them. That I'm the one causing her such pleasure.

The base of my spine tingles and I move my hand between her thighs to press against her clit. Rolling my thumb against it, I start to fuck without restraint. Her breasts bounce with each thrust and her cries become screams.

"Liam!" she cries out my name when she comes around my cock.

"Fuck, yes. Come on my cock, Emily. "

Seconds later, I come with a deep moan and collapse onto her. Our breaths are labored and the sound of her heart pounding against my ear fills me with contentment.

Once I've caught my breath, slowly pulling out, I lift myself off the bed. Light streaks of pink paint the condom. My emotions are all over the place from the trust she placed in me.

"Stay there."

I stride to the ensuite and dispose of the condom. Opening her cabinet, I grab a washcloth. After running it under some warm water, I reenter the room.

Emily is curled up under her blankets with her mouth slightly ajar. As gently as possible, I pull them back and shift her body so I can clean between her thighs. Light streaks of red mark the inside of her legs and the cloth when I swipe the material between her folds.

She whimpers softly in her sleep, and I know she's going to be very sore tomorrow.

After I've ensured that she's cleaned up, I place the blankets around her and kiss her forehead. I reluctantly move my lips away from her skin and move to get dressed.

I gaze over her sleeping form from the door as I make my way to exit. Despite wanting to curl up next to her, I can't. I can't let Declan or Conor know what has just happened. They'll kill me and I can't risk them being angry with Emily.

With one last look, I leave the room.

CHAPTER 10
Emily
RUSSIA

Pain erupts in my eye and cheek when Nikolai punches me. When I don't give him the reaction he wants, he hits me again. This time, harder and I can't hold back the whimper that leaves my lips.

My hair is brutally pulled into his grasp, and he jerks my head back so forcefully, I'm surprised I'm not decapitated.

"How dare you think you can tell me no! I own you." He growls. Droplets of his spit land on my face.

Today is the first time in a few days that Nikolai has made a move to rape me. I'm not sure what came over me, but I told him no. I fought him when he tried to force me and now, he's beating me for it.

His hand wraps around my throat and I'm shoved against the wall. He lifts me until the tips of my toes barely reach the floor. I claw at his hands when he tightens his hold.

"I own you, *Suka*. If I want to fuck you, you'll lay there and take it. If I want to have my friends fuck you, you'll lay there and take it. You will take everything I give you and be fucking grateful you're still breathing."

My lungs burn and my head pounds from the lack of oxygen they receive. I can't muster even a whimper in response.

I roughly collapse onto the concrete floor when he releases my throat. My fingers rub against where he dug his fingers into my flesh.

Despite my better judgment, I shoot him a glare which causes him to laugh and then land a kick to my ribs. The crack is instant, and I cry out in agonizing pain.

"Take her to the hole. It seems like she needs to be reminded of her place." He says to the guard in the room before he leaves. The door slams shut behind him and the force reverberates through my body.

I fight through my pain when the guard hauls me up to my feet and pulls me out of the room. His grip is unyielding but still, I fight and claw at every inch of skin I can reach.

He descends into the bowels of the basement and panic coats my very soul.

The Hole is a single, windowless room deep within the basement. There are no guards down here. No light. Not even the sounds of scurrying mice can be heard. It's a Hell I've experienced plenty of times and each time, a piece of me is carved out.

"Please, no. Please. I'm - I'm sorry." My heels scrape against the concrete when I dig into it. The guard completely ignores me and continues his path toward Hell.

The silence is petrifying. It's as though we've entered another dimension. One that is absent of all things.

Not even the door makes a sound when it's pulled open. I'm thrown into the darkness and land on my hip. I shriek when the pain shoots down my leg and into my toes.

I scramble to get to my feet and dart to the door, but it's slammed shut before I can stop it.

My fists pound against it repeatedly as I scream in panic.

"You can't leave me down here! Please! Please! I'm sorry!"

I slump down onto my knees when no one comes to release me. I press my head and hand against the cold metal of the door as tears fall freely down my face.

"Please…" I cry quietly.

I'm met with nothing but silence.

I wake on the dirt floor to the sensation of someone's fingers caressing my face. I can't see anything, but I can feel it. No, I can see *him*.

"Liam?" I whisper into the void.

"I'm here, *Féileacán*." The gentleness of his voice coupled with his calling me butterfly, causes unbearable grief to course through me. I'm never going to see him again. I'm never going to get the chance to tell him that I love him.

"Liam… I – "

"Shh," he silences me.

I feel the ghost of his touch on my skin, and I lean toward it. His scent invades my nose and absorb as much of it as I can. I don't know if he'll ever come back as the Liam I love. As *my* Liam.

"Everything will be okay, *Féileacán*."

My lip quivers and I softly shake my head. "I don't see how."

I feel his presence sitting next to me against the concrete wall I'm leaning against.

"Do you remember the day in the garden when we watched the clouds?" he asks.

"How could I forget?"

I remember that day so vividly as if it happened just yesterday. The smell of freshly cut grass and wildflowers flow through my senses and I can feel the soft breeze against the strands of my hair.

That was the day Liam gifted me with a butterfly necklace to replace the one I had lost.

A small smile spreads across my face when I picture how his eyes softened when he watched my reaction to the necklace. It quickly became one of my most prized possessions.

My hand moves to play with the pendant, only to be reminded that it was ripped away from me when I was taken. My eyes burn when tears begin to fill them.

"Don't cry, *Féileacán*."

I swipe at my cheeks, "The necklace is gone, Liam. They took it from me."

The sensation of his arms wrapping around me warms my skin, but only slightly.

"The necklace isn't what's important, Em. The feelin' is. The happiness you felt that day. That moment. That's what's important. Hold on to that."

"Why?" I ask in a broken whisper.

"Because you need to hold on. I'm comin' for you."

I let out a humorless snort.

"I'm comin', Em. Just hold on."

I can feel his presence begin to flicker in and out. I know my time with him is coming to an end. I feel his lips press against my forehead and I choke out a sob.

"Please don't leave me here alone, Liam." I reach out a hand, but it falls onto my lap. Mocking me for even trying because he's not really there.

"Keep holdin' on." He whispers.

And then he's gone.

"WAKE UP!"

I shoot up to the demonic scream that fills my ears. My heart is racing and my body trembles with uncontrollable fear.

My head whips around, trying to find the source of the sound. Do I really want to know? No, but I can't fathom *not* knowing who or what made that sound.

The energy of the room becomes heavy with the promise of overpowering cruelty.

My heart lurches into my throat when my eyes meet glowing red ones boring into me from the top corner of the room. I press myself tightly against the wall, trying to make myself smaller.

The eyes move lower, and I can make out the dark figure in which they inhabit. Fear, unlike anything I've ever felt, dominates every cell in my body.

"Who – who are you?" I stutter.

The chuckle that the creature let out, makes my blood curdle in my veins.

"Why, I'm *you*."

I'm frozen in place. My muscles refuse to move as I watch the creature crawl down the wall. When it reaches the ground, its body twists in broken movements until it stands in a hunched position. Its height is otherworldly.

"I'm what is living inside you, right now."

Its voice skates down my body like ice and I shiver. I whimper when it smiles and reveals sharp, jagged teeth that are dripping with a black, sticky liquid.

My eyes slam shut. "You're not real. You're not real. You're not real." I mutter.

The creature laughs loudly, and it pounds into my head. It echoes against the walls of my prison. I can't contain the trembling of my limbs or the coiling of my stomach.

I can feel its face sitting just centimeters from mine. The putrid stench of death permeates the air.

"I'm as real as you are breathing."

When I don't answer, its claw grazes my flesh.

"Look at me." It demands.

I shake my head violently.

"Look. At. Me." It emphasizes each syllable with an anger-filled growl.

I shake my head again and tears scorch my skin when they slide down my face.

"LOOK AT ME." It shrieks.

My eyes fly open as the feel of something slithering over my arms and legs. Dark shadows wrap around me and trap my body where it sits. I thrash against them but it's no use.

A hand with long, skeletal fingers grips my jaw and I'm forced to face the creature.

Its eyes pierce into my very soul but I'm at its complete mercy. My body refuses to cooperate when I try my damned hardest to close my eyes.

"You think that boy will come to save you? You're *nothing*. He didn't even fight for you. He threw you away like the disgusting, sad excuse of a woman you are. He will never come for you."

"Pl – please let me go," I beg.

Its head tips back and it laughs demonically before disappearing.

The shadows release me, and I scramble away from the wall and toward the direction of the door.

My fists pound and pound until they scream in pain. My throat is raw from my terror-filled shrieks. I have no tears left to stream down my face.

"Please let me out! Please! Please!"

CHAPTER 11
Emily
2 YEARS AGO

"Boo."

I jump and let out a yelp at the sound of Liam's voice inches from my ear. Spinning around, his face is gleaming with a wide grin.

Playfully, I slap his chest. "You scared me!" I scold.

His hand wraps around my wrist and he pulls me into him. I go willingly, and he cups the back of my head. His lips meet mine gently before he presses our foreheads together.

"I missed you," he whispers.

"I missed you too."

Liam was sent with Finn on an assignment and has been gone for the past two months. We've spent hours texting and talking on the phone, but nothing tops the feeling of being in his arms and having his lips pressed to mine.

"How were your photoshoots?" he asks, before plopping himself on my blanket in the garden.

This has become *our* place. Liam knows if he can't find me in the house, I'm here. He'll spend as much time as possible with me until he's pulled away for work.

My heart soars with each touch of his skin on mine and each wink he shoots my way.

We've had to hide our relationship from Declan and my father. He's still pushing me toward Ryan but since my father hasn't gone out and said it's for an arranged marriage, I've put little effort in talking to him.

Declan would murder Liam if he ever knew about us. His bloodlust is reaching scary levels, and I don't dare put Liam in his sights. It seems as though Declan spends more time in his cellar than anywhere else. He always looks crazed until after he's been down there.

"What are you doin'?" Liam asks, jutting his chin toward the journal in my lap.

I slam it shut and slide it under my lap.

"Nothing. Just writing."

His eyes fill with amusement, "writin', eh? Let me see."

When he goes to reach for the journal I quickly jump to my feet and run away from him.

Because of his height and my lack of it, he catches me within seconds. We fall to the ground and Liam twists to take the brunt of the force.

"You can't see what I'm writing," I giggle when he tries to sneak the notebook out of my hand.

"And why not?"

"Because it's my journal. It's private."

His eyes soften, "Okay."

He cups the back of my head when I move to kiss his lips. Our tongues move slowly against one another. I feel him hardening beneath me and it causes a moan to slip out of my mouth.

Before I can react, Liam flips us so I'm now lying on my back in the wildflowers and he's above me. His erection grinds against me and I whimper with need.

"Do you think you can be quiet so I can fuck you here in the garden, *Féileacán?*"

"Yes. Please, Liam." I roll my hips against him to try and apply pressure to my aching pussy.

My clit throbs and my pussy clenches with the heat of his hand sliding down my curves. I thank the heavens I decided to wear a white sundress today because I don't know if I could wait long enough to take my pants off.

He pushes the fabric of my dress up until my soaked panties are exposed. The feel of his fingers pressing against my aching pussy makes my hips buck.

"I love how wet you get for me, *Féileacán.*"

His fingers push my panties to the side and then he rams two of his fingers into me. Liam covers my mouth with his hand when I cry out.

"Shh, remember to be a good girl for me and stay quiet. We wouldn' want your da or Declan to find us, would we?"

I shake my head and he removes his hand.

"Good. Now ride my hand."

My hips roll and Liam continues to pump into me. The wet sounds of my pussy fill the air and it's nearly impossible to hold in my moans.

The front of my dress is pulled down and Liam latches onto my breast. His tongue flicks my hardened nipple in between nips and sucks. My hips roll faster, and he finger-fucks me harder and harder until I explode.

He covers my mouth with his and swallows my cries of ecstasy.

After I've come down from my high, Liam grips the fabric of my panties and pulls. It digs into my hip until the material gives away and rips. Liam tosses it aside.

His belt jingles as he works to free himself from his pants. His cock weeps precum and he roughly strokes himself while watching me with hooded eyes.

"Spread your legs for me, Em. Show me my pussy."

My knees fall to the side, and I shiver from the sensation of the breeze caressing my soaked slit.

"Fu*ck*, Emily. I wish you could see how unbelievable your cunt is."

The skin of my cheeks feels hot as the blush spreads over them. The mouth of this man will never cease to make me feel this way.

The stretch of my pussy when he presses his cock into me is incredible. Every time we come together like this, it's perfect. He's perfect.

I bite down on his shoulder to stifle my moans as he thrusts in and out of me. He moans in my ear and my pussy becomes an ocean of arousal.

His fingers slide into my hair which is now littered with wildflowers. Wrapping his fingers around the strands, he pulls my head back.

"This pussy belongs to me, do you understand? No one, and I mean *no one* will ever get to feel how tight you are. No one will ever hear you moan the way I do. You belong to me, *Féileacán*."

I nod rapidly.

"Say it."

"I belong to you. Only you, Liam."

He groans and his lips crash against mine. His kiss is punishing. Claiming.

My orgasm explodes through me before I even register it coming.

"That's it, baby. That's it. You come so beautifully for me, don't you?"

He fucks me through my orgasm and then fills me with his cum with a grunt. His head is pressed against the curve of my neck as he fills me to the brim.

When he pulls away, I feel his cum slipping out of me. Liam watches in awe before he scoops it up and pushes it back in.

"My cum stays inside you."

I bite down on my bottom lip and nod.

We pull out the flowers tangled in my hair before making our way down the path to the house.

Nothing could ruin this moment for me.

CHAPTER 12
Liam
2 YEARS AGO

As we near the house, I fall a couple of steps behind Emily. Her eyes fill with sadness for a moment before she pushes the emotion aside. We push through the door and step into the foyer.

Some of the guards eye me as we walk toward the kitchen.

Trying to hide my feelings for Emily is becoming more difficult with each passing day. I'm lucky that Declan is so consumed with his torturing that he hasn't caught on to us seeing each other.

When Caetlin found me outside the party, she gave me a knowing look before making me follow her to Emily's room. I wasn't expecting her to push us toward each other, but she said she knew I was meant for Emily just by looking at me.

I'm not sure what that means but I believe it. Emily is mine.

Entering the kitchen, we're greeted by Rhys and Declan sitting at the counter while Niall prepares food for them.

Declan eyes me for a second before his gaze flicks to Emily. She averts her eyes and moves toward the refrigerator. Rhys peers over Declan's shoulder and shakes his head at me in disapproval.

Shite.

"I just came to see if either of you needed anythin'." I shove my hands into my pockets and maintain a relaxed pose despite the crackling of anxiety coursing through me.

"How thoughtful of you," Rhys says with a sarcastic tone.

"Fuck off," Declan says with a flick of his wrist.

I force myself to avoid looking at Emily before leaving the kitchen.

"Feckin' eejit." One of the guards says with a shake of his head.

Fucking Emily outside was clearly a bad fecking idea. I shouldn't have let lust cloud my thoughts. There's no telling who all knows now.

I stand with my gun raised at the target in the privately owned shooting range. Once the center of the target is in my crosshairs, I unload the magazine.

My position doesn't falter in any way from the gun's recoil. I've long since mastered the art of firearms.

I never miss.

Moving in quick, trained movements, I reload the gun and unload the magazine into another target and then another and another.

The gun is hot by the time I finish firing. It lands with a thud when I set it on the table in front of me.

Slow clapping to my left pulls my attention from reloading another weapon.

"Excellent form," Rhys says with a smirk.

"What do you want?" I ask.

"Just seeing if my guess is correct." He steps toward me, and I raise a brow.

"You're fucking Emily, aren't you?"

I glare at him, and he shakes his head, letting out a huff.

"You either got some balls on you, or you're fecking stupid."

Shoving the magazine into the new pistol, I ignore Rhys and get into position. My heart pounds in my ears from how fast my blood is coursing through my veins.

Taking a deep breath, I release it slowly and press on the trigger. The bullet goes flying with a loud *bang!* And hits the target directly in the center.

Like I said. I never miss.

Rhys steps up to my left and takes the gun from me.

I let out an annoyed growl and spin to face him.

"Piss off."

"You're treading very dangerous waters, my friend." He levels me with his deep green eyes.

"I haven't the slight clue what you're talkin' 'bout."

"Don't bullshit me, Liam."

I swing my arms outward in annoyance. "What do you want from me?"

"Stop whatever you're doing with Emily before Declan or Conor finds out."

"No."

Rhys has me by a good three inches, so I raise my chin slightly to meet his eyes when he steps close enough for our noses to nearly touch.

"You're going to get yourself killed."

Anger flows freely through my body and I clench and unclench my fists.

His eyes bounce between mine and I watch as the realization hits him.

"You love her." He says.

"Aye." I nod.

He shakes his head, releasing a disappointed sigh, before stepping back.

"You're fucked. Conor will never accept it. She's set to marry Ryan Monroe."

My heart collapses the moment the words leave his mouth. "What did you say?"

His eyes fill with sympathy. "Conor is going to announce her engagement to Ryan Monroe in one month. Why do you think he's been having her spend so much time with him?"

I knew we were on borrowed time, but I didn't realize it would come to an end so soon. We've only just started.

She's mine.

My teeth threaten to crack from how hard I clench my jaw. Every muscle in my body is pulled taut.

"This marriage will allow Conor to launder his money through the Monroe Banks without catching the attention of the Feds. It's happening whether you want it to or not."

I rake my hand through my hair and then down my face. Turning away from Rhys, I tip my head back and let out a sigh.

I need to pull away now if she's going to accept the marriage. She's going to fight and if Conor learns it's because of me, he'll kill me, and I can't have Emily feel responsible for that.

My chin falls to my chest, and I shake my head slowly. Rhys comes up behind me and sets a hand on my shoulder. He gives it a gentle but firm squeeze.

No. She's mine.

"No," I say firmly, shrugging him off.

"What do you mean no?" Rhys asks.

Spinning around, I meet his confused face with determination.

"She's mine. I'm not lettin' her go."

He snorts and looks at me like I'm an absolute moron. "Then I guess be ready for Declan to skin you or Conor to shoot you between the eyes."

I don't give him the satisfaction of a reaction out of me. Instead, I push past him and head to Conor's study.

It's about time I lay my claim on Emily. Consequences be damned.

CHAPTER 13
Emily
RUSSIA

The coppery taste of blood coats the inside of my mouth and throat. Every cell in my body screams in agony with each movement I try to make. My brain feels like it's repeatedly throwing itself against the inside of my skull.

I've been fighting as much as I can against Nikolai and his beatings are becoming more violent. I've spent more time in The Hole than I have anywhere else. The only times I'm allowed out are to shower and when Nikolai wants me for his pleasure.

The demon that lurks, follows me everywhere now. It always hovers in the corner of every room. Watching me. Taunting me.

The demons that plagued me in the past hold no comparison to the cruelty this demon provides. It's no longer faceless or shadowy.

Its angular face matches my own but where mine is from lack of nutrients, its face is sinister. Evil. Its voice is one that brings your nightmares to reality and it's impossible to block out. It's impossible to ignore the terror it forces into my body.

The never-ending Hell of this place is something no living being should ever succumb to.

My scratching has worsened. Not to mention my appetite. My stomach is in a constant state of hunger that I've become accustomed to. Sometimes, I don't even notice it anymore.

The scrapes of fabric that make up the sad excuse for a dress they provided when I arrived, now sit on my body like a drape. I'm deathly.

But still, I hope. I still trust that the ghosts who promise salvation are not being deceitful.

I idly trace my forefinger along the cracks of the concrete wall I lean against. I've traced over markings that I can unfortunately tell are tally marks. I've counted them – there are one-hundred and fifteen.

Whoever made those markings spent either the number of days spent in here, or that is the total number of times they've been locked in. Either way, it's horrific to think about.

The scrapped concrete digs into the skin of my fingers as I continue to trace the lines.

How many women have been here before me?

How many never left?

That thought causes me to sit straighter and more on edge. Despite not being able to see inches in front of me, I still scan the dark space.

Anxiety simmers below the surface at the thought of seeing the faces of those who were trapped here in the past.

I remain unmoving as I wait for any indication that those ghosts are going to taunt me.

When nothing happens, my shoulders lower – only slightly. I'm still nervous that they will make themselves known when I least expect it.

I lean my head against the wall, feeling the cold of the stone press against my brow. My eyes flutter closed, and I begin humming a lullaby my ma would sing to me during the nights when sleep evaded me.

I can feel the soft caress of her voice flow gently over my skin. Her light floral scent begins filling my nose and I drift off to sleep.

Raising my cupped hands, I blow as much warm air as I can into them to warm my frigid skin. The tips of my fingers are beginning to lose feeling and they have begun to turn a pale blue from lack of circulation. The temperature outside plummeted with the impending winter and so did the temperature in The Hole.

I wrap the rough fabric of the dirty blanket around my legs and tuck the ends over my feet. My teeth have been chattering uncontrollably and my jaw is beginning to suffer because of it.

I'm not sure how long I've been down here. I'm not even sure what time of day it is.

"*Féileacán.*"

The whisper is so faint, I nearly miss it.

"Liam?" I whisper in the darkness.

"Stay alive, *Féileacán.*"

My cracked lip quivers slightly and I swallow the lump that has lodged itself in my throat.

"Stay alive."

I don't speak. I can't.

I'm fighting to stay alive. To hold on. I've been beaten because of my fight.

At what point does it stop being worth it?

Am I even worth it?

I can make out a soft glow just in front of me. Its shape is tall – like Liam – my heart starts to speed up. Slowly, I push the blanket away from me and use my shaky limbs to prop myself up on my knees.

The hard stone digs into my knees and I wince, buckling slightly.

The figure steps closer and lowers itself to my level. I let out a choked sob Liam's face appears. I bring my hand up and try to touch him, only for my hand to fall as it passes through his ghost.

71

Tears stream down my face at yet another reminder that he's not real, that I've truly lost myself in my mind and my hallucinations are altering my reality.

His hazel eyes watch me for a moment before he slowly begins to fade.

"No! Pl — Please don't leave. Please... don't leave me here alone." I cry and I try to grasp onto anything to ground his spirit.

"I'm coming, *Féileacán.*"

And then his ghost evaporates into nothing.

I swear the crack of my soul is audible. Lifting my hand, I rub my frail chest to try and relieve the pain of my heart.

It doesn't help. This pain is too tangible. Too deep-rooted within my body.

"Please... Come back." I whisper.

My eyes flutter as the tears continue to fall freely.

CHAPTER 14
Emily
2 YEARS AGO

I stand facing my father in his study with Declan and Rhys flanking me. Their faces are emotionless but the energy in the room has me on edge.

"We will be announcing your engagement to Ryan in one month."

Every inch of my body freezes, my heart falls, and the air in my lungs instantly disappears.

No. No!

"What?"

"You'll be moving to the city penthouse in anticipation of the engagement."

"Why?"

My father lets out an exasperated sigh as he walks to the wet bar and pours himself a glass of whiskey. Looking into the glass, he swirls the amber liquid slowly without speaking.

Bringing the glass to his lips, he tips the glass back and swallows the whiskey in one swig.

"You knew this was coming, *mo stór*. This marriage will immensely benefit this organization. Ryan is a good man. He will treat you well."

My eyes burn and my vision begins to blur.

My father's face softens when he sees my tear-rimmed eyes. Setting the glass atop his desk, he strides over to me and pulls me into his arms.

His large hand cups the back of my head for a moment as he gives me a tight squeeze.

Pulling back, he cups my shoulders and offers me a small smile.

"Everything will work out as it is supposed to. You will have a good life with Ryan. He comes from a good family."

I don't want Ryan. I want Liam.

The words almost spill from my lips, but I swallow them down. I need to see Liam. I need to talk to him about this. We need to find a way to fight for us.

"Go pack your things. You'll be moving to the penthouse today."

My blood drains from my face and I step out of his embrace.

"Today?! I don't want to go anywhere, Da."

His face steels. My Da is not standing in front of me anymore. This is Conor Moore – Leader of the Irish Mafia.

"This is not up for discussion. Go pack your things."

He dismisses me by turning his back and walking to the other side of his desk. His face remains stoic when he sits in his seat.

When I don't make a move toward the door, he raises his brow in challenge, daring me to defy him.

I shake my head in disappointment and my face morphs with pain. When I spin on my heels, Declan's eyes reflect sympathy. I'm not sure what is worse: the stone face of my father, or the face Declan has aimed at me.

The first tear slips from my eyes and rolls down my cheek. Without another word, I leave the study.

"You need to talk to him, ma! He's sending me away. I don't want to go. I don't want to marry Ryan." I sob into my phone. My mother listens silently on the other side.

"I've tried convincing him, *mo stór*. He will not budge on this."

I pace back and forth and run my fingers through my long strands.

"Have you spoken to Liam? Have you told your father about him?"

I sigh into the phone. "No and no."

"Emily, you need to speak to both of them. Liam will need to decide if he's going to follow orders or stake his claim. Your father needs to know that your heart belongs to another."

"I've sent Liam a message and told him I needed to speak with him. And Da won't listen. He simply tells me that Ryan is a good man and will take care of me."

I swipe at the tears that stream down my face.

"Oh *aingeal*, stand up to him. Put your foot down and tell him that you will not marry. Demand his attention. Make him listen."

"I'm not like you, ma. I can't just walk into a room and command men. I don't know how to without feeling like I'm going to throw up everywhere." I swing my free arm out in slight annoyance.

"Unless you stand up to your father about this, he will not yield." Her voice is stern.

A soft knock interrupts my response.

"I need to call you back." I hang up before she has a chance to answer.

Quickly, I clear my cheeks of the tears that have stained them and walk to the door.

Liam steps inside my room when I open it. I throw myself into his arms and begin to sob.

"What's goin' on?" He asks, his voice full of concern.

"My da is announcing my engagement to Ryan in a month and he's sending me to live in the penthouse."

His face doesn't show any hint of surprise and I pull away from him.

"You knew?" I whisper.

His eyes bounce between mine for a moment and then he nods.

"You knew and you didn't do anything? You didn't tell me? Did you even fight for me?"

He steps closer and I step back.

"I just found out, Em. I was on my way to speak to your da when I got your message."

He takes another step, and this time, I don't pull away. His arms wrap around me, and my cheek presses against his tee.

"What are you going to do?" I ask.

He pulls back and cups my face. His callused thumbs brush against my skin.

"I'm stakin' my claim." He says before his lips capture mine.

CHAPTER 15
Liam

2 YEARS AGO

"Come in." Conor's muffled voice sounds from the other side of his study's door. Turning the knob, I push it open and step inside.

Conor sits behind his desk with a cigar in his mouth. His blue eyes assess me from head to toe.

"I wondered when you'd muster up the balls to speak to me."

"Sir?"

His smile is anything but friendly. He takes a long drag of his cigar before blowing the smoke upward. His eyes never straying from mine.

"I know about you and Emily." His face darkens.

"Sir, I love her." I raise my chin and straighten my spine.

He slams his hand against the surface of his desk when he stands.

"You were both told that you cannot be together and yet, you deliberately disobeyed me." He growls.

He straightens his grey suit jacket and then sits back down. Leaning against the back of the chair, a smile plays on his lips.

Pulling another drag from his cigar, he crosses an ankle across the opposite knee.

"I'll admit, you both did a fine job keeping what you had a secret. But of course, you, being a stupid fuck, had to go and defile her in the garden. Did you truly think that would go unnoticed?"

I fecking knew that would come back to bite me in the arse.

I clench and unclench my fists on my sides. Though I'm feeling nauseated, I maintain eye contact with him.

"I love Emily and I'm not goin' to let you take her from me."

Untamed rage fills his face, and he circles the desk. He storms over to me. Before I have a chance to react, he lands a swift and strong punch to my gut.

With a grunt, I grip my stomach and hunch over.

The hard, cold metal of his pistol is pressed against the back of my head, and he lowers his mouth to my ear.

"Listen and listen well *fíochmhar*, you work for me. When I tell you to jump, you don't ask me how high, you jump. You don't question me or defy me. I fucking own you." He seethes.

Blood fills my mouth from how hard I bite down on my tongue. The gun is pressed harder into my head, and I grunt.

"This marriage is happening whether you want it to or not. I won't hesitate to order Declan to skin you alive if you continue this. You're a good shot, Liam but your value is easily replaceable."

I know Conor loves his daughter. I know how gentle he is with her, but I also know he does not make idle threats. He will teach Emily a lesson through me. He'll break her... because of me.

"Don't think that I won't make an example out of you because of Emily. Don't mistake my love for her as me being soft. I *will* kill you and make her watch if I have to." His spit lands on the side of my face with each word he growls. "Have I made myself clear?"

I swallow tightly and then nod. He pushes the gun harder into my head before stepping away. I stand upright with my hands at my sides.

"Emily is moving to the penthouse – but I'm sure she's already told you – you are not to go there under *any* circumstances." He levels me with a glare. "You are going to break her heart. Make her hate you. I don't give a shit. She is going to marry Ryan and you are going to make sure she has no lingering feelings for you."

My chest feels like it's caving in on itself.

How can I do that when she means everything to me?

"And if she refuses?"

"She doesn't have a choice."

I stare at Conor. Truly stare at him. He would really force his daughter to marry someone for power? He was always known as the one to put his family above all else.

But this? Why this?

"You're filth. Nothing but a replaceable pawn in my family's empire. Even if Ryan wasn't in the picture, you are not worthy of my daughter."

There it is.

He'd rather hurt Emily than allow me to be with her.

"The only reason I haven't already killed you is *because* of Emily. But mark my words, Liam. You disobey me again and I will make sure your death is slow and painful."

I stare at the wall, refusing to meet his eyes. His glare burns into me.

My body vibrates with anger, resentment, and grief. What I have is being ripped away from me and I can't do anything about it.

"Get the fuck out." He growls.

I walk solemnly toward the garden. Conor's words replay in my mind in a continuous loop. As much as I'd like to deny it, it's true. I'm replaceable in this world.

There will always be another grunt who can do his dirty work. There will always be someone who can shoot a gun with accuracy such as mine. If I die, someone new will take my place as if I wasn't even in it to begin with.

Emily deserves more than I can give her.

The truth is a slap to the face. Emily does deserve more than I can give her. We've both known that. We've just been running from the inevitable.

Ryan is a wealthy man who is going to run an empire of his own. He can provide her with the life she desires. I can't.

Emily sits atop a white throw blanket in the center of her wildflowers. She's writing in her journal with pursed lips and lowered brows. Strands of her red hair, brush over her cheeks with the soft breeze.

Sadness fills my heart.

I have to do this. I have to let her go.

The weight on my chest increases with each step I take.

Consequences be damned? Fecking Liar.

This is different. I can't stake my claim knowing she can and will have a better future with someone else. I can't allow my insignificance to burden her.

Emily spins around to face me when she hears the soft thump of my boots on the grass.

She smiles and her eyes are warm. It guts me.

Shutting her journal, she sets it aside and rises to her feet. I stop just a few feet away and her brows pull inward.

"Are you okay?" She asks, flicking her eyes from me, the space between us, and back.

"We need to talk." I swallow the lump forming.

What a fucking cliché.

When she takes a step toward me, I take one back. Confusion covers her face, followed by wariness.

"What's going on, Liam? Did you speak with my dad?"

"What has been going on between us is over." I try my damned hardest to keep my voice level but it's fucking hard.

She jerks her head back. "What?"

"We're over, Emily."

Her head starts to slowly shake, and sadness fills her eyes.

"What happened with my dad, Liam?" her voice cracks.

"We both knew we were on borrowed time, Em. You're going to be married soon. This needs to stop."

"What... What happened to 'staking my claim'? What happened to that?"

Make her hate you.

"I didn't mean it. You're not mine to claim."

She flinches like I've struck her and my heart breaks. It's hard to fucking breathe.

"You don't mean that. You can't mean that." She whimpers, the tears gathering in her eyes before falling down her freckled cheeks.

I turn my gaze toward the wildflowers to avoid watching her heartbreak. I watch as a butterfly lands on a bright yellow flower. Its wings are a light orange that darkens on the outer edges. It sways with the breeze for a moment before flying off.

"Emily..." I return my eyes to hers. She watches me with pained blue eyes.

The words are trapped in my throat and refuse to come out.

She deserves more. She will get more with someone else.

"We both knew this relationship wasn't goin' to lead to a happy endin'. Conor refused to let us be together from day one. Let's just accept it for what it is and move on."

Anger flares in her eyes and she balls her hands into tight fists.

"You're a coward. You're not even going to fight for us? What was the point of being with me in the first place?" she says through gritted teeth.

"There is no reason to fight for somethin' that isn't even worth it."

Each word tastes like acid. None of this is true. Emily is worth everything, which is exactly why I need to let her go. She deserves the world, and I can't give it to her.

"Not worth it?! Are you serious, Liam?" She shouts, her voice echoing.

Closing my eyes, I take a deep breath in through my nose and exhale through my mouth. The world feels like it's spinning from the force of my blood pumping.

Make her hate you.

"I don't want you, Emily. You were just a way to pass the time." My voice is void of emotion.

She presses a palm to her chest as if she's in physical pain, and I struggle to remain unmoving. Every fiber in my being screams for me to comfort her and beg for forgiveness.

"Liam... I – please..." she stutters.

I gently shake my head, peering at her through pleading eyes to understand that this is for the best.

"Don't make this harder than it needs to be, Emily."

"Whatever my dad told you, whatever he threatened, fight it. Fight for *me*. Pl – please, Liam. Fight for us." She sobs, her face streaked with her makeup.

"No." My teeth are seconds from shattering as I clench my jaw. I open and close my fists.

"Why are you doing this?!" she shrieks. "Why?!"

"Emily... Stop. This thing between us is over. Accept it. Move on. Marry Ryan. I. Don't. Want. You."

With those parting words, I walk away from the best thing to ever happen to me.

CHAPTER 16
Emily
2 YEARS AGO

Is this what dying feels like? I can't breathe. I can't think. My heart is falling to pieces with each step Liam takes away from me.

Why is he doing this to me? To us?

"Liam!" I scream.

His steps don't falter.

Once he's out of sight, I fall to my knees. My chest physically hurts from the pain of my heart, and I rub my hand against it.

He didn't fight. He didn't even try.

What did my father say to him that made him give up on me so easily?

Did I really mean so little to him?

The sky darkens as the clouds begin blocking the sun, and the wind picks up. My hair whips around in swirls of red. The skin around my eyes burns from the ongoing river of tears that fall.

The temperature drastically decreases but is still not as icy as the blood flowing through my veins.

My fingers brush against the butterfly locket that Liam gave me, and I move my hand to wrap my fingers around it. The metal burns my skin at the reminder that this is reality. Liam threw us away.

"I. Don't. Want. You."

His words sear my ears like hot coals. Burning away the sweet nothings he used to whisper to me.

I turn toward my journal sitting on the throw blanket. The letter I was writing mocks me from the closed leather that binds the pages. He'll never know the love I have for him. He'll never read the words I poured my soul into. He didn't give me a chance to even tell him what he means to me.

My stomach churns, the contents quickly climbing up my throat. I run to the nearest tree and heave everything I've eaten today onto its roots.

I stand straight and wipe my mouth with the back of my hand and release a ragged breath to slow my galloping heart.

Fine... If he can throw everything away like it was nothing, then I guess moving on and moving to the penthouse is my only option.

Even if the pain is unbearable.

Steeling my back, I walk over and pack up my things before making my way back to the mansion.

My bags are loaded into the trunk of Declan's SUV. He watches me with pity-filled eyes and it's an effort to ignore him.

It didn't take me long to pack what I needed. The quicker I leave this place, the quicker I can get away from Liam.

"Em, everything will be okay." Declan steps over to me and pulls me into his arms.

My eyes burn as I hold back my emotions. I've cried so much in the last few hours; I don't know how I still have tears to cry.

Declan is oblivious to the reason behind my heartbreak. I'm not vindictive enough to tell him about Liam. To confide in my big brother that the love of my life doesn't love me back.

He'll kill him before I even finish the sentence.

Declan kisses my temple lightly then he pulls away.

"Come on, the traffic is going to be shit right now." He reaches for the passenger door and opens it for me.

I turn toward the mansion doors in time to see Liam and Rhys walking out. He doesn't spare me a glance as he hops into the SUV, and they speed away.

Another fissure in my heart shatters.

Thunder rumbles in the dark cloud-filled sky and then it begins to downpour. Within seconds, my hair is drenched and sticking to the sides of my face and my neck.

"Em?"

I turn back to Declan who raises a brow and gestures his chin toward the opened door.

Soundlessly, I slide into the leather seat and buckle my seatbelt.

Declan closes the door and then walks around the front of the SUV to the driver's side. Buckling himself in, he shifts the car into drive, and we coast down the driveway.

When he turns his head to peer at me, I turn to stare out of the window. The trees that line the gravel road are a green blur as my vision becomes unfocused.

"Is marrying Ryan really going to be that bad? Has he hurt you?" He grits that last question.

I shake my head but don't say a word.

"Talk to me, Em. You're being too quiet."

85

I've been able to confide in Declan as much as a younger sister can to her older brother. But I can't talk to him about this. I can't hide the pain that I have within me.

"I'm fine." I say with little emotion in my voice.

I hear him release a sigh and then a hand is wrapped around mine. I peer down at it, studying the skeleton fingers he has tattooed over his.

Liam has a rose tattooed over his hand. I loved to trace the lines with the tips of my fingers when we'd lay in the wildflowers. When I asked him why he got it, he shrugged and said because he wanted to.

All of Declan's tattoos have some sort of meaning. From the owl he has across his throat, to the stupid worm he has on his knee. He was sixteen when he and Rhys bought a tattoo gun and tattooed each other.

I feel the tears start to gather in my eyes and quickly blink them away. All of my recent happy memories include Liam in some way.

How do I let that go?

"I'm fine, Dec. Really. Ryan is... Ryan is great." I plaster a fake smile on my way.

Declan gives me a pointed look that tells me he knows I'm hiding something. But he doesn't push – and for that I'm thankful.

With a gentle squeeze, he releases my hand and continues driving toward the penthouse.

The elevator *pings* and the doors open to the vast entrance of the penthouse. The contrast between charcoal and white fills me with nostalgia. When Declan bought this place a couple of years back, I made him remodel everything and threatened to castrate him if he made it a typical-looking bachelor pad.

I'm glad to see he kept it that way.

I haven't been to the penthouse in at least a year. I had no reason to. I also had no desire to see or hear Declan with his next fuck.

But I guess now, I won't have a choice.

My phone chimes with an incoming text, and I pull it from my back pocket.

Ryan Monroe

> Would you like to have dinner with me tonight?

Ugh.

"I'm having Jackie over tonight."

I don't bother hiding the disgust that mars my face. Jackie isn't *bad*, per se, but she's an airhead who walks around like she owns the place. She's also a whore.

Okay, that's mean. Declan is also a whore, and I don't really judge him for it.

I quickly reply that I'd love to, even though I don't. I don't want to be here with Jackie. She'll bother me about looking like shit the whole time.

"I'm going to go out to dinner with Ryan. I'm going to get ready now."

He nods. "Alright, I'll see you later then."

I nod and then make my way down to the guest room.

My bags sit on my bed when I step inside my room. The plush carpet quiets my steps the further I walk inside.

Unzipping the first bag, I pull out a white pantsuit and lay it on the mattress.

I need to wash off this depressing day.

Setting out the rest of my outfit, I head to the ensuite to shower.

CHAPTER 17
Liam
2 YEARS AGO

Bang! Bang! Bang!

The recoil reverberates through my arm, but my stance remains solid. Each bullet meets the target with trained precision.

The Russians' methods of attack are becoming more creative. But we're more violent. More calculated. We know exactly where to hit them and when.

I've killed dozens of those slimy fucks since I walked away from Emily. The distraction is needed but it barely tames the ache in my chest.

She hasn't returned to the estate since she left.

Not once.

Last night, I overheard Declan mention that she's been spending more time with Ryan. I know I pushed her toward it, but it doesn't lessen the hurt.

Growing up around the Irish Mafia, I've always found a sort of peace with pouring my frustration into shooting a gun. The control and concentration cause my mind to blank, and I focus solely on hitting my target.

But now? Nothing but Emily brings me peace.

And I let her go.

It eats away at my heart that she is going to build a life with someone who isn't me.

Bang!

The head of the target explodes into hundreds of broken pieces. Changing my stance, I hit the one next to it. Then the next. And the next.

Tonight, Conor is having a banquet to announce her engagement to Ryan. I've tried finding an assignment to avoid being present, but I'm being forced to watch because Conor knows what Emily means to me.

Rhys shakes his head at me in disappointment any chance he can, and it pisses me the fuck off. Fuck him. Fuck Conor.

I drop the pistol and move to a semi-automatic rifle. I fire until the magazine is empty, and the barrel is hot.

"Liam."

Turning my head, I peer over my shoulder at the sound of Declan's voice. He nods his head for me to follow.

I set the rifle down and then stride to his side.

"What's up?" I ask as we continue down the path toward the guardhouse.

"Looks like you need something to get your anger out. We're training."

I open my mouth to deny his assumption but quickly shut it when he side-eyes me.

The guardhouse is a large apartment building on the far end of the property. It houses any of the guards that don't have houses or apartments of their own.

Me included.

The building has a massive sparring gym on the lowest level that is used for hand-to-hand combat training.

As we enter the space, my senses are invaded by the smell of sweat, rubber mats, and blood. The sounds of the men grunting and punches landing on bare skin fill my ears.

"Let's head to the mat on the far end." Declan slaps a hand against my back and then strides to the mat he indicated. I follow close behind.

Once we've reached the end of the mat, Declan and I tug off our shirts and boots. As we walk to the center, some of the other men take notice and make their way over.

Declan bounces on the balls of his feet with his fists up – protecting his face.

"Alright, Liam, let's see what you got." He says in a mocking tone.

I twist my neck from side to side, roll my shoulders, and take my fighting stance. My fists are loose when I raise them to just below my nose.

I meet Declan's eyes for a second before throwing a right hook. He dodges it and jabs me in the ribcage. I grunt from the force and jump back.

Dropping down, I swiftly sweep his legs from under him.

The ground shakes from how hard he hits the mat. Moving quickly, I straddle him and slam my fist into his face with enough force to cause his head to bounce off the mat.

He gives me a wide bloody-toothed grin before slamming his head against my nose. I feel the crunch and fall back.

"Feck!"

"Shouldn't have left yourself open like that." He cackles.

I growl and spit out the blood that now flows down my face.

He spits the blood from his mouth and then we collide once again.

We continue to grapple on the floor – fists and elbows meeting flesh – before Declan manages to pull me into a triangle chokehold. One thigh presses down on the side of my neck while the opposite cages my other arm and shoulder across his pelvis and stomach. His hold tightens, squeezing me like a vice. I grit my teeth from the pressure building in my skull due to the circulation being lost.

"Get yourself out of it, Liam." Declan orders.

My eyes feel seconds from popping out of their sockets.

Using my trapped arm, I drape it over his hips, lock my hands together, and press down. In rapid succession, his hold loosens, I bring my knee upward, and ram it into his side.

When he lets go, I push away. The blood rushes to my head, and my vision is momentarily blurred.

"Good." Declan praises through panted breaths.

He stands and I remain seated on the mat. My nose is still throbbing from his head crashing into it. Sweat streams down my chest and back.

Someone tosses each of us a rag, followed by a water bottle, and we wipe the blood from our faces.

"You good?" Declan asks with a raised brow, gulping water.

"I'm grand," I say between panted breaths.

He gestures toward my face with a nod. "Go get your nose checked out by Dr. Robbins."

I nod and he reaches out a hand to help me up.

We clap each other on the back before walking out of the gym.

CHAPTER 18
Emily
2 YEARS AGO

The closer we drive to the venue where my father is hosting the banquet, the harder it is to breathe.

It's been a month since I moved to the penthouse. A month since Liam walked away from us. A month of shoving my feelings down so I could tolerate Ryan's presence.

And each day has been just as hard as the last.

Tonight, my engagement will be announced to the underground world. I'm hoping with everything in me that Liam won't be here. I won't be able to handle seeing his face while knowing I'm to marry someone else.

"I. Don't. Want. You"

His words echo in the back of my mind. Cutting deeper into me as if he'd just said them.

I need to remind myself that he walked away. That *he* left *me*. He ripped my heart out and threw it in the dirt without hesitation. Without any sign of regret.

I meant nothing to him.

Ryan sits next to me with his face buried in his phone — as usual. Aside from talking about himself nonstop, he's *pleasant* to be around.

Ugh.

I don't want to be with someone *pleasant*. I want to be with someone who lights a fire within me that is so bright, you can see it from outer space.

I want someone who needs me as much as I need them. Someone who takes the very breath from my lungs and breathes it back in.

Only that will never happen. Not for me.

I watch the city lights fly past my darkened window. My fingers wring anxiously with each passing mile.

"Why are you so fidgety?" Ryan says, startling me.

I flatten my palms on my knees and look over to him.

"Oh, I'm just excited for tonight." My cheeks burn from how wide my fake smile is.

He studies my face — his completely emotionless - and then nods in satisfaction before turning his eyes to his phone again.

His lack of attention makes it much easier to hide how I'm truly feeling. I can play the pretty trophy on his arm if he wants me to. I can't play the lovesick woman my dad thinks I'm going to be.

I could work harder to establish some kind of deeper connection, but I don't want to. He also doesn't seem to have much of an interest now that the arrangement is official.

The driver turns onto the private road toward the venue and my heart gallops in my chest.

It's fine. Everything's going to be. I'm fine.

My hand instinctually reaches up to wrap around the necklace I haven't been able to take off.

I feel Ryan's eyes on me and when I turn toward him, his stare is on my hand around the locket. It lingers for an uncomfortably silent moment before he meets my gaze.

I offer him a tight smile and then let my hand fall to my lap. My skin feels clammy, and I struggle to keep my breaths calm.

He continues to watch me, wordlessly.

Ryan has never asked me about the necklace, but he knows it's different than the one I used to wear.

The car comes to a stop and Ryan's door is opened by a young man in a black suit. Ryan clears his throat and then slides out. He holds his palm out for me to take and I do.

His skin lacks the rough texture of calluses that Liam has and another wave of sadness washes over me. I force the emotions down and smile up at Ryan as I slide out of the car.

He places a kiss on my temple and then positions his hand on the small of my back. Together, we stride inside the venue.

The ballroom is beautifully decorated with an array of white, gold, and black. A large crystal chandelier hangs in the center of the ceiling, giving the entire space a higher level of elegance. The women are dressed in floor-length gowns made of expensive fabrics. The men wear tailored black suits that either emphasize their muscular builds or large mid-sections. The staff wear white suits and carry silver trays of hors d'oeuvre or champagne.

Soft jazz music plays in the background amidst the quiet conversations and the clinking of glasses.

I discreetly scan the area for any sign of Liam and breathe a sigh of relief when I don't see him.

A waiter walks up to us, and Ryan takes two glasses of champagne – offering me one.

"Thank you," I say quietly with a dip of my chin. I sip on my drink; the crispness of the bubbles and the slight fruitiness help to distract my mind.

"Is everything okay?" Ryan asks, bringing the edge of his glass to his lips.

I look up into his eyes, which are filled with hesitant curiosity.

"Of course, why wouldn't it be?" I say with a slight raise of my brow.

He tips his head slightly and narrows his eyes.

"You've been acting like you're seconds from bolting as soon as we got in the car."

I place my hand on his biceps and give it a small squeeze.

"Everything is fine. I'm just excited about announcing our engagement." I'm unsure how my voice remains unwavering, but I thank God it does.

He brings his hand to cup my cheek, bringing his face inches from mine.

"Good. Tonight is going to be perfect."

His lips touch mine and I force my body to relax into his touch. We haven't slept together and I'm dreading the day he expects that of me. At some point, I will need to accept that my body doesn't belong to Liam anymore.

His lips are firm yet soft, but the kiss doesn't make my heart race. It doesn't make my head swim in a cloud of lust. My stomach doesn't flutter like it does when someone else's lips are on mine.

He let you go.

My spine tingles with awareness and I pull away from Ryan so quickly, I stumble back. He catches me by my arm and furrows his brows.

My head whips to the right and my eyes clash with Liam's. His hazel eyes swim with rage before he schools his features. Bruises are splotched over just about every inch of his beautiful face. My heart threatens to burst out of my chest and run to him.

Oh God. He saw me kissing Ryan.

You owe him nothing. He pushed you to Ryan.

My mind and heart fight for control. Logically, I know kissing Ryan isn't wrong. He's supposed to be my husband. But emotionally, letting anyone but Liam touch me feels like a betrayal.

Liam snaps his gaze away from mine and strides to the open bar. My chest constricts and I swallow tightly.

"*Mo stór!* You're here." My father's voice cuts through the crowd. Clearing my throat, I straighten my dress and lean into Ryan's side.

He wraps his arm around me and pulls me in closer.

A huge smile spreads over my da's face when he sees us standing so close.

"Hi, Daid," I say quietly, and he pulls me into his arms. When he pulls away, he nods to Ryan.

"Evening, Ryan."

"Evening Conor," Ryan reaches out a hand which my father accepts. They shake firmly.

"Come. Come. Let's have a seat and eat before we make the announcement. Emily, your mother is here. She's at the table."

Shit.

It's been easy lying about how I'm feeling over the phone or text, but she's going to take one look at me and know I'm full of shit.

CHAPTER 19

Liam

2 YEARS AGO

The burn of the whiskey going down my throat does absolutely nothing to tame the rage that courses through me. Seeing Emily in Ryan's arms, seeing his lips on hers, instantly boiled my blood.

I wanted to stalk over to him and rip him limb from limb.

She's mine.

Only, she's not. And after tonight, there will never be a chance for that to change.

A hand grips my shoulder and I turn to see Rhys taking a seat on the stool next to me.

"You going to be a sulking bitch all night?" he holds a finger up, gesturing to the bartender.

"Piss off, Rhys." I shrug him off.

"Don't be pissed off at me for your own stupidity. I'm not the one who got involved with someone I shouldn't have." The bartender sets his glass of whiskey down and Rhys nods in thanks.

"I'm fine," I respond through gritted teeth. I toss the rest of my whiskey back and slam the glass onto the bar top.

"Obviously," Rhys snorts.

"What the fuck do you want me to say, Rhys? I let her go and now I have to accept it for what it is. She's not mine." I run my fingers through my hair.

Rhys leans forward and I turn to meet his gaze.

"Then quit sitting over here feeling sorry for yourself." he jabs a finger into my chest. "You were warned to stay away, and you didn't listen. You pursued her, knowing it wasn't going to go anywhere."

"I –."

"No." he cuts me off. "You knew Conor wouldn't accept the two of you and you still went for it. You were selfish and Emily got hurt in the process."

Anger laces his tone, and he jabs me again.

"You're damn lucky Conor didn't kill you and Declan still doesn't know about any of it. But get your shit together, Liam. Emily isn't a game."

"I know she's not." I seethe.

"Then cut the shit. If you let her see you like this, then she's going to hold on to something that can't happen. Let. Her. Go."

"I did let her go," I growl.

He glances to his left and then sits up straighter. He clears his throat and then flares his eyes slightly. I straighten my spine and peer over my shoulder.

Declan is sauntering toward us with Jackie on his arm. She's clutching onto him like he's going to disappear if she doesn't.

"Sup, Dec," Rhys says with a lift of his chin. "Jackie." He offers her a tight smile.

"Hello, Rhys." She smiles at him seductively. Her eyes flick to me and travel down my body, searching for a spot to sink her talons in.

"And you are?" she purrs.

I glance at Rhys who subtly rolls his eyes.

"Liam," I answer.

"I love your accent, it's very sexy."

"Uh..." I look to Declan who appears completely unfazed at her obvious flirting. "Thanks." I grimace.

Rhys chuckles and then stands. He tips his whiskey back and then sets the glass down.

"Come on, kid. Let's go sit down." He slaps me on my back and then walks through the crowd.

It's physically painful to avoid looking in Emily's direction. She sits at the table adjacent to mine and I'm excruciatingly aware of every movement she makes. I know she's more than aware of me because every time I shift, she stiffens.

I try my damned hardest to pay attention to the conversation at my own table, but I keep being distracted by every caress Ryan makes to Emily's skin. Every time he leans over and whispers in her ear. Each time she grasps onto his bicep and chuckles.

It's tearing me apart from the inside.

Caetlin has glanced in my direction a few times throughout dinner, but her expression is unreadable. I wish I knew what was running through her mind, especially since she is the one who had a hand in my and Emily's being together.

Conor makes sure to meet my eyes every so often and when he does, he'll glance at Emily and then smirk.

The bastard is a cruel motherfucker and I hate him for it. I hate that I can't have the one thing that I truly *need* in this life like I need air.

Conor and Caetlin stand and make their way to the front of the tables. Conor is handed a microphone. The feedback grates through my ears and the crowd quiets.

"Thank you all for coming tonight. I'm sure you're all wondering why Caetlin, and I requested your presence." He gestures toward Ryan who stands and reaches his hand out to Emily.

She peers over at me from the corner of her eye, and I avert my gaze. From my peripheral, I see her place her hand in his and stand. He places his hand on the small of her back and they walk toward her parents.

"Tonight, we're here to announce the union of The Moore and Monroe Families." He smiles widely and everyone around me claps.

I bite down on my tongue until the tangy taste of blood fills my mouth.

Emily looks uncomfortable standing next to Ryan, and I resist the urge to throw her over my shoulder and run out of here. Every cell in my body is screaming to tell Conor to fuck off and take her away.

You're replaceable. Nothing.

The gun tucked in my shoulder holster burns into my ribs. Calling for me to shoot Conor, Ryan, and even Declan. To show them that Emily is mine.

Ryan holds out his hand and Conor hands him the microphone. Holding Emily's hand in his, he faces the guests.

"The marriage between Emily and I will not only greatly benefit both our families, but also create new opportunities for all of those who work with us. Our union is a step into a new age for the underworld." He looks over to Emily who is watching him with a smile.

I know that smile. It's the fake one she plasters on her face to hide her emotions inside. The one she uses when she's about to burst into tears.

Feck.

I shift in my seat as the need to go up there grows.

Rhys kicks my foot and I whip my head in his direction. He flares his eyes in warning and then glances over at Declan who is watching his family.

"To Ryan and Emily." Conor's voice booms through the microphone once again. The crowd raises their glasses and repeats "To Ryan and Emily."

A loud gunshot echoes through the room, and I watch in horror as Conor's head is thrown backward. Blood splatters across Caetlin's face.

Bang!

Another shot sends Ryan to the ground like a damned tree.

Everything moves in slow motion. People scatter, tables are overturned, blood sprays, and shots continue to fly through the air.

Emily. I need to get to Emily.

I pull both of my guns from their holsters and shove my way through the chaos.

"Emily!" I shout over all the noise around me.

The room is a blur of colored gowns, tablecloths, and blood. So much fucking blood. Bodies drop like dominos but there is still no sign of Emily. Terror fills my veins with each second that I don't hear her reply.

I shoot a man in the chest who is climbing through a broken window and continue trudging through.

"Liam!" I hear her shriek and I feel her panic in my bones.

A massive guy comes at me like a freight train, but I quickly raise my weapon and shoot him between the eyes. His body crashes into the table directly in front of him, sending everything flying.

Declan is racing out of the room with his ma in his arms. Her frantic eyes scan the carnage. When they meet mine, they widen, and she points somewhere over my shoulder.

I spin around and spot Emily's red hair in the crowd. My mind can't navigate the panic and relief I feel from seeing her. I don't glance back to Caetlin or Declan before I take off in her direction.

"Emily!" I shout again, hoping she can make her way toward me. My body is jostled left and right by people colliding with me.

"Argh!" someone growls just before pain erupts on my cheek. I'm thrown to the ground from the sudden hit. One of my guns is kicked from my grip by a woman running.

I blink rapidly to clear my blurred vision and then look up. Another man with a buzzcut and a scar that cuts diagonally across his nose grabs onto the collar of my suit and hauls me up. He rears back and punches me on the other side of my face.

I grin at him and bring the gun I didn't lose to his abdomen. He pauses his next hit and looks down. Before he gets a chance to return his eyes to mine, I pull the trigger. I stumble slightly when his grip loosens but raise my gun and shoot the next bullet through his face.

His body doesn't meet the ground before I push toward Emily.

She comes into view and untamed rage coats every cell in my body. Her head whips to the left from the massive man slapping her face. She cries out in pain and falls to the ground.

"Hey!" I shout. My gun is already pointed at him and the moment his eyes meet mine, I shoot. The bullet flies through the air and lodges itself into his skull. His head is tossed back and his body collapses onto the ground with a loud *thud*.

I re-holster my gun and run to Emily. Crouching down, I slide one arm under her leg — the other under her arms — and lift her to my body.

"I've got you, *Féileacán.*" She clings to me, nails digging into my skin, and I run out of the building.

CHAPTER 20
Emily
RUSSIA

Scratch. Scratch. Scratch.

Blood trickles from the wound I've dug into my thigh like a broken faucet. And still, I scratch.

The voices in my head haven't stopped – not once – since I woke this morning. Ma. Declan. Liam. Da. Each of their voices has echoed on a continuous loop.

"Today is the day," they've taunted. *"Your pitiful existence is about to end."*

Every one of their taunts make it unbearably hard to not see some truth to them.

What if this really is the end of my life?

What if my suffering is finally going to be over?

Would I even care?

Today marks day ten of being in The Hole. The longest I've been placed here and if I hadn't gone insane before, I am now. Logic has no place here after I started seeing the faces and hearing the voices of women who have said they were also locked in this Hell.

Their cries of pain and suffering seep through the concrete walls and into my very soul. They are becoming part of me at this point.

Scratch. Scratch. Scratch.

My nailbeds scream in protest from the constant strain. I haven't been able to find anything I can use to cut into my skin to give them a rest. I've traced my palms over the walls repeatedly – hoping to find a large enough crack to pull a chunk from. It was no use.

Shuffling to my left causes every muscle in my body to tighten.

Nonono. Please, no.

Despite the darkness surrounding me, I watch as tendrils of black vines travel up the wall. They spread across the concrete, growing thicker and taller by the second.

I can't contain the tremors that force their way through my body. I clench my jaw until I fear my teeth will shatter. The vines continue to grow, drawing closer and closer. I'm already plastered against the wall, but I push against it as if it'll absorb my body and shield me from what's to come.

The cries of the women from the past slowly fill the air. The misery and sorrow that seeps into my soul from those sounds cause my chest to feel seconds from caving in.

So much wretched agony is harbored within these walls. Within the very foundation of this building. I'm sure the grounds are saturated with just as much suffering.

My heart is beating so rapidly, I don't know how I haven't had a heart attack yet. Despite constantly being haunted by these signs of past lives; my psyche goes into a panic every time.

I feel the sensation of my hair being moved and I jerk away.

It's not real. It's not real.

Something that sounds like metal scrapping on the concrete sounds from within the darkness; followed by the sound of a whimper.

"Please, help me," a woman's plea flows through my body, and goosebumps spread across my skin.

I slam my hands over my ears and close my eyes.

"You're not real. You're not real. You're not real," I mutter repeatedly. The air in the room is thick with desperation, hopelessness, and death. So much death.

I hear the muffled sounds of metal clanking and screams through the barrier I created with my hands.

The hairs on my arms stand on end as the sensation of eyes watching me coats my skin.

"Go away. You're not real," I whimper.

A shriek so loud, it shakes me to my core, breaks through my barrier and I choke down a sob.

Then... nothing.

All the sounds and feelings that have flooded my system cease all at once.

My mind is no longer my own and I don't know how much more of this torture I can handle.

I'm pushed into the communal showers after my twelfth day in The Hole. The dim lights of the room burn my retinas and it's hard to keep my eyes open. I can't decipher if the faces I see are from past or present.

The icy water pelts my skin. My teeth chatter violently, and I wrap my hands around myself.

"You get five minutes," the guard growls but his beady dark eyes still travel down my body in hunger, and I choke down the bile I feel climbing up my throat.

I lather myself with the small bar of soap and scrub my skin until I'm satisfied that I've taken off the first layer. There are a few young women in here with me. Their faces are shadowed in deep-rooted sadness and their eyes are red-rimmed and downcast.

The fissures in my heart widen every time I've seen the others. Their bodies are painted with bruises in different healing phases and are pale from lack of sunlight and malnutrition.

I lather the soap in my hair and the suds tangle my strands. Tipping my head back, the water cascades down my hair and washes the soap away. I run my fingers through it and feel the sharp pain of the roots being ripped from my scalp. The intertwined strands create a spider-like mass that falls to the floor.

I stare at the pile and my eyes burn from tears gathering and grief growing in my heart.

Feeling the loss of hair seems so pathetic considering the entire situation I'm in. How could I feel pain from the loss of something that will grow back? But the more I think about it, the more I realize it's more the loss of another piece of myself because of this place.

"Time's up," the guard grunts and we jump at the sudden sound of his voice.

He throws us old towels that are littered with holes and stains. The material scrapes against my skin with each pass. Once we're relatively dry, we're handed a *clean* set of ragged clothes that smell of mildew. The fabric sticks to my damp skin.

We walk behind the guard as he takes everyone to their cells. I'm the last to be locked up. The palm of his hand presses between my shoulder blades and he pushes me with a force that causes me to stumble and fall. The concrete digs into my knees and I wince.

I bite my tongue to refrain from crying out. I won't give him the satisfaction of seeing how his treatment affects me. The door slams behind me and I hear the sound of the lock engaging.

Only then do I let the emotion break through, and a tear slides down my cheek.

CHAPTER 21
Emily
2 YEARS AGO

I cling to Liam's neck as he runs toward the SUV. The scent of his cologne is mixed with the coppery tang of blood and my stomach twists at the stench.

They're dead.

My dad and Ryan are dead.

The scene replays in my head in a never-ending loop. Shock and heartache overwhelm my system.

I'm struggling to grasp the reality of what happened.

"Are you hurt?" Liam says. His voice is thick with panic and concern.

I silently shake my head. I can't gather the ability to speak. The words are trapped deep within me and refuse to rise.

He gently sets me on my feet and opens the passenger door. My eyes remain locked on the ground as he guides me toward my seat. My movements are on autopilot when I climb into the vehicle.

Liam reaches over and buckles my seatbelt. When I'm safely buckled, he brings his eyes to mine. My eyes flutter at the concern that radiates through him. The comfort that the swirls of green and amber bring is accompanied by pain.

"I'm so sorry, Emily." His fingers caress my cheek tenderly and my lip quivers.

When I don't respond, he presses a soft kiss on my forehead and then closes the door. I watch as he rounds the hood of the car and climbs into the driver's seat. Turning the ignition, he shifts into drive, and we make our way away from the venue and away from the bloody madness inside.

The drive home is a blur. My emotions are in absolute mayhem. I'm so overwhelmed by them that I sit staring out of the window in a frozen state. Liam drives in silence but every so often, I feel the tingle of his gaze on me.

"Em?"

I close my eyes at the sound of his voice and swallow the lump that is choking me.

"I'm here if you need me." He says softly, and I feel the burn of tears gathering in my eyes.

I don't want to find comfort in him. I won't be strong enough to have him push me away again.

When he reaches a hand toward mine, I gently pull it away without turning to face him. The energy between us is strained and I want to escape it as soon as possible.

I feel my muscles slightly relax with each mile we put between us and the city. The skyscrapers transform into open plains and green forests. The vehicle jostles as it drives from the paved road to the gravel road leading to the estate.

I see the path leading to the garden and my throat tightens. Grief fills me and I struggle to hold back the sob that wants to break through. Everything is different than when I was here last and it's heartbreaking.

How can a place that once brought me so much joy cause me so much sadness?

The car comes to a stop in front of the mansion. Declan and Rhys are standing at the bottom of the steps in tactical gear, barking orders to the men who are loading weapons into a truck.

My heart begins to race at the thought of them going back.

I'm pushing the door open and running toward them before Liam has a chance to turn the ignition off.

I throw myself into Declan's arms when I reach him, and he envelops me.

"You're okay. Everything is going to be okay." He murmurs against my hair, and I sob uncontrollably.

"Where's ma?" I ask as I pull away from him.

He scans my body for injuries before replying.

"She's inside. She's working on getting information about who would have leaked our location. There weren't many people who knew about the banquet."

"How is she?" I whisper.

Sadness fills his eyes, and he gives me a small smile. "She hasn't stopped long enough to let it set in."

I nod in understanding. The sudden loss of my father in such a violent way, no doubt, has led my ma to push her emotions down. Instead, she's going to retaliate before the shock wears off.

I feel Liam step up behind me and my body tingles in awareness. I avoid turning around and instead turn to Rhys who pulls me into a tight hug. He cups the back of my head and plants a kiss on my temple.

"I'm glad you're safe, kid."

With a fine squeeze, he lets me go and steps back. His eyes glance over my shoulder and harden before he peers down at me and smiles.

My brows pull inward, and I study his face. But of course, Rhys's poker face shows no indication of what he's thinking.

"Liam, get ready to head back with us. We're not going to give those fuckers time to meet at another location."

My chest constricts.

He's going back too?

What if I lose him?

I flex my fingers and try to mask the anxiety that grows. Rhys is studying me and sends me a soft smile when I meet his eyes. Understanding it etched in them.

Does he know?

"Please be careful," I say to Declan and Rhys. I'm indirectly addressing Liam, but still refuse to face him.

"Of course. Stay here with ma. The property will be on lockdown until we confirm they won't come here."

Every assignment they go on has a risk of them not coming back. But this one feels different. Declan isn't just going for revenge. He's going as the new leader of the Irish Mafia. This is his chance to show the underground that he's in charge and what he's capable of.

"Just... Please come back." I choke on a sob.

Declan pulls me back into his arms and I hold onto him tightly. We hold each other for a long moment before he pulls away and kisses my forehead.

"I'll see you later."

He and Rhys turn on their heels and make their way to the train of blacked-out SUVs.

"Em," Liam whispers.

I blow out a deep breath before spinning to face him. His hair is disheveled, and his clothes are covered in blood splatter. The bruises from his eyes have spread across his cheeks.

My palm tingles with the want to touch him but I force myself to stay still.

"*Féileacán —.*"

"Don't call me that." I hold my hand up, interrupting him.

His eyes flick between mine and his shoulders slump.

"Emily... I'm so sorry about your *daid.*"

I rub my front teeth with my tongue while nodding. The fact that I can't confide in Liam like I used to, sends a new wave of hurt through me. He was my everything and I was nothing but a hole for him to fill.

How could I have been so stupid?

He steps toward me and my muscles lock. He gently pushes a strand of my hair behind my ear and my lip quivers. I stare at his chest to avoid meeting his eyes.

"Look at me, Em."

My heart drums through my ears and I feel each pound throughout my entire body. I close my eyes and shake my head.

When his callused fingers caress my cheek, I can't help but lean into his touch. A tear slips from my eye and slowly falls down my face.

"I can't do this." I push him away from me and run up the steps to the mansion without looking back.

The hurt that crossed Emily's face at my nearness nearly brought me to my knees.

I did that.

I broke her heart and she'll never trust me like she used to. How could she? I'm the one that pushed her away... I told her I didn't want her. I made her feel used and then tossed her aside.

I'm a fool.

"Let's load up!" Rhys shouts and everyone begins climbing to the trucks and vans.

Someone tosses me a bulletproof vest and I nod my thanks before putting it on. With a final glance at the mansion, I hop into one of the SUVs.

The convoy of vehicles speeds down the road toward the city. Declan has already called in a favor with the local PD, so we have an unobstructed route to the club where the Russians often lurk.

We come to a screeching halt in front of the club, the doors are shoved open, and we pile out with our guns raised. The two bouncers guarding the entrance don't have a chance to react before bullets are lodged in their skulls and they crumble to the ground.

"All right everyone, look alive, and watch your six." Declan's voice rings through our comms.

Finn and Rhys order groups to surround the perimeter while I lead the group with Declan who will be breaching the front doors.

"Everyone in position?" Rhys asks and replies of confirmation follow.

"All right, let's move."

We quickly open the door and creep inside. The stench of cheap cigars, sweat, and sex fill the air. The thrum of the bass reverberates through my chest as we stalk down the darkened hallway. Women dressed in bikinis that barely cover their tits and pussies press against the walls with wide eyes.

I bring my finger to my mouth, gesturing for them to keep quiet, and they nod rapidly. Once we've passed them, they scurry away on their sky-high heels.

"Avoid killing any women, if possible," Declan says through the comms.

"Aye," we reply.

The hallway opens to a room shadowed in red and blue lights. A scrawny woman is dancing naked on a stage directly in the center of the room. The place is filled with men smoking cigars and nursing clear liquid that I assume is vodka. I fire at the man closest to me – hitting him in the back of the head – he slumps over and his head smacks against the table.

The room is thrown into a warzone as the Russians stand and draw their weapons. A bullet whizzes past me and hits the man behind me in the chest. I quickly check that he's good before returning fire.

Glass shatters, tables are overturned to be used as shields, and shouts in Russian and Irish are exchanged in quick succession.

I fire until I have no choice but to reload. I crouch slightly next to the bar and change the magazine before rising to my feet and firing again. Declan and Rhys are pushing through the carnage, heading toward the hallway leading to the backrooms in search of Vladimir.

This isn't a fight. This is a massacre.

Just as it should be.

"On your left!" someone shouts, and I turn in that direction just as an excruciating burn slices across my arm.

"Shite!" I grunt and look down at the wound in my left arm. It seems like the bullet went through, so I ignore the pain and fire back. *I fucking miss* and he ducks behind a table.

"Shite," I mutter under my breath.

I crouch behind an upturned table closest to me and press my back against the underside. I'm panting from the adrenaline coursing through me. Screams from the women ring in my ears and I feel the thump of bodies meeting the floor.

Blood flows down my arm, staining my shirt, and dripping down my fingers.

Feck. I need to stop the bleeding long enough to finish this.

Finn kneels next to me and rips the bottom of my shirt. He quickly wraps it around my arm and knots the ends. The blood saturates the fabric, but it will have to be enough for now.

"Get your ass back out there," he orders and then takes off back into the fray.

I haul myself up and rejoin the fight.

When the final body has dropped, we start working to remove our wounded and dead.

The pain in my arm has reduced to a low ache, allowing me to lift men from where they've fallen.

"Vladimir escaped before we could reach him," Declan growls through clenched teeth once we've returned to the estate. The doctors and surgeons on our payroll are tending to the severely wounded. Those of us who returned to the estate are working to unload the remaining weapons. The others are continuing to clear out the bodies of our men.

The local PD has given us an hour to clear out before they swoop in, so everything is still a blur of men running around and orders being barked.

A sudden wave of dizziness hits me, and I stumble, falling against the van.

"Whoa, are you okay?" Tommy, one of the newest recruits, holds onto my shoulder to help me avoid falling to the ground.

"Yeah, I'm good. Just got dizzy all of a sudden." I wince when I push off the vehicle.

The dizziness hits again but this time, I fall to my knees.

"We need a doc!" Tommy shouts, but his voice sounds miles away. My vision begins to blur and a sharp pain spreads along my thigh. I look down and see that my jeans are coated in blood that I had assumed belonged to someone else.

"Emily," I mumble before I black out.

CHAPTER 23
Emily
2 YEARS AGO

The voices of men shouting and car doors opening and shutting flow through my open window. I watch as they move in an orderly fashion to unload the weapons and help the doctors take the wounded to the lower-level hospital we have on the estate.

When I spotted Liam, Declan, and Rhys stepping out of their SUVs, I released the breath I had held since they left. They were covered in blood, their hair disheveled, and their faces showed signs of their underlying fatigue. But knowing they were unharmed and alive made it so much easier to handle the chaos.

I know better than to go down there and check on them right now, so I watch them from my window.

After my ma was finished barking her own orders, she retreated to her room and hasn't emerged since. When I had gone to check on her, she was curled up on the bed, lying on my father's side. My heart ached at the sight. I can't even imagine the pain she must be feeling.

I silently laid with her for a while, just holding her as she cried.

What do you say to someone who just lost the love of their life?

I can offer nothing to provide any comfort besides my company. Once she had fallen into an exhausted slumber, I slipped out of bed and waited for the men's return.

I'm still wearing the dress from the banquet and am still covered in blood. I couldn't find the strength to wash away the reminders of what happened today. It felt *wrong* to erase the evidence of what Vladimir's men did until Declan returned with their blood on his skin.

Now that I've seen proof of their retaliation, I decide it's time to wash away the day.

I step into the ensuite and see my rumpled appearance. My reddened cheek is still tender from where the man's hand struck me. Dried blood is splattered across my face and my hair is in knots.

With an exhausted sigh, I slide the straps of my dress off my shoulders. The material bunches at my feet and I step out of it. Stripping the rest of my clothes, I walk to the walk-in shower and turn on the water.

My muscles begin to relax at the feel of the scalding water sliding down my body. I stand for several minutes, blocking out the outside world, and enjoying the sound of the water droplets pattering against the tile.

I'm still struggling to comprehend that my father is truly gone. I won't ever get to see him again. Declan will be the leader now.

How will that change him?

Will he force an arranged marriage on me?

"Ugh." I let out a low, frustrated groan and then pull the shampoo bottle from the built-in shelf. The fruity scent envelops me when I squeeze the liquid into my palm and create a lather. After I've massaged it into my hair, I tip my hair back and rinse out the suds. I then squeeze a generous amount of conditioner into my palms and then comb that through my hair with my fingers.

My favorite body wash is scented similar to my hair products, and I breathe in the familiar scent of berries. After rinsing myself off, I turn the knob to shut off the water and then grab a plush towel from the hook just outside of the shower.

Wrapping it around my body, I grab another and knot it around my hair before making my way to the walk-in closet.

Despite not living here for a month, a large number of my things remained so I choose a set of matching forest green sleep shorts and a tank to wear to bed.

I struggle to collect my thoughts as I lather myself with body lotion and then follow with my skincare routine. My movements are muscle memory and I'm not even sure I've blinked since exiting the shower.

A soft knock brings me back to reality.

"Come in," I say as I put my things away in their respective spots.

Declan steps into my room. His steps are muted by the plush carpet. Exhaustion is etched on every surface of his face.

I quickly make my way over to him, but he holds up his hands before I get a chance to hug him.

"I'm filthy, Em. I just wanted to come in and check on you and ma."

"I'm okay... I think. Ma is sleeping but she cried for a while."

He nods in understanding and then sighs, combing his fingers through his sweaty strands.

"I'll be meeting with the organization and our allies in the coming weeks. We need to discuss my transition to leadership," his eyes pivot between mine for a moment.

"I don't want you anywhere near my office when they're here."

I furrow my brows and tilt my head. "Why?"

"Right now, everyone is going to be circling around, waiting for me to fuck something up, or a weakness so they can take over. You and ma are that weakness."

A chill travels down my spine and I can't repress the shudder that escapes.

"O-okay," I stutter.

Declan steps closer and cups the nape of my neck before bringing his forehead to mine.

"We're going to be okay, but right now, I need you to stay hidden as much as possible until I show them who they answer to."

I nod against his sticky skin and release a sigh.

He pulls his head away from mine and stares at me for a moment. When he opens his mouth, another knock interrupts whatever he was planning to say.

Rhys walks in and pulls me into his arms. The smell of sweat, dirt, and blood fills my voice and I cringe.

"I just showered," I grumble.

He chuckles but the amusement doesn't reach his eyes.

"Anything to report?" Declan asks, pulling Rhys's attention from me.

"Liam is in surgery as we speak. The bullet nicked his artery but wasn't too severe."

I go rigid.

"Liam was hurt?"

Rhys looks into my eyes with an odd expression I can't read before nodding and returning his gaze to Declan.

"He was shot in the leg and lost a lot of blood but he's fine," Declan says from behind me.

"He'll be up and moving in no time," Rhys adds.

The desire to go to Liam's side is almost uncontrollable. I want to see him with my own eyes and ensure he's truly okay. I know I can trust Declan and Rhys but the fear of not laying eyes on him outweighs that logic.

"Get some rest, it's been a hard day for all of us." Declan finally pulls me into his arms and kisses my temple. Rhys does the same, and they both leave me standing in the center of my room.

Do I go see him?

Will he even want me to?

With a huff, I toss myself onto my mattress and land on my back.

"Why did you have to make me fall for someone that doesn't even want me?" I say to whatever God will listen.

Of course, there is no answer.

After what feels like forever, I decide it's best if I don't go and see him.

It's best if I truly accept that he doesn't want anything to do with me.

I just need to convince my heart to accept it.

CHAPTER 24
Liam
2 YEARS AGO

It's been two weeks since Conor was killed, and I haven't seen Emily since his funeral services a week ago. She wouldn't make eye contact with me... Not that I expected her to. But still, I hoped she would. I struggle with wanting to push for something more and leaving her be.

Rhys is right. She's not a game. But I can't help but replay Conor's words in my mind.

"You're filth. Nothing. Replaceable."

Although her engagement with Ryan is officially over because of his untimely death, I can't allow myself to be with her, especially not after everything I said.

She deserved so much more than I gave her and ripping out her heart? Fuck, she didn't deserve the words that I said. She didn't deserve to be left in the rain to cry.

The battle that raged throughout my body when she screamed my name was unbearable. I had to get away from her as fast as possible before I said, 'fuck it' and stayed with her.

Fuck. My mind and heart can't fucking decide what to do.

I'm in crutches for a few weeks while I heal, so searching for Emily on this vast property has been difficult. I know she's likely been spending the majority of her time in the garden, but I can't navigate the terrain with these damned things.

I want to speak with her and ensure she handles the recent events okay. But would she even want me to? She doesn't look at me and avoids being in the same room as me.

The fact that our relationship is completely destroyed is slowly killing me. I swear I can still smell her when I lie in my bed and feel the gentle caress of her lips on my chest or neck. I can still hear her soft and sweet laugh.

I'm so fucked.

As I hobble through the front doors of the mansion, I hear her chuckle from the kitchen and stop short in the foyer.

Now is my chance to see her. To speak with her.

I tap my fingers along the handles of the crutches, contemplating what I should do.

My body is moving before I officially decide.

I hear Niall speaking with her and her chuckles fills my ears once more. My stomach flutters at the sound. Her laugh is one of my favorite things about her. It's a melody that I could listen to for the rest of my life and never tire from.

As the kitchen comes into view, Emily is seated on a stool in front of the kitchen island. She's in a tight pair of jeans and a pale pink knitted sweater. Her red hair sits atop her head in a messy bun with strands that frame her beautiful face.

Niall spots me first.

"Morning, Liam. How are you feelin' today?"

Emily's shoulders go rigid, and I internally wince at the sight.

"I'm grand, Niall."

I head toward Emily and sit on the stool next to her. She shifts slightly away from me.

"How are you, Em?" I ask quietly.

"Niall, I think I'll go eat in my room." She ignores me completely and stands.

I reach out and grasp her wrist to keep her from leaving.

"Why you avoidin' me, eh?"

Her face is void of emotion as she pivots her eyes between mine, but I can see the pain in her swirls of ocean blue.

"I have nothing to say to you, Liam." She pulls her arm to try and escape my hold, but I tighten my grasp.

I open my mouth to say something but shut it when I hear the sound of footsteps making their way toward us. I quickly drop my hand from her wrist and turn toward the counter.

Emily lets out a disappointed huff and from my peripheral, I see her shake her head.

"Morning boss," Niall says with a nod.

"Good morning, Niall. What do you have planned for breakfast today?" Declan replies.

I tune out the rest of the conversation because I'm so focused on Emily. She still hasn't left but she has taken a seat on the stool farthest from me.

Declan claps a hand on my shoulder and squeezes it.

"And how are you feeling, Liam?"

Niall sets a mug of black coffee in front of me, and I raise it in Declan's direction. "Just grand."

"Just a few more weeks and you'll be rid of these damned things." He gestures toward my crutches.

"Aye, and I can't wait."

Caetlin steps into the kitchen and we all greet her. She decided to stay a while to help Declan's transition to leadership. Her face has paled, and her cheeks are thinner, but when she is out of her room, her poker face is unwavering.

I don't know how she does it. If I had lost Emily... No, I can't even think of that. Losing her in such a permanent way would be my undoing.

Emily stands and walks over to Caetlin. They hug each other tightly for several seconds before pulling away. Caetlin strokes Emily's cheek gently and nods at whatever Emily whispers to her.

"How are you, mam?" Declan says and pulls her into his chest.

"Oh, you know. Just grand." She lets out a humorless laugh and steps away from Declan.

"It's good to see you, Liam."

It is?

I have no doubts she knows that I broke Emily's heart, so I'm surprised she's not ripping me apart.

"It's always good to see you, Caetlin." I nod.

She smiles warmly at me and then makes her way to the table where Niall is setting down a cup of tea and her plate of breakfast.

The tension coming off Emily rises, and I struggle to breathe. If I can't have her romantically, I'd still like to be her friend.

Ha! That's ridiculous. Being her friend is not possible.

I turn to meet her eyes and she averts her gaze to her plate of food. The need to touch her and breathe her in is suffocating.

Even with Conor gone, I can't see Declan accepting my love for her. He'd likely tell me the same thing his father did. That I'm not worthy of her.

"Thank you for breakfast, Niall." Emily says and then all but runs out of the kitchen.

I sit for a beat before pushing to a stand. Tucking the crutches under my arms, I follow Emily without a word to the others.

I'm huffing and sweat beads down my back by the time I've made it through to the garden. Emily is sitting with back to me. Her knees are tucked up to her chin and her arms are wrapped tightly around them. Her bun has been taken down so her soft strands down cascade down her back.

124

"Go away," she says without turning in my direction.

"No. We need to talk."

She snorts but doesn't respond.

I hobble toward her and sit next to her on the grass. She closes her eyes and avoids looking at me. There is a gentle breeze that pushes a small strand of her hair in front of her face, and I reach out to push it behind her ear.

Her eyes tighten and she lip twitches as though she is holding back a sob.

"Look at me, Emily," I whisper.

"What do you want, Liam?" she mumbles.

"I want to make sure you're okay... with everything that has happened."

She looks up at me and I see the anger in her eyes.

"You mean like how you shattered my heart and then a month later my fiancé and father are assassinated in front of me?" she huffs out a humorless laugh. "I'm great!"

"I didn't want to hurt you."

"You don't get to say that to me after telling me I was nothing but a hole to fill and you don't want me." She pulls away, but I see the pain spread across her face.

"It's for the best." I try to reason.

"Just... Please leave me alone." Her lip quivers and it takes everything in me not to pull her into my arms.

"I still want to be here for you, Emily. I want us to still be friends."

Her face contorts with anger, and she shakes her head.

"I don't want to be anything to you after what you've said and done. Not after you tossed me aside like trash."

The tears start to form, and I swallow tightly.

"I'm going to Ireland when my ma leaves and I don't want to hear from you ever again." She stands and leaves me alone in the garden.

CHAPTER 25
Emily
RUSSIA

"Let me out! Please! Let me out!" I shriek with each pound of my fist on the metal door. The black tendrils have morphed into millions of spiders that are climbing along every surface of the room and making their way toward me. One climbs up my leg, and I smack it repeatedly, but it continues its path up my body.

I feel one land on the top of my head, and I scream and thrash until I no longer feel it in my hair. I continue to fight off the crawling arachnids, smashing them, and pushing them off my body as best as I can.

As quickly as they came, they disappear.

I pant and press a hand against my chest. My heart is beating a mile a minute and sweat flows down my brow.

"It's okay... I'm okay... They're not real..." I repeat each word and release slow, steady breaths. My teeth chatter as the adrenaline begins to subside.

"They'll come back." A voice says in my ear, and I cry out. I crawl as fast as possible to the closest corner of the room and shove my body as close to the wall as possible.

"You're not real. You're not real. You're not real," I repeat over and over.

A deep and terrifying laugh echoes in the room before silence descends. I clamp my hand over my mouth and sob. I sob until I have no tears left to cry. I sob until I feel lightheaded and I'm trembling from all the emotion I've purged.

My breath bellows out in a small puff of white that I can barely make out in the darkness. My eyes have been adjusting to the lack of light which I guess can be seen as a good thing. Me? I know it's a sign that my vision is no longer what It used to be.

I knock on the door again and again until my hands ache and my voice is hoarse from begging to be set free.

"Please..." I croak.

I wake to the sound of the deadbolt unlocking and shoot up to a seated position. I press my back against the wall and hold up my hand to block the blinding light that spills from the doorway.

A large figure walks through the threshold, and their boots thudding against the concrete sends a jolt of fear down my body.

I've come to recognize who enters cell by the sound of their steps... and I don't know who this man is.

His shoulders are so broad that there is barely any space between him and the doorframe. He towers at such a staggering height that I'm left paralyzed with fear.

"Get up," he growls.

When I don't make any attempt to move, he stalks toward me and grips my arm so tightly that I worry the bone will snap. He hauls me to my feet, and I whimper at the aggressive manhandling.

"I said to get the fuck up."

He drags me behind him, and we exit the room. I squint as my eyes struggle to adjust to the sudden change in lighting. The silence up the steps is nearly as deafening as the cries I hear when I make it to the top.

I'm not sure where he's taking me but the alarm bells in my head haven't stopped ringing since he stepped into my room.

"Where are we going?" I risk asking. He mutters something in Russian under his breath but doesn't respond to my question. His hold on my arm tightens. I can already feel the bruises taking form.

My weak legs struggle to keep pace with his long stride and when I unfortunately stumble, he whips around and grips my hair in his fist. My neck is forced to crane back to its absolute limits, and he brings his face centimeters from mine.

His dark eyes snake down my body in obvious disgust before he grunts and pulls away. He continues to drag me down the hallway with doors on either side.

I keep my eyes down to avoid looking into any of the open rooms. The torturous cries of pain and agony ring through my ears with each step we make, causing the cracks in my heart to expand. Silent tears travel down my cheeks, and I can't control the tightness of my throat from nearly suffocating me.

We come to a stop at a wooden door on an upper level of the building. The man knocks three times and then the door is opened.

Pressing his massive hand against my back, he pushes me into the room. I try to scan my surroundings, but everything is blurred. My soul shatters at the confirmation that my time spent in the dark has deteriorated my vision.

The man pushes past me, stepping further into the room.

I track his movements with cautious eyes. My body is tense, and my heart is hammering against my chest.

He takes a seat on a large couch that is in the center of the room. He splays his arms on the back of the sofa. He slouches and opens his legs, getting comfortable.

"Come." He commands, his voice has a thick Russian accent.

I nibble on my bottom lip, tearing skin until the tangy flavor of blood touches my tongue. Timidly, I shuffle closer to him. My trembling fingers play nervously with the frayed fabric of my dress.

Once I am standing in front of him, he reaches over and grabs onto my hips. I squeak when he pulls me to straddle him.

No. Please no. Not again.

He slides his meaty hands into my hair and grips it tightly at the root. I wince at the sharp tug as he pulls my head toward him. He traces the column of my neck with his nose and breathes in deeply.

He reeks of sweat, vodka, and blood. My stomach twists at the combination of smells. My entire body is trembling with fear.

"Fight it."

Every muscle in my body goes ramrod straight at the sound of Liam's voice.

A bite to my neck brings my attention back to what is happening, and I whimper at the pain. The man's large hands move from my hair to my thigh and travel up my skin. When I try to pull away, he digs his fingers into my flesh, and I cry out.

The door opens behind me, and I peer over my shoulder to Nikolai stepping in.

He smirks and says something in Russian that I don't understand.

My clothes are ripped off my body and I try to cover my breasts, but the guard swats my hands away before biting down on my nipple. I cry out and then whimper when he lets go.

"Fight, Féileacán." Liam growls.

I sense Nikolai stepping behind me and the man wraps his hands around my hips to lift me enough that I am exposed to Nikolai. He hums in appreciation and then I feel the scrape of his finger at my back entrance.

"Are you ready to be fucked by both of us, *kukla?*"

"No, please no." I beg and try to scramble off the guard's legs.

The sound of belts clinking followed by zippers being pulled down fill my ears and my body goes into a panic. I scream out and thrash when I feel Nikolai's cock start to breech my back entrance.

He presses his palm against my back to hold me in position and thrusts.

The sharp pain of my flesh ripping causes me to shriek in agony and tears flow down my face. The guard groans in Russian as he presses against my other entrance before he thrusts upward.

"FIGHT!"

"I… I can't…" I cry as they alternate their thrusts.

They alternate their violent thrusts. Their hands, squeezing and kneading my flesh. I try to fight them off but I'm too weak. Too frail.

My cries of pain only seem to arouse them further.

"Emily, fight them!"

I feel Liam's presence but I'm too deep in my abuse to truly hear his pleas.

Nikolai finishes first and fills me with his cum. He bites my shoulder before pulling out. His release oozes out of me and he smears it into my skin. The guard increases his thrusts and then holds me tightly as he finishes his assault.

He throws me to the couch, and I bounce off and land on the ground. I suppress a yelp when pain erupts in my hip. I curl into myself and sob into my hands.

"Clean her up and then lock her in the pit" Nikolai orders as he buttons up his pants. He straightens his clothes and fixes his hair before striding out of the room.

CHAPTER 26
Emily
1 YEAR AGO

The birds sing their songs, and the butterflies and bees travel from flower to flower around me. The smell of the wildflowers flows through my nose, but they don't bring me the comfort they used to. Instead, they make me angry. Liam has ruined the only place that gave me a sense of peace.

After I told him that I would be leaving for Ireland, he hasn't spoken to me. He still watches me whenever we're in the same room, his eyes fill with longing when I meet them, and it hurts.

He wants to be friends. How could I be friends with the one person who brings my soul to life while also killing me? How could he possibly ask that of me?

I need to leave this place. I need to leave Liam behind and move on. I can't be around him without feeling physical pain from it. As much as I have tried avoiding him, *he's fucking everywhere.*

"You're so stupid," I whisper to myself and shake my head slowly. "You fell so hard and so fast without any thought of whether he loved you back and look where that got you."

I rub my chest as the ache increases.

Back at the mansion, the staff are collecting my belongings and loading them into the SUVs to be taken with us to Ireland. I've opted to sit out here until it's time to go. I don't want Liam to try and talk me out of this.

My ma has been giving me looks of sympathy over the last few months. She sees my heartbreak all over my face and can't do anything to help just as I can't help the grief she's hiding.

Ever since Declan took over, he's been hunting for Vladimir. According to some spies that were planted in Russia, Vladimir denies having anything to do with my dad's assassination.

I call bullshit.

My father was the only thing standing in Vladimir's way and controlling the docks for his sex trading. When my father denied Vladimir the chance to transport his women from those docks, he was angry and had been working to dismantle the warehouses in the area.

If he thinks Declan will consider mercy or any future allegiance, he's sorely mistaken. Declan is out for blood, and I don't see Vladimir having any chance of surviving him.

The sound of muffled footsteps comes from behind me, and I tense. I know it's Liam without turning around, just like I know he's not going to leave until he's said what he needs to.

I turn around from where I am seated on the grass, and he stops short.

"Hi," he whispers.

I don't respond. I simply stare at him with a brow raised.

He sighs and runs his fingers through his hair. My fingers tingle with the need to reach for him.

"Are you really going to leave without saying goodbye?" he searches my eyes from where he stands.

I shrug, "I have nothing to say to you." I move to stand, and he steps closer. I clench my fists at my sides when I stand to my full height.

"Emily, you don't understand. I *had* to let you go despite how much I want you."

My hands tremble and I feel the burn behind my eyes.

"Do you expect me to believe you? You had no problem telling me how I was nothing to you, had no problem watching me fall apart when you told me I was just something to pass the time. I gave you everything, all of me, and you... you *left me* in the rain crying, breaking for *you*." I close my eyes as the first tear falls. "You don't get to tell me that you want me, Liam when I *begged* you to fight for me and you did nothing."

His eyes search mine for a moment and then he nods, pulling his bottom lip into his teeth.

"You're right. I don't. You goin' to Ireland is the best option. I can't be anythin' more than a friend to you and you don't want that, so..." he shrugs.

I let out a humorless chuckle and shake my head at him in disbelief.

"Even now, you give me up so easily."

"What do you want me to do, Emily?!" He yells and holds out his arms.

"Nothing! I want nothing from you anymore! You're free to fuck whoever you want, whenever you want, and I will do the same in Ireland. Find someone to *pass the time with*," I say in quotations. "You didn't fight for me then and you're clearly not going to fight for me now. And that's okay because I'll find someone who will."

I move to stomp past him, but he wraps his hand around my bicep, stopping me.

"Let. Me. Go," I growl and try to pry away from him.

He tightens his grasp. His eyes moving over every inch of my face as though memorizing the details.

"I'm sorry."

"Fuck you, Liam. Fuck you."

He releases my arm and I storm down the path to the mansion.

CHAPTER 27
Emily
1 YEAR AGO

I've been in Ireland for a few days and finally mustered up the courage to go on a *date*. Declan promised that he's not going to force an arranged marriage on me and for that, I am partly grateful. Some part of me wants to have another arranged marriage so then I will have no choice but to move on from Liam.

The bastard still haunts my memories and dreams despite being thousands of miles away.

Maybe if I give myself to someone else, I'll finally be able to love someone who will love me in return.

So, tonight. That's what I plan to do.

Maybe it's foolish. Okay, it's definitely foolish. But Liam is so embedded into my being that it's suffocating me.

Loving him is destroying me.

I coat my eyelashes with a layer of mascara one final time before twisting it shut. I run my fingers through my natural curls and straighten my pale blue sundress. The fabric flows beautifully down my curves, stopping just below the knee. I've paired it with white sandals that have a high enough heel to lengthen my legs.

My freckles are on full display and have darkened from the amount of sunlight I've been getting since moving here, so instead of covering them with make-up, I've opted for a more natural look and only put on mascara and some lipgloss.

With one last look in the mirror, I shut off the light and exit the bathroom.

"Ma, I'm leaving!" I shout from the foyer.

She comes into view and walks down the steps.

"You look beautiful, *mo stór*," she says, pulling me into a hug.

"Thank you, ma. We're going to be walking around the Farmer's market before going to dinner."

She nods with a smile. "Perfect. Now, remember, Ronan and Lorcan will be keeping their distance but will be watching."

I inwardly groan and she levels me with a disapproving look.

"It's for your own safety and you know this. You've had guards follow you your entire life."

"I know, I know. It just seems unnecessary to have two men watching me."

"Emily..." she sighs. "*Leanbh*, these next few months, if not years, are going to be very dangerous with Vladimir and we need to keep our wits about us."

I nod in understanding.

Things with Vladimir are in an odd state of limbo. He continues to maintain his stance of not having anything to do with my father's death. I don't know anyone who would have enough Russian help to attack us that wouldn't be Vladimir, but that's Declan's job to find out.

Here in Ireland, though. It's been quiet. We've had no words of any attacks here and no confrontations with any of Vladimir's men. There have been rumors of a new Russian mafia forming that is outside of Vladimir's control, but I don't know enough about it to know if it's true.

"Go on this date, and just make sure you stay safe." My ma pulls me into another hug before leaving down the hallway.

I can't put my finger on it, but there is something about this man that doesn't sit right with me. When we first arrived at the market, he was very sweet and attentive, it was nice but now, he's becoming a little too comfortable invading my space.

I discreetly scan the area and meet the eyes of both Ronan and Lorcan. They both nod and then disappear into the small crowd.

"So, Emily. How long do you plan to be in Ireland?" Fionn asks as we stop at a stand with freshly baked bread.

"I'm not entirely sure but I do hope to stay a while. I haven't spent much time here since I was a girl."

He nods and then checks his watch for the umpteenth time since we arrived.

"Am I keeping you from something?" I ask, my eyes gesturing to his watch.

He chuckles and it sends a creepy sensation down my spine.

"No, of course not. I just have someone coming that I'd love for you to meet." He smiles at me, but it doesn't meet his eyes.

Something is wrong.

I turn to look for Ronan and Lorcan again but don't see them.

Fionn's phone chimes and he pulls it from his back pocket. He quickly replies and puts it away before looking me in the eyes.

His stare is cold, his body language is no longer welcoming. He glances over my shoulder and then a wicked sneer spreads across his face.

I take a step back and tense when I feel the hard, cold metal of a gun pressed to my back.

"If you scream, I will shoot." A deep voice with a thick Russian accent says in my ear.

My eyes frantically scan the area for Ronan and Lorcan but they're still nowhere to be found.

"You'll see your precious bodyguards soon." Fionn chuckles.

A large hand wraps around my bicep, and I'm roughly escorted away from the Farmers' Market and to a small alley where a white van is parked.

"Bag." Fionn holds out his hand with a bored expression.

My heart is pounding against my chest, and my stomach threatens to spill its contents.

I slide the bag off my shoulder and place it in his hand. He dumps its contents. He picks up my phone and searches through it.

"Tell her you've been offered a photoshoot tour with your modeling agency, and you will be leaving immediately. *Do not* give any hidden messages or pull some shite that will indicate something is wrong."

My brain whirls as I try to keep up with what he's demanding.

He shoves the phone in my hands. When I peer down, my mom's name is on display. All I have to do is press *call.*

The cold press of a gun to my temple sends my body into motion and I press the button.

"Speaker." Fionn grunts.

Doing as he says, I listen as the phone rings. The moment my mom's voice fills the speaker I suck in a breath.

"The date is over already?" she teases.

Fionn's jaw ticks, his glare a clear warning.

Swallowing the tightness in my throat, I adjust my sweaty grip on the phone.

"Ha." I laugh nervously, "I'm actually calling to let you know I just received this a-amazing news from my agent. They're offering me a spot on their US tour." I blurt the words out, feigning enthusiasm as panic coats every cell in my blood.

"Oh, *mo stór!* That is a wonderful opportunity. Go! Go! We've had quite the eventful life recently and I think this is exactly what you need."

I can almost physically hear my heart shatter in my chest.

"Are you sure?"

The gun presses harder into my head and I wince.

"When would you need to leave?" My ma asks.

I clear my throat.

"I actually need to leave immediately, which is why my date ended early."

Fionn nods in approval. I close my eyes as the first tear spills out of the corner of my eye and down my cheek.

"Oh." She says, the word extending. "How long are you expected to be gone?"

I open my mouth but then shut it quickly.

I'm never going to come back... am I?

My eyes flick to Fionn and he slowly shakes his head before looking at the other man who holds the gun to my head.

"Um... Right now, there isn't an end date." Each word leaves a sour taste in my mouth.

"Mmm." She hums.

I'm trembling as I wait for her reply. I hope she'll make a fuss about not knowing how long I'll be gone. I'm hoping she demands that I stay so then she'll know that something is wrong.

"I think it'll be a good chance for you to find some kind of escape from reality." Her words are like a punch in the gut. My stomach churns. "Make sure you keep me updated on your trip."

I sniffle, unable to hold back the tears.

"Oh, Emily." Her voice softens. "I know it's been hard… very hard, these last few weeks. But everything will be okay."

Fionn motions with his hands for me to speed up the conversation.

"I- I'll talk to you soon, okay, ma?"

"I love you, *mo stór*."

"I love you too."

When the call ends, Fionn rips the phone from my hands and pockets it.

"Take off your jewelry." The man holding me at gunpoint orders.

I hesitate. My necklace has a small tracker in it. I can't let them take the one chance I have of someone finding me.

Fionn's hand connects with my cheek before I have a chance to register what is happening. My head whips to the side and I press my palms against the sting.

"Jewelry. Off." He growls. This time, I don't hesitate to remove everything. I place them into his waiting palm. My eyes fill with tears as I watch his fingers wrap around the necklace Liam gave me.

The van's door opens, and I freeze as I come face to face with Lorcan and Ronan. Their faces are stoic, clearly expecting to see me.

"Get in." Lorcan orders.

I'm shoved forward, forced into the van, followed by Fionn and the other man.

"Where are you taking me?"

Fionn turns around and looks at me with a smile that is anything but pleasant. "You'll see."

CHAPTER 28
Liam
4 MONTHS LATER

Bullet after bullet goes flying through the air, meeting their mark. My ears continue to ring from the explosive that was detonated. The bodies are piling, and it seems never-ending. Blood coats every surface of the building but it's not enough.

It will never be enough.

I want the blood of every person involved in tonight's event to spill.

"Move! Move! Move!" I order as we make our way through the chaos. We kill every person in our way. Every one of them is vile and doesn't deserve to draw in another breath.

Emily was fucking *missing* for months, and I didn't know. I didn't *fucking know*. I shouldn't have given her the space she demanded. I shouldn't have let her leave for Ireland. *I shouldn't have walked away.*

Rage and desperation flow through my veins at an alarming rate. Every second that passes is another second that Emily is locked somewhere in this God-forsaken place.

Declan and Rhys assigned me to come through the front with Cormac's men rather than accompanying them through the basement. I wanted to object but we would have lost precious time to get to her and I refuse to allow her to continue to suffer.

"There are women and children coming up through the halls, make sure you don't shoot them!" Declan shouts through the comms. Moments later, the hallways are flooded with skeletal frames running in tattered clothes.

My heart drops at their appearances. Emily likely looks just as sickly and I'm struggling to stomach it.

"Make a path for them to run out," I order and the men behind me follow suit.

I continue through the carnage, shooting with the precision I'm known for. I follow the path the women and children are running from. With my gun still raised, I walk down the long and dark staircase that leads to the lower levels.

I can't hear anything but the sound of my heart pounding with each step I take. The temperature drops the lower I get and the smell of blood, sweat, piss, and sex begins to invade my sinuses.

At the end of the stairwell, I freeze. Cells upon cells make up the majority of the space along the walls. There are random holes in the ground with grates over them. Declan and Rhys are shouting for Emily and Paige.

In my peripheral, a man tries to barrel into me, but I quickly spin, raise my gun, and shoot him in between the eyes. He drops to the floor and slides until his dead body stops at my feet.

"Declan!" Emily's shriek sends my body into motion and I'm running in Declan's direction. I don't bother shooting at anyone since the rest of our men have now entered the basement.

I come to a screeching halt when I see Emily in Declan's arms. Her cries of relief quickly turn into cries of agony and grief when Declan asks where Paige is.

"Declan!" Rhys shouts and we turn to see him carrying a limp Paige in his arms. Declan hands Emily over to me and I pull her into my arms.

She clings to me and sobs.

141

"Féileacán," I murmur. Her frame is so small and frail, I'm afraid I'm going to break her.

I repeatedly stroke her matted hair and watch as Declan presses his forehead to Paige's.

After a moment of him sitting like that, he lays Paige on the concrete floor and begins chest compressions.

I don't register the conversation Rhys and Emily have as I watch him continue to alternate between chest compressions and breathing air into her lungs.

Emily is trembling in my arms, and I pull her in closer to try and warm her. She looks up at me and I clench my jaw at the sight of the swelling and bruises that litter her beautiful face.

"Oh, Emily..." I whisper and her lip trembles. Her eyes are no longer bright. Her skin is ashen. Her cheekbones and shoulder bones are frighteningly prominent.

"She's alive!" Declan yells and Emily begins to sob into my chest.

"I'm here, *Féileacán,* I'm here." I lay my cheek on her head and resume stroking her hair.

Declan stands with Paige's body in his arms and leaves after ordering Rhys to bring any survivors to his cellar at the estate.

"Let's get you out of here," I say to Emily and scoop her into my arms. She's so alarmingly light that I don't know how much longer she would have survived before dying from starvation. She leans her head against my shoulder, and I carry her out of the basement.

Part Two

CHAPTER 29
Emily
PRESENT DAY

"How are you feeling today, Emily?" Dr. Morrison asks. Her glasses are perched on the bridge of her nose; hair meticulously styled in a bun at the base of her neck. She watches me with a warm expression, but I don't feel any warmth from it. I don't *feel* anything but the desire to end it all.

I started therapy after Declan begged me to when Paige and I were rescued. Paige has been making improvements without it and killing those who hurt us, and everyone else seems to think that I am too because of my therapy sessions.

In reality, I'm on the edge of putting a bullet in my head or even finding the closest cliff to jump from.

I straighten my spine and send her a small smile.

"I'm okay," I lie.

She nods before jotting something down in my file.

"Are you all set to get your new glasses?"

I let out a sigh and nod.

"My eyesight isn't improving. The doctor recommended I get a seeing-eye dog sooner rather than later."

She frowns and then a sympathetic smile forms on her lips.

"There's nothing they can do at this point?"

I shrug. "I think I might see a new doctor to get a second opinion, but I don't know."

She nods again and jots something else down.

"And the hallucinations?" she asks quietly.

I twist my fingers in my lap and avoid looking to my right where a woman in tattered clothes has been standing for the last fifteen minutes.

She's not real. She's not real. She's not real.

I can't control it when my eyes flick in her direction. Dr. Morrison follows my line of sight and then turns back to me. Her eyes soften and she nods with a sad smile.

"Okay," she whispers.

I sniffle and rub my nose. Dr. Morrison hands me a tissue which I take with a trembling hand.

"Are you still taking your medication as prescribed?"

No.

"Yes."

She studies my face for a moment, and I try to school my features so she can't find the lie.

"I think I need something stronger to help with my sleeping," I say.

"Okay, has it been getting worse?" she asks as she writes in my file.

"I don't sleep anymore." I nod.

"Not even with the anxiety medication we prescribed last time?"

I shake my head.

She sighs. "Okay, and you understand that we'll likely need to start something that will likely sedate you?"

I swallow through the tightness forming in my throat before nodding.

"Okay, we'll try a medication called Ambien. This is a sedative that will help with your sleep but it also has a higher risk of being addictive so we will need to monitor your usage closely." She peers at me over her glasses with a pointed look and I nod.

She nods and then goes over the precautions of the medication and the schedule I'm to follow for using it.

"Let's check your weight before you go."

I stand and nervously walk to the scale she keeps in the corner of her office. I stop just short of it and peer down at the black surface. I know I haven't gained anything. I've likely lost some weight instead.

"Emily," Dr. Morrison's voice startles me, and I spin to face her. She looks from me to the scale and back.

"I ..." my mouth opens and closes like a fish as I try to find the words to say.

"Get on the scale, Emily..." she says as though I'm a caged animal.

I turn back to the scale. Slowly I lift my foot and slip off my shoe, then the other. I let out a deep breath and then step on.

The digital screen counts down from five as it measures my weight. When the number appears on the screen, my shoulders sag, and I dip my chin to my chest.

Shit.

"Emily, if you continue to lose weight, I'm going to have to refer you to get a feeding tube placed." Her voice is saturated in disappointment and worry.

My eyes remain on the number until the screen clears.

"How about we set a goal to have you gain three pounds by your next visit in 2 weeks?"

Three pounds. Three fucking pounds.

I can't do it. I can't. Food is nearly impossible to stomach. I eat and immediately feel the need to vomit so I avoid it as much as possible.

Dr. Morrison steps to my side and I turn to meet her eyes. She reaches out and strokes my back gently.

"You're not alone, Emily. You have so many people who love you and want to see you improve. I know you can do this. Three pounds might seem like an impossible number, but I know you're capable."

I chew on the inside of my cheek for a beat and then nod. Stepping off the scale, I put on my shoes and make my way to my bag.

"Thank you, Dr. Morrison. I will try my best. See you next time."

She smiles softly and I leave the room.

Liam sits in the waiting room, and I suck in a deep breath. He's been nearly attached to my hip since I was discharged from the hospital. I love and hate it. We talk but for me, it's forced. I don't want to talk. I want nothing more than for him to stop looking at me like he can fix me.

My heart still sings for him, and I hate it. I hate how much I love him; how much I *need* him like my body needs oxygen.

I haven't told him that he's one of the reasons I stayed alive in Vladimir's trading. I haven't told him that on the days I wanted so badly to give up, his presence kept me going.

And I never will.

He looks up from his phone and smiles wide when he sees me watching him. He stands and pockets his phone as he makes his way over to me.

"How did it go?"

I plaster on a smile and nod.

"Great. Really great," I say.

His eyes bounce between mine and I avert them before he can spot the lie.

Liam has always been the one who could read me without any difficulty whatsoever. The last thing I need is for him to know just how *not* okay I really am.

CHAPTER 30
Liam

She's lying. I know she's lying. But what do I say that won't cause her to spiral? That would cause her to push me away? She thinks I can't see the lies she tells me, but I can read Emily's expressions better than anyone else. I *know* Emily... And I'm losing her.

When we brought her home a few weeks ago, she started making remarkable improvements right away, and I immediately knew something was off. No one else sees the times she stares blankly at the wall or the counter. No one sees the way she reacts to things that aren't really there.

No one sees that Emily is trapped in her mind and can't find a way out.

I thought maybe taking her to the garden and doing things she used to do would help but she refuses. She spends so much time locked in her room alone. I don't know what she experienced, and I expected major changes in her, but I wasn't prepared for the isolation she seeks. She very rarely wants to be around anyone.

Even her interactions with Sarah and Paige are *off*. Sure, she'll laugh and smile, but it never reaches her eyes.

Her eyes haven't brightened since the day I carried her out of that basement and it's eating at me.

I don't know how to save her. Don't know how to free her from the demons that haunt her.

But I'll be damned if I don't find a way to.

I hold out my hand and she stares at it for what seems like minutes before finally sliding her palm into mine. The warmth of her skin brings me some sense of peace because she's actually here. She's alive.

We walk to the SUV in the parking garage, and I open her door for her. She glances to her left and tenses.

Following her line of sight, I see nothing that would cause her reaction.

I never do and fuck if I don't want to be the one to take away her trauma. To break the chains that bind her in darkness.

"Emily..." I say gently and she spins to face me.

Fear flashes through her eyes before fading away to her usual blankness that I've come to loath.

"Sorry," she mumbles under her breath before climbing into her seat. Once she's settled and buckled, I shut the door, walk around the hood of the SUV, and climb into the driver's seat.

Emily is staring at the dash with an odd expression on her face.

"Are you okay?" I ask, but she doesn't react.

She continues to study the surface before tipping her head slightly to the side and furrowing her brows. After a moment, she shakes her head as though clearing her mind, and then faces me.

"Huh?"

I scan her face; my heart is heavy with grief for the Emily I used to know. I smile tightly then let out a deep breath before starting the ignition and pulling out of the parking garage.

The drive back to the estate is quiet, I can feel Emily's eyes on me every so often, and I can't help but do the same to her.

"Are you hungry?" I ask.

"No," she says, shaking her head.

"Are you sure? It's been a while since breakfast."

"Yeah, I just want to go home."

cMy heart constricts. She always just wants to be home. And I get it. I really do. I just wish there was more I could do to help her with what she's going through.

Emily doesn't say a word as we pull up to the estate. She's fleeing from the SUV before I even shift it into park. The vehicle shifts from the force in which she slams the door. I watch as she takes the steps two at a time before going inside.

With a sigh, I turn the ignition, lean back into the seat, and scrub a hand down my face.

Maybe I could speak with Declan about her?

No. I can't do that. Paige is also still recovering, and he thinks Emily is doing well. I also don't want anyone else to get in my way from being the one to help her.

A knock on the glass startles me from my thoughts. My pistol is unholstered and drawn before my mind catches up. Rhys holds his hands up and frowns at me.

I click the safety back on and holster my pistol. With a sigh, I push open the door and step out.

"Sorry," I mutter when I step in front of him.

"Not a good session, I take it?" he asks, tipping his head.

I rub the back of my neck with my hand and stare up at the sky.

"No, it's not that. She seemed really good after seeing Dr. Morrison. It's just... She wants to be alone. All the time." I hold my arms out before letting let fall to my side.

When I meet Rhys' eyes, they soften, and sadness fills them.

"She was gone for a long time, Liam. We don't know all she's been through and there is a huge chance we never will. Give her some space."

Space? Letting her out of my sight is almost physically painful. My anxiety skyrockets and it's hard to breathe. Letting her lock herself in her room is astronomically difficult even when I know it's what she wants. I gave her space in the past and she was taken, and I didn't know. I can't let that happen again.

I refuse.

"I can't do that."

A sympathetic smile spreads over Rhys's face.

"I get you're worried about her, we all are, but she clearly needs to process everything and you breathing down her neck isn't going to help."

"That's not what I'm doing."

"You are though. You follow her everywhere. I'm sure she's feeling trapped by it."

My heart stops and my muscles lock.

"I don't know how to leave her alone, Rhys. I walked away from her before and now that she's back... I just... I don't know what to do."

He nods in understanding and lets out a sigh.

"I think it's best if you give her some space for a few days. I think it'll be good for both of you."

I rub a hand on the scruff that lines my jaw and rub my tongue along the front of my teeth.

"Alright... we'll see if that will help."

"Good. Now, come on. I need you to come check out the Manhattan warehouse with me."

He slaps my back as he strides toward the passenger door.

I once again, climb back into the SUV and back out of the driveway.

CHAPTER 31
Emily

I knock back a handful of pills and chug the glass of water that was set on my nightstand. I stumble toward the window and look over the ground of the estate. The moonlight lights the grounds in a soft glow.

The Ambien has been working wonders for my sleep. I don't dream. I don't have the voices dancing in my head throughout the entire night.

It's an escape.

Something that I hope never leaves.

I've been emailing with Dr. Morrison over the last three days, and she recommended I start writing in a journal again.

She wants me to write something good that happened each day.

There isn't anything I can find good.

I'm breathing and I don't want to be.

It's a struggle every day to find something – anything - to make me feel something other than this cloud of agonizing emptiness that surrounds me.

I had spoken with my ma earlier today and she apologized profusely about not knowing I was missing. She explained that she was in communication with what she had assumed to be me. My social medias had been hacked and apparently there were regular postings of me modeling in photos and various cities I had supposedly visited.

Hearing the depth Vladimir's men had gone to hide my disappearance was daunting.

I don't fault my mother for not noticing our interactions were fabricated. She's grieving the death of my father. I wouldn't have expected her to be able to see the deception when her heart and mind were clouded by that substantial loss.

After telling my ma about the betrayal of Ronan and Lorcan, she and my uncle Cormac hunted them down and executed them before they were able to escape Ireland.

Good riddance.

My body begins to relax as the medication flows through my bloodstream. I walk on wobbling legs to the ensuite and strip my tank and shorts. I stare at myself in the mirror and cringe at the sight.

The blackness that circles my eyes has set up a permanent residence on my face. My eyes are glazed over due to the medication.

I reach over and dig through the top drawer of the vanity until I find what I need. I take the razor apart, leaving just the blade in my palm.

The metal shines with the promise of peace. The promise of continued silence in my mind.

I look at myself in the mirror once more and bring the sharp edge up to my hip. I wince when the blade begins gliding through my flesh. The warm blood pools before sliding down my body.

With one cut made, I line the blade along my skin and make another parallel to the first.

My forefinger groans in protest as the blunt side of the razor cuts into it. I welcome the additional pain with open arms.

Anything to help make me *feel*. Anything to silence the voices. Anything to distract me from the reality of my life. Of the reality that I survived something I shouldn't have.

The blade clinks to the floor with I release it from my grasp. Bringing my fingers up to my hip, I smear my blood across the canvas of my flesh.

I bring my bloodied hand up and as I look into the mirror, I swipe it across my reflection.

Releasing a deep breath, I step into the shower and turn it on. The cold water shocks my system before heating up and warming my skin. The cuts in my hip sting as the water flows over them.

As the medication takes full effect, I struggle to stand, and the world begins to twirl on its axis. I use my hand to stabilize myself before sliding down the wall and onto the floor.

The cold tile is a stark contrast to the heat of the water.

I lean my head against the wall and stare blankly at the water droplets collecting around my feet before they travel down the drain.

I'm not sure how much time has passed when Ingrid's gasp startles me.

"What are you doing?" she sputters with wide eyes.

My head feels incomprehensibly heavy when I try to turn toward her.

She shouts but in my muddled state, I can't make out what it is.

The scent of musk and spice fills my nose.

Liam.

The icy water is shut off and a towel is draped over my shoulders.

"Come on, Féileacán," he whispers as he bends to lift me into his arms.

My head lulls against his shoulder. I can hear the steady beat of his heart and something inside warms.

That's just the medication.

"I'll help her get dressed. You go." Ingrid tells Liam as he sets me on the bed.

I raise my eyes to meet his which are filled with such concern and sadness. My eyelids feel heavy, and they close before I can fight it.

I feel the heat of Liam's body shift closer and then the warmth of his lips on my forehead. My body unconsciously leans into his touch. Somewhere deep inside my heart cracks.

He releases a deep breath before stepping away. My dazed and blurred vision tracked his silhouette making its way to the door and exiting.

"Oh, *Leanbh*...What are you doing?" Ingrid whispers as she helps me dress in a clean tee and shorts.

The weight of my tongue makes it impossible to respond so I don't.

She helps me lay down and then tucks me into my blankets – not too tightly of course – and then switches the overhead lights off. The soft glow of the bedside lamp illuminates the room and I drift off.

I sleep well into the next day when Rhys steps into my room.

"Paige wants you to meet her in the cellar."

My brows raise and my stomach rolls.

"Why?" I ask.

He smirks but the amusement doesn't reach his eyes.

"She has an idea."

I nod and follow him out.

April 17

Something good that happened today...
I helped Paige kill a man.
The sounds of his bones breaking and his
screams echoing in my ears made me
FEEL.

The old Emily never in a million years
would have done something so gruesome.

I guess that's my confirmation...
The old Emily is _dead._

CHAPTER 32
Liam

Electricity spreads throughout my body as I stand outside Emily's door. The nerves I feel are overwhelming my system and I feel like I'm going to throw up.

I don't know what state she's going to be in when I cross that threshold and I don't think I'm strong enough to see her dazed and nearly unconscious from whatever medication she's taken.

I wasn't there when she killed one of Vladimir's men, but Rhys has mentioned it was a shock to see her release so much anger. Emily has always been gentle and relatively level-headed. To know she had that emotion trapped inside makes it even clearer that I need to help her.

I need to find a way to help her release what's inside before it locks her in a place she's never going to escape.

I straighten my shoulders and sigh before raising my fist and knocking on the door.

Silence.

I knock again.

When I'm greeted with more silence, I reach for the doorknob. It twists easily and I push inside.

Emily is seated with her back to me as she stares outside her window. Her hand moves rapidly against the outside of her thigh. Her posture is rigid, and I can hear her shallow, panicked breaths.

"Emily?"

She doesn't react to my voice or presence. Her hand continues to move in jerky yet quick movements.

Something is wrong. The atmosphere in this room is dark and depressing. It's suffocating and makes the collar of my shirt feel too tight. I pull at the material and try to breathe through the smothering sensation.

My steps are muffled from the plush carpeting, but I try to make some noise, so she knows I'm here. I don't want to put her into a panic.

"Féileacán?"

I peer down at her hand and see the blood that is spread over her fingertips and that gaping wound that is in her thigh.

"Emily, stop." I reach for her shoulder, and she jumps with a shriek.

She falls from her chair with a loud *thud* and pushes herself up against the wall. She slaps her hands over her ears and her eyes are closed.

"You're not real. You're not real. You're not real." She mutters under her breath and my heart breaks.

"It's me, Emily. It's Liam."

She shakes her head, her face scrunched in pain.

Blood runs down the side of her thigh and stains the white carpet.

I kneel in front of her. My heart constricting in my chest so tightly, it's physically painful. Her face is pale, sweat lines her temples causing the hairs to stick to her skin.

"Baby... You're okay. You're home." I whisper, trying to coax her out of where her mind has taken her.

She pauses and then peers up at me. Her eyes are haunted and glazed over.

"L-Liam?" she whispers. She's looking at me yet not *seeing me* as being truly here.

"I'm here, Em."

"Please don't leave me again. I don't want to be alone." Her lip quivers and she chokes out a sob.

"I'm not going anywhere, baby," I whisper and scoot closer.

"I don't want to die here."

Pain unlike anything I've ever known saturates my soul and starts to pull it apart thread by thread.

"*Féileacán*, you're home. You're not trapped anymore." I try to keep my voice from shaking but it's nearly impossible.

My beautiful Emily is shattering before my eyes, and I can't stop it.

She closes her eyes and slowly shakes her head.

I reach out and push a strand of her hair behind her ear and she flinches. When she opens her eyes again, they're wide and clear.

"Liam?"

I smile softly at her and stroke her smooth skin.

"I'm here, baby."

Her face crumbles and she throws herself into my arms. A broken sob escapes her. Within seconds the front of my shirt is soaked in her tears. She clings to me with all her strength. I wrap my arms around her small frame and kiss the top of her head before pressing my cheek against it.

The scent of berries fills my nose. She's missing the scent of wildflowers, and it sends another wave of sadness through my heart.

I pull back when I remember the wound on her leg, and I peer down. She sees what I am looking at and tries to pull the hem of her shorts over it.

"Why are you doing this?" I whisper.

She doesn't answer, simply dips her head with embarrassment, or is that shame?

"Emily, why are you hurting yourself?" I press.

Her red hair falls from behind her ear and umbrellas over her face.

"It quiets the noise," she mumbles.

My brows furrow but I don't say anything. I'm not sure what to say. She haunted and I don't know how to help. I don't know what to do.

"Can I help you get cleaned up?" I ask and she nods.

Gently, I scoop her up into my arms and she wraps her arms around my neck. Her body is trembling and there is still a light sheen of sweat along her hairline.

I stride to the ensuite and set her down on the countertop. She keeps her eyes trained on the ground.

I walk over to the cabinet and search for a first-aid kit. Once I've found what I need, I step in front of her and set the container on the counter.

"Em..." I whisper, but she shows no indication that she's heard me.

I grip her chin with my forefinger and thumb and gently raise her eyes to mine. Her eyelids flutter and there is glossiness in her gaze.

"I'm going to start cleaning your leg, okay?" I ask, keeping her from moving her eyes away from mine.

She studies my face and then nods slowly while chewing on her cheek. When I release her chin, she keeps her head up and watches my movements as I set the supplies out.

"This is going to sting," I say as I pour the antiseptic on a clean cotton pad. She doesn't react when I place it on her wound which causes me to pause and look up at her.

She's staring blankly at her leg; her eyes are vacant.

Feck.

I continue through the motions of tending to her leg. Once finished, I throw the garbage away and place my hands on either side of her hips, holding onto the counter.

"Do you want to talk about it?" I ask quietly.

She shakes her head and my shoulders sag.

"Tell me how to help, *mo ghrá*. Please," I plead.

"You can't..." she whispers. Her voice is emotionless.

I step closer to her, and her entire body tenses. Slowly, I press a kiss on the top of her head. Her body begins to relax after I do not remove my lips from her hair.

"Let me help you, Emily. Let me be here for you."

The back of my eyes burn as the emotions within me begin to overflow.

I peer down when I feel her press her palm against my chest. She stares at her hand and then clenches the fabric of my Henley.

"You're really here... Aren't you?" she whispers, more to herself than me.

I don't reply. I just watch as she explores my chest with her hand. She adds the other and then trails up along my neck and finally my face. I close my eyes and simply *feel* the softness of her touch along my skin. My body is buzzing, and my heart is beating erratically with each pass of her touch. Her fingers lightly trace my jawline and then my lips, where they stop.

When she pulls her touch away, I open my eyes.

"I'm ready to go to bed." I'm forced to step back when she hops off the countertop. She winces when her leg meets the ground and I realize it's the only time she's reacted to the pain.

I watch as she makes her way out of the ensuite. When I step through the doorway, she's pouring some pills into her palm.

"How much of that have you taken?" I ask and step toward her.

She mumbles something under her breath, but I can't hear what is said.

"Emily," I press.

"I take what I need," she says, keeping her back to me as she raises her hand to her lips and tosses the pills into her mouth. She swallows them dry before bringing the glass of water from her nightstand to her lips.

Her phone rings and she looks down at the screen for a second before sending the caller to voicemail.

161

"Please leave," she whispers and then climbs into bed.

I clench and unclench my fists as I watch her settle into bed.

"I'm here when you need me, *Féileacán*."

I stride to the doorway and exit her room.

CHAPTER 33
Emily

Sitting in the kitchen with Niall, I push my food around my plate. Liam has been encouraging me to step out of my room for at least an hour every day, so here I am. Spending my hour in the kitchen trying to force food down my throat.

He's been a constant since he came to my room last week. He's actually been helping me with talking. I mean, we don't talk about what happened to me. The only person outside of Dr. Morrison who knows what happened is Declan.

And the only reason he knows is because he wouldn't leave me alone about how isolated I am. He didn't understand and after weeks of hounding me, I caved and told him.

Of course, I didn't tell him everything but enough that he finally left me alone.

Liam's presence has surprisingly been welcome, and I look forward to the time I get to spend with him. There have been a few times that my body has reacted to him in ways that it hasn't in such a long time. When he sits close to me, I lean in and wish he'd press his lips to mine instead of my forehead.

Each night, I find myself mourning the loss of his presence and wishing he'd never leave.

It's been confusing the say the least.

Paige and Sarah step into the kitchen and smile widely when they see me sitting at the counter.

"Hi, Emily. How are you feeling?" Sarah says with a grin.

I straighten my shoulders and return their smile as best as I can.

"I'm doing really good, how are you guys?"

I feel the burn of Paige's gaze as she studies my profile. When I turn to meet her eyes, she smiles softly at me, but her brows are slightly pinched.

"We're good. Sarah came to rip me a new one about killing more men without her help."

I chuckle softly.

I haven't had a desire to kill any more people since that first man I helped Paige with. It felt amazing at the time to let go and allow my emotions to take control, but after the weight was lifted, all I saw were the women and children who suffered because of Vladimir.

Their stares were wide, and they looked afraid of me. I couldn't stomach it, so I didn't go back down to the cellar.

"Hello, ladies," Niall says as he wipes his hands on the cloth draped over his shoulder. "What can I get for you?"

Paige smiles warmly at him as she takes a seat next to me. Sarah takes the one on the opposite side.

"We wanted to come and see if we can talk you into making steaks for dinner."

"No need to talk me into it, Miss Paige. Your wish is my command." He dips his chin.

"Can I have him?" Sarah says.

I snort and then freeze at the sudden noise. It's the first time in weeks I've had a genuine reaction with someone who isn't Liam.

"Hell no, you can't. Niall is the best and refuse to lose him." Paige laughs.

Niall shakes his head with a huge smile spread across his face. Pink tints his cheeks when he spins around and sees Declan striding into the room.

Black smoke begins to spread across the countertop, and I tense. I try to ignore the dread that spreads over me and pay attention to Declan as he greets everyone but it's a struggle.

I roll my eyes when he looks up at me after essentially making out with Paige in the middle of the kitchen.

The smoke darkens and I lose myself in it. There is no sound around me. It's as though the entire atmosphere has been sucked into its murkiness with no way out. It begins to envelop me; I expect fear to invade my body, but it never comes. I don't feel anything. My body is completely frozen, I stare unblinking as the smoke continues to grow and grow.

Suddenly Declan's voice breaks through and I startle. He's staring at me, and I point at myself.

"Me?"

He raises his brows. "I am looking right at you, Em."

"Psh, yeah I'm completely good." I feign a relaxed posture and flick my hand out in dismissal.

When his attention is no longer on me, I find myself lost, once again, to the shadow that hasn't stopped growing. Time and space no longer exist. Just darkness and complete silence.

"All done, boss." Liam's voice breaks my trance, and my skin feels hot when I see him walking into the kitchen. My breath catches at the sight of his black Henley stretching over the broad plain of his chest and wrapping around his muscular arms. He's wearing black cargo pants and black boots, and it just adds another layer of sex appeal to an already gorgeous man.

I feel Declan's stare and when I meet his eyes, they narrow.

Shit.

I turn my gaze back to my plate.

Declan's voice is tense when he orders Liam to meet him in his office.

Shit. Shit. Shit.

It's not like anything romantic is happening between us but I don't know what Liam is going to do if Declan tells him to leave me alone.

He gave me up once before. Will he do it again?

"Don't worry."

I spin to Paige who is smiling softly at me.

"Worry?"

She peeks over my shoulder at Sarah and then meets my eyes once more.

"About Liam."

I avert my gaze.

"I don't know what you're talking about."

"Sure you don't," Sarah says and Paige glares at her.

"What? She's the one pretending that she's not completely in love with Liam."

Paige rolls her eyes and lets out an exacerbated breath.

"Ignore Sarah. I know that Liam has been a big reason you've been getting better. It's also one of the reasons I haven't been spending as much time with you as I did when we first got home. Liam loves you, Em. So don't worry about what Declan is going to do."

She winks at me and then spins around and leaves the room.

"She's right, you know," Sarah says once Paige is out of sight.

"About?" I ask.

"Liam loves you."

"We have a history, and he didn't admit to loving me then, so I'm not so sure his feelings are considered love," I say with a shrug.

Sarah studies my profile. "That's not what Rhys said."

"What do you mean?" I ask, sitting up straighter in my seat.

She smiles, her eyes fill with mischief.

"Ask Liam about it." She winks and pats my leg and then hops off the stool. Leaving me alone in the kitchen.

My phone vibrates on the counter. Ma's name flashes across the screen. I stare, unmoving until the screen goes black. A second later, the notification of a new voicemail pops up.

Sighing, I press *delete* without listening to the message. Hopping off the stool, I leave the kitchen and head toward my room.

CHAPTER 34
Liam

Anger continues to flow through my veins with each pound of my fist on the bag. My knuckles are swollen and bloodied, and my muscles scream in pain, but I don't stop. I can't stop. This is my punishment.

I fucking agreed to Declan's demand of stopping what has been going on with Emily, just like I did with her father and I'm bloody furious with myself. He's not wrong in saying she's been through enough.

I know she has. But over the last couple of weeks, she's started to put on weight, she's willing to leave her room and has actually been showing emotion.

It's been days since I've spoken with her because Declan keeps putting me on a bunch of assignments. My texts have gone unanswered, and it has me on edge. On top of that, she's still relying on medication more than she should and any time I bring it up, she all but eats me alive.

My arm gives out when it connects with the punching bag.

"Let it all out?" Declan's voice sounds from behind me, and I bite down on my tongue.

My arms hang loosely at my sides, and I twist my neck and roll my shoulders, eliciting popping sounds from the joints.

Declan is standing with his legs wide, and arms crossed over his chest when I turn around to face him.

"Do you have an assignment for me?" I ask, avoiding his question. I'm lacking patience for his bullshit right now and I don't need a bullet in the head today.

His eyes narrow as he studies me. "Not today."

I nod, then turn to where I set my water bottle. After I've quenched my thirst and wiped the sweat from my brow with a rag. I turn back to Declan.

"I mean this with the least amount of disrespect I can muster but fuck you."

His features harden but he doesn't say a word, so I continue.

"I walked away from Emily when your da was still alive and I regretted it. I can't do it again, boss. I can't." I shake my head. "Emily... Emily is everything. I can't live without her."

The sound of the door shutting draws mine and Declan's attention. Rhys walks in, his eyes pivot between the two of us and he raises a brow.

"All good?" he asks.

Declan ignores him and returns his attention to me. The tension in the room rises and the hair on the back of my neck starts to stand on end.

"I'm not lettin' her go this time." I keep my voice strong, and my chin raised.

"Oh..." Rhys's voice trails off as he steps up to Declan's side. He puts his hands in his pockets and watches Declan's features closely.

"What do you mean you walked away when my da was still alive?" Declan's voice is calm, but his posture is tight.

"Emily and I had a relationship two years ago. Your father found out and threatened to kill me in front of her if it continued." I shake my head in shame and let out a sigh. "I allowed my insecurities to get in the way of the best thing that ever happened to me then and I refuse to allow you to take her from me now."

"Dec –." Rhys starts but is interrupted when Declan holds his hand up. His jaw clenches and unclenches as he glares at me.

"I'll kill anyone who gets in my way when it comes to Emily. Including you."

Rhys's eyes nearly burst out of his skull.

"Is that a threat?" Declan finally growls.

I smirk. "It's a promise."

He steps into my space with his hackles raised but I don't back down. I maintain eye contact—something I should have done in the past with their da.

"You're not worthy of my sister."

"I know I'm not. But I will spend the rest of my life worshipping the ground she walks on."

"Dec, Emily has been doing better with Liam around."

Declan whips around toward Rhys who holds his hands up.

"I'm not saying to approve of this. That's your decision. All I'm saying is to watch her for yourself."

He huffs a breath, shakes his head, and then growls.

His fist connects with my face so fast that I don't have time to react. When I turn my head back to him, his pistol is raised and pointed at my head. I stand taller and move to press my forehead against the barrel.

His eyes flare in surprise.

Rhys stands completely still, waiting for Declan to make his move.

"Beat the shite out of me, carve into my flesh – feck – rip my eyes out of my skull. Nothing you do will keep me from making her mine." He presses the gun harder into my skin. "Do it. If you truly don't approve of this. Then do it. Because I promise you, right here and now, I'll fight for her until my last breath."

Declan's muscles shake with rage, but he lowers the gun. His icy glare remains in place when he leans into my face.

"We'll see." He says through clenched teeth and leaves the gym.

Rhys lets out a breath I didn't know he was holding and shakes his head. Walking up to me, he punches my arm and I grunt.

"You definitely got some balls on you kid. I thought for sure we'd have to clean for brain off the floor." He chuckles under his breath, but I don't laugh.

"I meant every word."

I unwrap my hands and stretch my fingers.

"I know you did. Now the question you need to ask yourself is, what are you doing to show Emily you're not pussying out this time?"

I glare at him from the corner of my eye.

In truth, I have no idea. I haven't spoken a word to her or seen her in days. Does she think I gave up like before?

Ignoring his question, I pack my things and head to my room.

I need to come up with a way for Emily to know that she is *it* for me.

April 30

I know I'm supposed to write positive things in this journal but today has just been... hard.
I hate smiling and laughing with everyone and pretending like I'm okay.

I'm an imposter in my life and it's killing me

Paige is the only one who understands but I can't bring her down with me so once again I pretend that everything is fine.
But in reality... I'm not okay...

CHAPTER 35
Liam

After receiving no answer to my last three knocks, I twist the knob to Emily's room and enter inside. She's sprawled over the top of her bed with a glazed stare pointed at her ceiling.

Anxiety fills my veins and I'm at her side in two strides.

"Emily?" I ask, pushing a strand of her out of her face. She blinks slowly before her eyes turn to mine.

God damnit. She can barely keep her eyes open.

I sit on her bed and pull her into my arms. Her head lulls lazily against my shoulder.

"What are you doing, *Féileacán?*" I whisper and press a kiss on her forehead. She mutters under her breath, but I can't make out the words.

My heart aches for her. She's in so much pain and looking for an escape in places that are just going to kill her in the end.

Shifting, I pull my phone from my back pocket and send a text to Paige. She enters a moment later with a glass of water.

Tears well into her eyes when she sees the state of Emily.

"Don't tell Declan. I got her." I say quietly and take the glass from her outstretched hand.

"Stay with her tonight." She says softly and I meet her eyes.

"Thank you, Paige. Really."

She steps closer and sets her hand on Emily's shoulder. She gives it a light squeeze before making her way out of the room.

"Baby, I need you to try and drink this." I peer down at Emily who watches me with her heavy gaze. "Can you do that for me?" I ask and she nods slowly.

Reaching over, I set the glass on her nightstand before adjusting our position, so she is sitting between my legs with her back against my chest.

Taking the glass, I raise it to her lips. Sluggishly, she leans forward, and I wrap my free arm around her torso to support her weight.

She groans as she drinks the ice-cold water. When she falls back against me, I place the glass back on the nightstand. I caress her arm with my fingers as I lean against the headboard. Her body is lax, and her breaths are slow.

What the hell did she take?

I search the room from where I sit but can't find the pills, I know she has. I'll have to wait until she's asleep to find them.

She hums and I pull her closer to me.

"I'm here, Emily. You're not alone anymore. You don't need to keep doing this." I struggle to swallow the lump in my throat.

I plant another kiss against her hair and breathe her scent in.

When her body relaxes further, I know she's fallen asleep. I gently shift to set her down on the bed. She rubs her face against my side and breathes in deeply. She hums and I swear a smile tries to spread over her face before disappearing.

My eyes roam over her face. Her cheeks have started filling out, but her skin is still pale from lack of sunlight.

Lightly, I brush my finger along the bridge of her nose. Warmth spreads over me as I trace the freckles that paint her skin. Her lashes are still as long as I remember. They flutter as her eyes move rapidly behind her eyelids.

Releasing a deep breath, I push off the bed and begin my search for her medications. I find them in a basket under the bathroom sink. Pulling it out, I set it on top of the counter and begin rifling through it. I don't know what any of these medications are for, so I search each of them up on the internet.

Antipsychotics.

Muscle relaxers.

Antidepressants.

A variety of eye drops.

The number of medications in this basket seems endless and my heart breaks the more of them that I discover.

Shite.

I grip the edge of the counter until my knuckles whiten and close my eyes. My limbs tremble and I fight to contain the emotional pain and grief that fill my system. I need to do something. But what? What could I possibly do for Emily to see that she doesn't need to rely on medication to survive?

When I go to place the basket back under the sink, I find a small box that seems out of place. I reach over and pick it up. It's light and I assume it might be empty, so I go to put it back. It slips from my grasp and falls. Loose tablets and capsules of unknown medications spill across the tiled floor.

What the fuck?

Some of these look like the ones in the bottles, others don't and it sends a wave of unease through my body.

Where in the fuck did she get these?

I pull my phone from my pocket and snap some photos of the medications before cleaning up and putting everything away. Striding back into the room, Emily lies in the same position as I left her.

I walk to the side of the bed that is closest to the door. Slipping off my boots, I take off my pants and tee before sliding into bed. Lying on my back, I tuck my arm under my head and drape the other over my stomach. My thoughts are in disarray with everything I've learned today.

Emily's phone pings and I move to check the screen.

Ma

> I love you, Emily. Please don't
> push me away. Call me back.

Furrowing my brows, I peer at Emily over my shoulder.

Emily has always been close with Caetlin. Why would she be pushing her away?

I set her phone back on the nightstand and lay back down. After spending hours staring at the ceiling trying to figure out what to do, I finally drift off to sleep.

CHAPTER 36
Emily

It's hot. Why is it so hot? I shift, trying to push the blankets off my body, but there are none. I shift again and hit something hard. My eyes fly open, and I sit up. My heart gallops in my chest, my throat closes, and tears instantly fill my vision.

"Hey, hey, it's okay. It's me." Liam's raspy voice fills my ears. Turning to my right, I see him sitting shirtless in my bed.

What the hell?

"Wh-what are you doing here?" I pant. My eyes drift down his chest and stop when I see a butterfly tattoo over his heart. My brows furrow and I raise my confused gaze to his eyes.

"What is that?" I gesture to the tattoo.

"You." He says softly.

"I don't understand." I shake my head.

I pull away when he reaches for me. "Liam, what are you doing in my room? In my bed?"

He sighs and runs a hand through his hair. "I came to see you last night and you were nearly comatose from whatever shite you took."

I scoff and roll my eyes. "That doesn't explain why you're in my bed." Anger begins to simmer in my blood.

"I wasn't goin' to bloody leave you in here alone and risk you choking on your own vomit or some shite like that."

My face contorts and I climb out of bed to put distance between us. My eyes involuntarily flick to the ensuite where my promise of an escape sits in bottles under the sink. Liam follows my gaze, and he pushes the blankets off himself.

His black boxer-briefs outline his morning erection and I avert my eyes before he notices my stare.

I internally groan in annoyance that I even looked.

He stomps to the bathroom and rips open the cabinet. He takes out my medication basket and the box I keep hidden in the back.

"What are you doing?!" I shriek when he begins rifling through the bottles and dumping their contents down the toilet.

"You're not going to keep popping pills to deal with your shite, Emily. It's time you find some other way to cope." He grits through clenched teeth.

I claw at his arms to get him out of the way but he's a fucking wall and completely immobile.

"Stop! Liam, stop!"

He spins around and grips my face with both hands.

"You're going to kill yourself, Emily!"

"Good! Then maybe I can finally be free of the fucking voices in my head. The fucking women and children that sit in this fucking room with me!" I scream as tears begin to spill from my eyes.

Sadness fills his eyes as he stares at me like he doesn't recognize me. His grip tightens when I try pulling away.

"Look at me, *Féileacán*." He orders.

Hearing him calling me *butterfly* in person is nearly as painful as hearing the ghost of him say it when I was trapped in *the hole.* My lip quivers and I close my eyes. I shake my head, avoiding looking at his beautiful fucking face.

"This has to stop, baby. You don't have to do this alone. You're not alone anymore. Let me fight this with you."

The simmer becomes boiling rage and I snap my eyes open. Glaring at him, I press my hands against his chest and shove myself out of his grasp.

I point my finger at him. "You don't get to say that to me. Ever. You had your chance to fight with me. *For me.* And you didn't, so take your plea and shove it up your ass."

I push past him and exit the bathroom. He is right on my heels.

He grips my bicep and spins me to face him.

"You have every right to be mad. I was a fecking eejit for walkin' away from you. But I'm not goin' to this time."

I laugh humorlessly and get into his face.

"Let me make this clear to you like you did to me. I. Don't. Want. You."

Of course, I'm fucking lying but I refuse to trust Liam with my heart again. Fool me once, shame on you. Fool me twice, shame on me. Only, Liam won't fool me twice. I've already been broken enough.

His face steels and he grinds his teeth. His eyes bounce between mine. They're filled with anger and regret, but I don't care.

He had his chance to love me, and he chose to let me go. Despite him being the reason I fought to stay alive, I'm not giving myself to him. I can't. I'm barely surviving as it is.

"I'm fighting for you now, Em. Let me."

I rip my arm out his grasp.

"No. I'll find someone who will fight for me the first time. Not after the damage to my heart and soul becomes irreversible."

His hackles raise and he steps closer, forcing me to take a step back. This dance continues until I'm pressed against the wall. He crowds my space and slams his hands against the wall, caging me in.

179

"You want to try and replace me, Emily? Fine. Go ahead. But know this..." he dips his head, bringing his lips inches from mine. "I won't hesitate to put a bullet in the head of every man who speaks to you."

A shiver skates down my spine and for the first time in two years, arousal saturates every fiber of my being.

Damnit.

Liam smirks arrogantly, obviously having seen how my body reacted, and then pulls away. Unconsciously my body leans into him, chasing his lips.

Liam looks me over, stopping at my chest. My thin tee doesn't hide the fact that my nipples are pebbled to near-painful points. I swiftly wrap my arms over my chest to hide the clear sign of my arousal.

Liam licks his lips and chuckles under his breath. He makes no attempt to hide his hardened cock as he steps to the side of the bed. Bending, he picks up his pants and slides them on, followed by his tee.

"Get ready. I'll be back in an hour. We're going to the garden."

What the fuck just happened?

My head is spinning at the rapid changes in conversation we had since waking up.

I frown. "I'm not going anywhere with you."

After slipping on his boots, he walks over to me and cups the side of my neck. His thumb strokes my cheek lightly and I find myself leaning into the feeling of his callused skin touching mine.

"One hour. Be ready." He says with a smile.

He presses a kiss to my forehead and then turns to leave the room. My jaw is slackened as I gape at the door.

I gasp when I suddenly remember what Liam was doing in the bathroom. I spin on my heels and run to see if any of my medications are still safe.

Nope. Only the *safe ones* remain.

Motherfucker.

CHAPTER 37
Liam

Returning to Emily's room, I knock before entering. She's not in the room but the sound of the shower tells me that's where I'll find her. I make my way over and freeze. Emily is crouched with her arms wrapped around her legs and her chin resting on her knees.

Instead of immediately trying to get her attention, I lean against the door frame and observe. She's as still as stone. The room is humid from the heat of the water and my upper lip begins to sweat.

From where I stand, I can see her lips moving but no words are said.

I frown and shift nervously. Her attention immediately spins to me, and I tense.

"The voices... they never stop," she whispers.

I remember her comment about the voices, and I swallow tightly. Pushing away from the door, I take the towel from the hook by the shower. Reaching in, I shut off the water and then drape the towel over Emily's body.

Bending, I scoop her into my arms, and she rests her head on my shoulder. The fabric of my shirt becomes soaked and sticks to my body. Instead of setting her on the bed, I sit and set her on my lap.

So many emotions rage within me that I can't focus on just one.

We sit in silence for an eternity. I close my eyes and listen to the sound of her breathing.

"I'll be right back," I say and plant a kiss on the top of her head before moving to set her down so I can stand. I walk over to her walk-in closet and quickly grab a pair of leggings and a sweater.

With it being early spring, the temperature outside is still chilly.

The clothes fall to the ground when I step back into the room. Emily is standing in front of the floor-length mirror that sits in the corner. She tips her head side-to-side, examining her naked reflection with an expressionless face.

I watch as sadness spreads over her face and her eyes gloss over.

"Emily?" I whisper, taking a step toward her, but she doesn't respond.

The light coming through her window reflects off something in her hand and my eyes flick to it.

It's a razor blade.

My stomach falls and I race to her just before the sharpened edge reaches her skin. I grip her wrist and spin her toward me. Her eyes are wide with shock as she stares at me.

"Don't," I say. My jaw clenches.

"I need to make them stop, Liam... Please let me make them stop." Tears well in her eyes.

Releasing her, I step back and rip off my tee. I grab her wrist again and bring the edge of the blade to my chest.

"Give me your pain, *Féileacán*. If you need to cut something, cut me. Don't..." I swallow the lump in my throat. "Don't hurt yourself anymore, baby. "

Her stormy eyes flick between mine. Hesitantly, she pushes the blade into my flesh. I hiss through my teeth as it begins to slice into me. Her gaze repeatedly jumps from my face to her shaky hand. The warmth of my blood sliding down my chest sends a chill down my spine.

After cutting into my chest a few times, she steps back. Her breaths are erratic, her pupils are blown when she peers at up me, and her hands are trembling.

Her bottom lip quivers and I cup the back of her head, bringing our foreheads together.

"I…" she pauses and licks her lips. My eyes track the movement, and my heart rate increases.

She moves closer to me and places her palm against the cut. She stares in fascination. The rise and fall of my chest intensify. The feel of her skin against mine sends my blood into overdrive.

"Liam," she whispers, and I close my eyes. I'm thrown into the past. Back to when Emily first entrusted me with her body. With her heart.

I release a deep breath and when I open my eyes, her gaze is soft.

"Don't say my name like that," I whisper. The corner of her mouth ticks as a smile tries to form.

She's remembering it too. Remembering us.

I brush the tip of my nose lightly against hers and she hums. My lips hover so close to her lips, all I need to do is shift and they'll press against hers.

Hesitance fills her eyes and I pull back. "What is it?"

She swallows tightly, her lips forming a frown. "I-They,"

"What?"

She closes her eyes and shakes her head. A tear rolls down her cheek. I don't know what's going on. What is causing this reaction out of her?

"Tell me, baby." I whisper.

"They took my body, Liam… They've felt it." Her voice breaks.

Understanding dawns on me and my blood boils with anger, but my heart cracks. Does she think this would change anything? Does she think I'd love her any less?

183

Taking her chin between my forefinger and thumb, I tilt her head. Her eyes flutter open, and they glisten with more tears.

"Listen to me, *Féileacán*. There is nothing in this world or the next that would change the way I see you, the way I want you. Your body is mine. Not theirs."

I swipe away the tear that falls from her eye.

"I'm dirty, Liam." She chokes out.

I shake my head. "I will never see you as anything less than perfection, Emily. You feel dirty? Let me wash away any remanence of their existence on your skin, in your mind, and in your soul. You belong to me, *with me*."

Her eyes flick between mine. They're sad but trusting. She nibbles on her bottom lip, never moving her eyes from mine.

Swallowing tightly, she whispers, "Kiss me."

I pull back and search her face. Her freckles appear darker as a soft-pink spreads over her cheeks. I move my hand to the side of her neck and caress her bottom lip with my thumb. She raises her hand and holds onto my wrist, staring at me with warm, welcoming eyes.

Slowly, I inch closer. Our breaths intertwine, becoming one. She sucks in a breath when I place the lightest of kisses on the corner of her mouth. I place another on the opposite side.

She moves her head, chasing my touch and it sends a thrill through my body.

My eyes flick down to her naked breasts. Her dusty-rose nipples are peddled and my cock doubles in size. It presses against the confines of my pants.

The tension in the air coils around us. It's so potent that I can taste it.

She gasps when I wrap my arm around her waist and pull her body into mine. My lips land on hers and I swear fireworks explode.

She immediately melts into me, and I groan when a small whimper escapes her lips. Our tongues move together effortlessly. Her hands explore my chest, the sting of the cut is a dull ache, but it only heightens this moment.

Bending, I cup the back of her thighs and pick her up. She wraps her legs around my waist, and I walk us toward the bed.

Without breaking our kiss, I kneel on the bed. Using one arm to support her weight, I use the other to push down my pants and boxer-briefs. I kick them off and they fall on the ground.

My cock is painfully hard and desperate to be buried in her pussy.

"Please... Please, Liam." she begs between kisses.

I lay her down onto the mattress. Her still damp hair spreads behind her. My eyes roam over her face and for the first time in so long, her eyes are bright.

Warmth seeps into my soul at the sight.

I pepper her collarbone, neck, and jaw with kisses.

Gripping my cock, I slide the head up and down through her glistening folds, coating myself in her arousal. She moans and arches her back. Her head digs into the mattress, her breasts are pushed into my chest.

My eyes roll when press into her pussy. She welcomes me by spreading her thighs wider and I take full advantage of it. Each inch that disappears into her cunt elicits whimpers and moans from her lips.

"Fuck, Emily. I've missed this. Missed you."

Once I'm fully seated inside her, I pause. Allowing her time to adjust to me.

"Okay. Okay." She says, nodding rapidly.

I pull back to the tip and when in a slow thrust, push back in. She tips her head back, mouth falling open, and a deep, satisfied moan falls from her lips.

CHAPTER 38
Emily

Blazing fire scorches my blood. I feel each vein and divot of Liam's cock with each slow thrust he makes. Undeniable ecstasy swims through me at the feeling of his body connecting with mine.

I can't find it in myself to think of the consequences of giving my body to Liam again. And honestly, I don't give a shit right now.

"Oh my god. Yes. Yes. Yes." I moan.

My hands reach down, and I grip his ass, pulling him closer. Encouraging him to fuck me harder. My core clenches when his breathy moan sounds in my ear.

"You feel as amazin' as I remember. Tell me this pussy is still mine."

I don't respond but the muscles that are wrapped around his cock contract in a silent answer.

I can always deny it despite my body saying otherwise.

His tempo remains unchanged, and my orgasm slowly builds. My clit pulses and swells with each thrust. Liam rolls his hips, causing his pelvis to rub my clit, and I explode.

Every muscle in my body grows taut and I arch into him.

"That's it. Squeeze my cock, Emily." He hisses. His hand envelops my hip and he pistons into me. The headboard hammers into the wall from the force of his body crashing into mine.

"Oh fuck! Fuck yes!" I scream. My eyes roll to the back of my head.

With one final thrust, Liam empties himself into me with an animalistic growl.

We lie wrapped in each other. Bodies sweaty, hearts pounding, and completely engrossed in our own bubble.

Liam slides out of me, his cum drips down my lips and down the seam of my ass. He watches in awe before scooping it up with two fingers and pushing it back in.

He looks up at me with a mischievous smile.

"My cum stays inside you."

A small smile appears on my face, and I bite the inside of my bottom lip. My cheeks heat as I recall the day he took me in the wildflowers.

Climbing off the bed, Liam heads toward the ensuite and returns a second later with a damp washcloth. He kneels in front of me and nudges my legs apart. I spread them for him, and he swipes the fabric through my folds.

I whimper and jolt upward when it makes contact with my still-sensitive clit.

"I guess going to the garden is no longer happening," Liam chuckles, slumping into the mattress after tossing the washcloth into the laundry basket.

I hum in agreement.

My limps feel like Jell-O. There is no possible way I could climb off this bed even if I wanted to.

"Come here," Liam says in a low voice. I turn toward him, and he motions to the top of the bed.

Spinning around, I trudge over, and he pulls me into his chest. He tugs the blankets over us. I release a breath, relaxing further into him.

My brows pull inward when the thought of what will come of this starts to trickle into my mind.

When Liam wraps his arms around me and presses a kiss on my head, I decide I'll worry about it later.

Right now, I want to simply live in this moment. Soak up the scent of Liam in my nose and believe that the last year of my life never happened. That Liam never left me, and I was never broken.

My eyes fly open, and I gasp. The room is pitch black and I hear the shuffling of something moving at the end of my bed.

Nonono. Please, not now.

My body trembles and I feel like the weight of an elephant is sitting on my chest. I can't breathe. Panic overtakes me. I try to scream but nothing comes out. My arms and legs feel like they're strapped down.

I turn my head to get Liam's attention but he's not there.

I'm alone.

Why did he leave?! Why are my lights off?!

The bed dips with the weight of something climbing onto it. My vision is blurred from the tears that flood my eyes and spill down my cheeks.

I try to open my mouth again, but nothing happens. The sensation of something pressing against my lips prevents me from doing anything. But there is nothing there.

What is happening?!

I feel an icy breath against my neck and slam my eyes shut. My head thrashes from side to side as I try to escape whatever is trapping me in this bed. In this room.

A deep, sinister chuckle sends terror down my spine.

I know that chuckle.

Nikolai.

No. No, he's dead.

Isn't he?

"Did you really think you'd be free of this place, Kukla?" *he laughs.*

I whimper and feel my bottom lip quiver.

The feel of his hand sliding up my thigh sends another wave of terror through my system.

My screams are muffled but still, I scream and scream. I continue to thrash my head. My heart beats against my chest and the sound is like a sledgehammer in my ears.

This isn't real. This isn't real. It's just my mind playing a sick and twisted game.

But it feels so fucking real.

Large hands grip onto my face and this time, I let out a shriek.

"Hey, hey, it's me. It's Liam, baby."

My vision clears. I'm still in my room. Only this time, it's not dark. I'm not alone. Nikolai is dead.

A thick layer of sweat covers every surface of my skin. My breaths are shallow, and my eyes are wide with fear.

"You're okay, it's okay," Liam whispers and I finally focus my eyes on him. He hovers above me. His eyes are filled with concern, panic, and sadness. His fingers swipe at the tears that haven't stopped flowing from my eyes.

My entire body is shaking as though I've been in sub-zero temperatures. My teeth chatter violently against each other.

Liam wraps his fingers around my hand and brings it to his lips. He places gentle kisses on my skin and then places my palm against his heart. It pounds against my hand.

"I'm here. This is real. Not what you saw or felt in your mind. What you're feelin' now is real, Emily."

I don't fight the sob that climbs up my throat. It bursts through me with such force that I swear the house shudders.

Liam sits on the bed and pulls me into his arms. He gently rocks us as he strokes my hair.

"P- please don't leave," I cry.

"I'm not goin' anywhere." He tightens his hold and presses his lips to my head.

CHAPTER 39
Liam

I sit with my back pressed against the headboard and watch the steady rise and fall of Emily's chest as she sleeps. Her lips are slightly parted, hair mess of red tangles. Her fingers clutch onto the blanket as though it'll be ripped away from her.

It took several hours for her to finally fall back asleep after waking from her nightmare. I lied awake until the sun rose, and when it shone through the window, I pulled the curtains to leave the room dark, aside from the lamp that sits on her nightstand.

My thoughts race as I try to come up with a way to help her sleep without resorting to medication. She hasn't started to show any signs of withdrawal, but I know it's coming soon.

I need to be prepared for it.

Leaning forward, I push away the hair from her forehead and press a light kiss to her skin before rising.

I need to go change before she wakes and sees me gone.

Swiftly and quietly, I exit her room.

As I make my way toward the front door, I'm stopped by the sound of Declan calling my name.

Stopping at the base of the staircase, I wait as he saunters over.

When he stops in front of me, his eyes flick up in the direction of Emily's room before he meets my eyes. Irritation rises in his features and his jaw ticks.

Straightening my shoulders, I stand taller, refusing to be intimidated by him.

"What are you doing?" he grunts.

"Goin' to get changed. I want to be back before Emily wakes up."

"You stayed in her bed?" he growls, shifting closer.

"Yes. And I'll continue to stay there until *she* tells me otherwise." I ball my fist, waiting for him to make his move.

He studies me with a scowl planted on his face.

"I don't approve of this."

"Seeing as I don't have a bullet in my skull, some part of you does." I shrug.

His lip twitches and satisfaction flows through me.

Despite what he says, and despite the fact that I'm not worthy of her, Declan is okay with my being with Emily.

"I stopped you to tell you to pick up a few gallons of hydrofluoric acid. Paige has one last person to take care of." He smirks when my brows shoot to my hairline.

"Does she plan to melt someone?" I ask.

"I have a feeling that's exactly what she plans to do."

I nod with an amused smirk and brows raised. Declan chuckles at my expression before sobering.

"As much as I hate to admit it, Emily can make her own decisions, and if being with you is one of them... Then I guess I'll have to accept it."

I'm working on making her see that but I'm not about to tell Declan that bit of information. He'd likely change his mind.

"I love her, Boss. I've always loved her."

He nods, rolling his lips inward before stepping past me.

"See you later tonight." He says over his shoulder, walking toward his office.

I watch until he's out of sight. Making a quick detour to the kitchen, I ask Niall to prepare breakfast for Emily then head to the guardhouse.

Emily is still asleep when I step inside the room. She's wrapped in her blankets in a tight ball. Her brows her pinched and her lips are pursed.

As if sensing my stare, she begins to stir. Muttering under her breath. I move closer and gently sit at the foot of the bed.

"Hi, baby," I whisper.

Her eyes flutter open, and she looks at me with a confused expression. She sits up and rubs her eyes. A small smile sweeps over her beautiful face the moment her vision is cleared.

"Hi." She pushes a strand of hair behind her ear.

I'll never get used to this woman's beauty. Every one of her features is absolute perfection.

"Did you sleep better?"

She shrugs and I frown.

A knock on the door pulls our attention. I stand and open it.

Ingrid is holding a tray with a plate of breakfast. With a brow raised, her gaze travels down my body in obvious suspicion. When her eyes meet mine and nods curtly, pushing the tray into my hands.

"Make sure she eats." With that, she saunters down the hallway.

I kick the door shut with my foot and then take the tray to Emily.

She lightly scrunches her nose before masking her reaction. Trying to get Emily to eat is like pulling teeth. She knows she needs it, but she'll eat as little as possible and then say she's full.

193

"Don't make that face," I scold playfully.

"I'm not hungry."

"You only just woke up; you need to eat."

I gesture with my chin for Emily to sit against the headboard and then set it on her lap.

"I'm really not hungry. I need to talk to you about something important though."

I tilt my head, brows furrowing.

"What about?"

Pursing her lips, she stares into my eyes. "I need that medication you threw out."

My body tenses and my jaw clenches. Despite her features being blank, her eyes are pleading.

"I can't sleep without them, Liam. I haven't had a nightmare like that since I started taking them."

"Emily, you were relying on that medication far too much. From what I saw under the sink, you weren't exactly taking them like you were supposed to."

Her eyes immediately fall to the tray.

"I'll do better," she mutters, pushing her utensils around with her forefinger.

As much as I'd like to trust her, I can't. Being a part of this world, I've seen my fair share of what happens when you don't take prescription medication as intended.

Addiction is a disease. It happens swiftly and silently. Slithering its way through every intertwined fiber of your DNA until it's too late.

Peering down at her, I lick my lips, trying to formulate a way to make her understand that what she's doing isn't safe.

"What would your doctor say about how you've been taking your meds, Em?"

Even with her head down, I can see the grimace that flashes over her face.

"Call her."

Her head whips up to me.

"Call who? Dr. Morrison?" She sputters.

I nod, picking up her phone off the nightstand and handing it to her. If she won't listen to me, then maybe speaking to a medical professional will help.

She nibbles on her lip as she stares down at the black screen. Her fingers are trembling but I'm not sure if it's from the beginning of withdrawal or nervousness of having to call her doctor.

With a sigh, Emily unlocks her phone and dials Dr. Morrison.

"Emily, hi. Is everything okay?" Dr. Morrison says when she answers the phone.

"Hi, Dr. Morrison. I was calling because I have a little issue that I need to talk to you about."

"Okay, would this conversation be better served in my office?" she asks, voice laced with hesitant curiosity.

"I stopped my Ambien. M- My use of it wasn't exactly... as I said it was."

The silence on the other line causes Emily to fidget and pull on a stray piece of fabric from one of the blankets on her bed.

"Just to make sure I'm understanding," Dr. Morrison says, "you are – or were – abusing your Ambien?"

Emily closes her eyes in shame and swallows roughly.

"Yes. I'm so sorry, Dr. Morrison. The medication was working with my sleep. I wasn't having nightmares; it was taking the voices away and the demons left me alone." Her voice cracks. "I wanted the feeling to stay so I started using it outside of the schedule you prescribed."

Her eyes flick to mine quickly before she resumes playing with the fabric.

"I –." she clears her throat, "I found someone who was able to get me a few other medications that I wasn't prescribed."

"What medications?"

She lists them off, some I recognize from when I went through her medications, others I don't.

"Emily, did you abruptly stop these medications?"

"I threw them out," I answer.

"And you are?" Dr. Morrison asks.

"Liam. I'm Emily's."

"Emily's what?"

"Just, Emily's."

Emily's eyes flash before narrowing at me, brows quirking.

"Okay well Liam, are you aware of the dangers of stopping medications abruptly?"

"I'm aware of withdrawal symptoms."

"There are other – very serious – risks with stopping medications, especially without the supervision of a *medical professional*." She chastises. "Emily, I want you to come into my office as soon as possible so we can discuss this further."

"Okay," Emily agrees, nodding, despite Dr. Morrison not being able to see her.

"And Liam?"

"Aye?"

"Do be sure to come with her."

I curse inwardly.

"Will do," I reply.

Once Dr. Morrison hangs up, Emily sets the phone next to her and then moves the tray from her lap.

Without meeting my gaze she says, "I'm going to get in the shower," and disappears into the bathroom.

CHAPTER 40
Emily

I let out a long sigh, feeling the warmth of the water cascade down my body. My heart hasn't stopped racing since I woke up and I feel the trembles down to my very bones.

I sense Liam before I see him. Turning my head, Liam is leaning against the doorframe watching me with his hands in his pockets.

"When do you want to go see her?" He asks.

I shrug. "I don't really want to."

Liam runs a hand through his hair, letting out a frustrated sigh.

"Emily, this is serious –."

"I'm not the one who tossed my medications in the toilet, Liam."

Annoyance builds in my body, and I don't bother pushing it down. I'm in no mood to be treated like a child. No mood to be chastised.

"I thought what I was doing would be the best thing for you."

He steps into the bathroom and begins undressing.

"Wh- What are you doing?" I ask, watching his muscles ripple with his movements.

My core pulses and squeezes, searching for something to grip onto.

Liam ignores my question, instead stepping into the shower with me. The space shrinks as his large frame fills it.

I crane my neck when he steps closer to me. His eyes travel down my body and the heat of them warms my blood. If it weren't for the water already making my skin flush, he would see just how much his stare affects me.

"Beautiful," he whispers, raising his hand to cup my face. His thumb strokes my bottom lip.

My eyes find the tattoo on his chest again and I lightly touch it with my fingers. He releases a deep breath, closing his eyes.

"Why did you say this was me?" I ask, stroking the intricate design of the butterfly wings.

"I might not have been with you, Emily." He cups my jaw, tipping my head to meet his eyes. "But you were always with me."

Goosebumps rise over my entire body. My pussy all but screams for his attention. Liam has always been able to draw primal reactions from my body.

A satisfied smirk spreads over his lips. His free hand caresses my thigh, moving upward at a snail's pace. I close my eyes, savoring the feel of his callused fingers rubbing against my skin.

"You're still mine, *Féileacán*." He whispers in my ear. His breath brushes over my sensitive skin and I shiver. When his fingers reach the apex of my thighs, I suck in a sharp breath.

He leisurely slides his finger through my wet folds. He hums, pleased with the evidence of my arousal.

"Still so responsive to me."

"Uh huh," I whimper, tilting my hips, opening up to him.

"Tell me you're still mine, Emily," he orders, voice husky with lust.

His thumb circles my clit, sending a bolt of electricity through my nerves.

"Tell me you'll let me take care of you like I should have the first time."

My hands move to sit on his shoulders, fingernails digging into his flesh as he continues to stroke me. My orgasm steadily builds, I'm a mess of whimpers and moans.

I whine in protest when he stops his movements.

"Why did you stop?" I pout.

"Tell me."

I study his face, seeing the unwavering desire and need in his eyes.

I give him the slightest nod.

"I need to hear the words, *Féileacán*."

Damn this man.

"I- I'm yours, Liam. I've always been yours."

Crashing his lips to mine, he fills my pussy with two fingers. He swallows my moan, growling as he pumps into me.

He curls the fingers of his hand that grip my jaw around my throat, and they tighten slightly. I tense, and he pulls his lips from mine.

"I've got you, Emily. I won't hurt you."

I swallow before pressing my lips against his. He groans, fingers picking up speed. They curl, rubbing that perfect spot inside my pussy and my legs begin to shake.

"Come for me, babe. Scream for me." He bites down on my neck and my orgasm explodes from my body.

The water begins to cool, and Liam quickly turns to shut it off before lifting me by the back of my thighs. Wrapping my legs around his waist, I kiss and lick the skin of his neck and shoulders.

His finger digs into my ass before he tosses me onto the bed. Landing on my back, I prop myself onto my elbows and watch as Liam pumps his cock, watching me with hooded eyes.

He pulls me by my legs to the edge of the bed before kneeling. He stares into my eyes as he lowers his mouth to my thighs, his warm breath skates over my skin and I moan at the sensation.

Smirking, he plants a kiss on each thigh and then moves to my pussy. Brows pinching, mouth falling open, I moan the moment his tongue meets my folds.

I slam my head against the mattress, fingers sliding into his wet strands. "Oh fuck," I whimper.

He licks, nips, and sucks on my lips and clit. Every stroke of his tongue causes my clit to swell. My lower stomach tightens, and I feel my heart beating in my pussy.

My hips grind against his face, and he hums in approval. He hooks his arms around my thigh and holds firmly, increasing his lapping at my pussy until I burst, his name falls from my lips with a scream.

He presses a kiss to my pulsing core and then moves to hover above me. His grinning face is glistening with my cum.

"I love the way you taste," he says.

He kisses me, the flavor of my release fills my mouth.

"Let me take care of you, Em." He says when he pulls his lips from mine. "Let me take care of you like I should have."

My throat tightens. Instead of answering, I slam my lips to his. Using one hand, I take his hardened cock into my grasp and line him up with my entrance. Liam presses into me and we groan when he fills me to the hilt.

I don't know if I can trust Liam with my heart again. I can't trust that he won't shatter it, completely obliterate it. And in truth, I don't want to risk it right now.

When I told him that I was his, I meant it. I always have been. It's never changed, and I don't ever see it happening.

Each roll of Liam's hips sends my eyes rolling into the back of head. His hands grip onto my hips, his mouth moving from my neck to my shoulder, then down to my breasts. He pulls my nipple into his mouth and flicks his tongue over it.

My legs fall open wider, encouraging him to fuck me harder. Our bodies slap against each other, echoing in the room. My screams combine with his groans until we both reach our peak.

He releases into me with my name leaving his mouth and it sends me over the edge.

"Oh fuck! Liam!" I scream. Legs trembling, body tightening, my orgasm bursts out of me like a freight train. My pussy gushes, squirting my release all over Liam and the bedsheets.

"Shite, *Féileacán*," He groans, squeezing my hips tightly.

He pulls out slowly, the mixture of our cum spills from my core. Liam watches, his eyes filled with satisfaction.

His gaze flicks to mine. "You already know what I'm going to say," he says before scooping our combined release and pushing it back into my pussy.

I gasp when he gently caresses my still-sensitive pussy.

Getting off the bed, I head to the ensuite. After relieving myself, I dress in black leggings and an oversized knit sweater. Walking back into the room, Liam is already dressed in the clothes he had on earlier.

He sits facing me at the end of my bed.

"Come here," he gestures for me to sit next to him. Striding over, I sit cross-legged on the mattress.

He watches me, brows slightly pinched. His eyes are filled with nervousness.

"What?" I ask, pushing a strand of hair behind my ear.

"I meant what I said, Em. I want to take care of you like I should have in the past."

I chew on my bottom lip, and he reaches out, using his thumb to pull it from my teeth.

"I'm fighting for you. And this time, I'm going to win."

I peer at him through lowered lashes. My heart rate begins to speed up.

"I trust you with my life, Liam. But I can't trust you with my heart."

"I'll do whatever it takes to win back your heart, Emily. If I need to walk through Hell to do that, I will."

I lower my gaze to my hands and pick at the nail polish. "You know nothing of Hell, Liam," I whisper.

Taking my hand, he places it on his lap. Using his fingers, he traces circles on my palm. The feel of his skin tickles mine but it's also comforting.

"We both have our versions of Hell. I want to know yours. I want to fight yours."

I close my eyes when the burning behind them rises. I don't want to cry anymore. I'm so tired of crying. So tired of feeling lost.

Just... tired.

"I know you don't trust me. That's my fault for pushing you away. There are no amount of words I could say that would express how sorry I am. How regretful I am." He takes my chin between his forefinger and thumb, forcing me to look at him.

"I should have said this before but I'm saying it now." His eyes pivot between mine and they soften. "I love you, Emily. I've loved you for so long that my heart is bound to yours."

I feel the first tear slide down my cheek. Liam watches it for a moment before using his thumb to swipe it away.

"You don't need to say anything right now. But I know. I know that you love me."

Words are lost to me. I've dreamt of hearing him say that to me for so long, especially when I thought I'd never hear them.

He intertwines our fingers and pulls me toward the door. "Let go to the garden before I need to leave on an assignment."

CHAPTER 41
Liam

The closer we get to the garden; the more tense Emily becomes. Her face is drawn tight and her hand trembles in mine. Another piece of my heart fractures. Seeing that a place that used to mean so much to her – to us – is a place she's dreading visiting.

Stepping into the clearing, Emily pauses and scans the space. The wildflowers have started to bloom with the warming of the weather, songbirds chirp wildly – as if to celebrate her return.

She takes a hesitant step forward and reaches out toward the first flower. The moment her finger caresses the soft petal, a small smile forms on her lips.

I release her hand and place my hands in my pockets. I watch as she moves from flower to flower.

Every so often, she will take in a deep breath. Soaking in the different smells that she once loved so much.

She moves through the foliage, toward the center of the garden and falls onto her knees. Her head falls to her hands and her shoulders bob as she begins to cry.

As much as I'd like to walk over and comfort her, she needs this.

When her breaths become less erratic, I step forward. She looks over her shoulder, her eyes are bloodshot, and her face is stained with tears.

I kneel next to her, and she leans into my side, resting her head on my shoulder. I wrap an arm around her.

We sit in a comfortable silence. The sounds of the garden surround us in a calmness that I don't think Emily has felt since being rescued.

"I'm scared," she whispers – nearly inaudibly.

I rub my hand up and down her arm. "Being scared is okay, it means what's to come is going to push you and help you grow. Help you become stronger."

She burrows herself closer to my side and I squeeze her tightly.

My phone dings in my pocket. Pulling it out, I see a message from Declan of an address for where I can pick up the acid he needs.

"Do you want to go inside? I have to go pick up some things for Paige and Declan."

She shakes her head and pulls away from me. "I think I want to stay out here for a little while longer."

When she looks into my eyes, they're brighter than they've been in a long time and my heart expands at the sight.

"I will be right back." I kiss her temple and stand.

She looks up at me with tired, but soft eyes.

"I love you, *Féileacán*."

She smiles and it's filled with warmth, but her eyes show the hesitance she has to say it back.

That's okay.

I'll win back Emily's heart and this time I'll never let go.

"Any reason you need so many gallons?" The stocky bald-headed man asks, hauling the hydrofluoric acid into the van.

"If you weren't given that information then you don't need to know." I answer.

He holds his hands up, "I meant no harm. Just curious is all."

"Well don't ask. Curiosity killed the cat after all." I say pointedly.

He nervously glances at my gun that I have on full display in my shoulder holster. Swallowing tightly, he lugs the final gallon into the van. I slam the door shut then hand him the envelope with his payment.

"Pleasure doin' business with you." He grunts when I slap a hand against his back.

Climbing into the van, I head back to the estate.

The drive takes longer than I expected due to the shite fucking traffic in the city. I'll never understand traffic in the US. What is the purpose?

Of course, traffic does happen in Ireland but nothing of this scale. I've also learned what road rage is and struggle not to shoot people in the fecking face because of it.

I flex my fingers on the steering wheel and let out a frustrated breath. This driving at a snail's pace is testing my fecking patience.

I just want to get back to Emily.

Finally, after nearly an hour of sitting at a standstill, I'm able to make it out of the city and toward the estate.

My head is a swarm of emotion as I listen to *Save Me* by Jelly Roll on the radio. The lyrics resonate with everything Emily is going through and it hurts. She's trapped so deep within her mind that she truly thinks she'll never be able to escape. Sometimes it seems like she doesn't want to.

I don't regret tossing her medication down the toilet. She needs to see that she can survive whatever torments her. She needs to see that it's okay to be scared but she needs to fight. That's the only way she'll be able to overcome her suffering and truly *live*.

My phone pings when I pull into the driveway of the estate.

Declan

Where are you?

Me

Unloading the acid now.

A moment later, Rhys and Declan are walking around the mansion from the outdoor entrance to the cellar.

"Hey, Liam." Rhys greets, bending to lift a gallon.

"Liam, I need to speak with you before we head down there."

I turn to Declan. His face shows signs of his mood.

"Boss?" I square my shoulders, maintaining eye contact with him.

He shakes his head with a low chuckle. "Calm down."

My shoulders relax, only slightly.

"I've seen how different Emily is when you're around versus when you're not. I wanted to deny it when I shouldn't have. It's clear as day how you care for each other. Just…" he clears his throat. "Take care of her." He meets my eyes and I see the love he has for his baby sister.

"I'd die for Emily."

He scans my face and then nods. "Good. I expect nothing less for her."

He moves to pick up two gallons of the acid and then strides toward the cellar entrance.

Rhys smirks at me then follows Declan.

Smiling, I bend and pick up the remaining two gallons then head inside.

"I want one." Sarah says, spinning around to look at the near empty cellar.

"A cellar?" I ask.

"Yup," she says, emphasizing the 'p' with a pop.

"Why does that not surprise me?" Paige snorts and I chuckle.

She smirks at us. "I need something to give me more dopamine."

We burst in laughter.

Sarah is a ball of unhinged energy and needs constant stimulation. If she doesn't, she turns into this destructive maniac.

I love her for it.

Her and Paige are the sisters and friends I never knew I needed.

Rhys and Declan enter the room, each holding gallons of acid. When Liam steps in behind them, I stand taller and a blush spreads over my cheeks.

When he looks at me, his hazel eyes light up and he smiles softly at me.

I spent a few hours sitting in the garden after he left, and it was so peaceful. There were no shadows, no crying women or children, no Nikolai. I stayed as long as possible before Declan shouted for me to head to the cellar with him and Paige.

Rhys and Liam head toward the room at the back of the cellar where there are cells. Aleksei – the man who mutilated Paige – saunters in a second later with his head held high.

A disgusting smirk spreads over his face when he sees Paige. Declan knocks him unconscious before he walks over to her and cups her face, whispering encouraging words in her ear.

Liam and Rhys work on suspending Aleksei by his wrists from the chain that hangs from the ceiling.

"Wake him up," Paige says.

Liam moves to pour some acid into a bucket and then throws it onto Aleksei's limp body. He wakes with a scream.

"Morning sunshine, glad you could rejoin us." I bite my lip as heat spreads over my body.

Something about seeing Liam this way sends arousal through my blood. I press my legs together, trying to relieve the need in my core.

I don't know what Liam has done to me, but my libido has reappeared, and it seems to increase each time I see him.

His eyes find mine and he winks at me. He sets the bucket aside then strides over.

"What are you thinking about, *Féileacán?*" His breath caresses my ear and I shiver, goosebumps rise on my arms.

"Are you wet, Emily?" his hand presses against my lower back and I feel the burn of it through my sweater.

I moan quietly, avoiding drawing attention to us. Liam moves to stand behind me. His cock bulges in his pants and he presses it into my ass. I arch my back into him, and he groans.

I'm brought back to reality by the screams of Aleksei. The acid falls from the ceiling. His body begins to dissolve as it splashes onto his skin.

I grimace at the smell of burning flesh and acid.

Paige leaves the room without saying a word. Declan follows soon after.

"Let's get out of here." Liam's pinky hooks with mine and he pulls me toward the door.

"Lay down," Liam says as soon as we step into my room. He pulls his shirt off in a smooth motion as I lower myself on the bed. Lying on my back, I prop myself on my elbows. Liam watches me through hooded eyes as he removes his belt and unbutton his pants.

My breaths become shallow and my heart thuds rapidly in my chest. He hooks his thumbs at the hem of his boxer briefs. His cock is hard and thick, precum leaks from the tip.

My core pulses, begging to be filled with him. To be fully sated by him and only him.

Standing at the end of the bed, Liam bends and slides my leggings and panties down my body. He bunches up the fabric of my panties, bringing them to his nose, he inhales deeply.

"Fuck, Emily. I'll never tire of your smell."

Queue my pussy becoming the Nile River.

He tosses my clothes on the floor then grips my ankles. I yelp in surprise when he tugs, my ass nearly falling off the edge. My legs unconsciously spread for him.

"Good girl," He hums, pleased that I'm presenting myself to him.

The fabric of my sweater rubs against my hardened nipples and I moan. They're so sensitive that I can't stop myself from reaching up and removing the sweater.

Liam takes his bottom lip between his teeth and tips his head. The intensity of his hunger gaze roaming my naked body nearly forces an orgasm out of me.

"You're stunnin', baby."

"Liam, please," I whimper. My hips begin to roll of their own accord.

He kneels in front of me, his callused hands slide up and down my calves. I'm burning up, completely wanton, and needy beyond words.

"Please. Please. Please." I beg through panting breaths.

He chuckles and then I moan loudly when his tongue presses against my slickened core. I run my fingers through his hair and tug him closer. He groans, feasting on my pussy. Giving me pleasure so delicious that I can't focus on anything else.

"Oh my God, yes." I cry out, riding his face.

Two fingers probe my entrance before plunging into me. The thickness of his digits stretches me. My orgasm builds and builds until I explode like a nuclear bomb. My screams bounce of the walls and my hips roll and roll from the intense pleasure that flows through me.

Liam removes his fingers and rubs at my clit until I'm a squirting mess.

"That right, baby. Give it to me." He growls.

Once my high descends, Liam grips onto my ankles and spins me around. He quickly grabs my hips and pulls me back until I'm on all fours.

He sinks into my pussy; the slow stretch sends my eyes rolling back.

Fully seated, Liam grips onto the back of my neck and shoves my face down. He pulls back and slams into me. My pussy clenches and he growls.

"You like that? You like me forcing you to take my cock?"

"Only you." I pant, gripping onto the sheets.

"You're mine." His thrusts are so deep, so perfect that another orgasm starts to build.

"I feel your cunt tightening, baby. You like being called mine, don't you?"

I moan loudly. I couldn't form a coherent sentence even if I tried. Everything about this is animalistic – claiming. My pants become erratic; my hips start to jerk. I fall into a haze of ecstasy when my orgasm takes over.

Liam wraps his hands around my hips and using them for support as he fucks me into the mattress. He fucks me through my orgasm until he fills me with a deep growl falling from his lips.

He slumps over my back. Our bodies are slick with sweat and we're both a panting mess.

Pulling out, Liam peppers my back with kisses before standing. He says nothing as he scoops up his cum and pushes it back inside me. I smile and hide my face in the blankets.

He swats my ass with his palm, making me yelp, and then strides to the bathroom. A second later, he returns with a washcloth and cleans my swollen pussy.

He pulls me into his chest when he lays down. The sound of his heart beating against my ear lulls me to sleep before I have a chance to fight it.

May 11

The voices weren't so loud yesterday.

CHAPTER 43
Liam

Parking the SUV in front of Dr. Morrison's office, I remove the keys from the ignition and turn to face Emily. She chews on his lower lip as she stares out the windshield.

"Ready?" I ask, pulling her attention to me.

Her eyes flick to the building again before returning to mine. She gives me a small nod.

"Wait right there," I say, climbing out the vehicle. I round the hood and open the passenger door. Offering my hand, Emily places hers in mine and climbs out.

I intertwine our fingers and we stride inside.

Dr. Morrison sits across from us with her chocolate eyes narrowed at me. Her lips are pursed as she studies me closely. She has a file resting on her laps and she taps the end of her pen in a repetitive pattern.

She's spent the last fifteen minutes lecturing me about messing with Emily's medications – though not all of them were truly hers.

Emily hasn't said much since we arrived. She keeps peering over her shoulder to the back corner of the room. I placed my hand on her thigh after she looked the third time. That seemed to relax her just a little bit.

"I hope we understand each other, Liam." Dr. Morrison says, peering over the rim of her glasses with a brow raised.

"Yes ma'am."

She gives me a curt nod before looking at Emily.

"I'm very proud of your progress thus far, Emily. You should also be proud of yourself."

Emily dips her chin and gives her a shy smile.

I squeeze her thigh lightly and wink at her when she looks over.

Dr. Morrison looks down at the file on her lap and then nods.

"Let's get a weight for you before we discuss your medications further." She moves to stand and strides over to the scale.

Licking her lips, Emily nervously stands and walks over. I stay on the couch and watch as she slips off her shoes. She takes a deep breath then takes a cautious step onto the small black platform.

A few seconds later, wide smile spreads across Dr. Morrison's face. "That's amazing, Emily!" she says, clapping her hands together.

Emily stands straighter and looks over her shoulder at me with a smile.

"Thank you, Dr. Morrison. I couldn't have done it without Liam's help." She gestures toward me, but I shake my head.

"It was all you, *Féileacán*."

Dr. Morrison smiles at me and then wraps an arm around Emily's shoulders. "Whatever the reason, you're doing phenomenal."

Emily peers at the corner but relaxes when whatever she saw earlier is no longer there. I pull her close to my side when she returns to the couch. She melts into my body, setting her head on my shoulder.

I stroke her arm with my hand as we listen to Dr. Morrison go over the steps to gradually – and safely – stop her medications without severe side effects.

There are some that she will continue to take until she's in a more comfortable mental state, but the goal is to no longer need any medications.

Once the appointment is over, we stand from the couch. Dr. Morrison hugs Emily tightly.

"You've got this, Emily." She whispers in her ear before pulling back.

She meets my gaze and then peers over the rim of her glasses. "And I trust we don't need to have another discussion about stopping medications abruptly?"

I chuckle, holding my hands up. "No, ma'am."

"Good. I'll see you in about a month, Emily. Email or call me if you need anything."

"Thank you so much, Dr. Morrison."

Emily wraps an arm around my bicep and intertwines our fingers. I give them a light squeeze before bringing them to my lips and kissing the back of her hand.

"Anything you'd like to do today?" I ask when we reach the car.

"I'd actually like to go home to sit in the garden." She takes my offered hand and climbs in.

"Yeah?"

This is great. Absolutely great. The fact that she wants to spend time not only outside her room, but in the garden sends my heart soaring.

She smiles at me, her dimple on full display, and nods. "Yeah. I think I need the fresh air."

A grin widely before shutting the door. I climb into the driver's seat, turn the ignition, and then drive out of the parking lot.

The energy as we drive toward the mansion is light. Emily has a soft smile the entire time. She faces the passenger window and watches as the city passes by.

Her phone rings in her purse. Pulling it out, she sits and stares at the screen with her brows furrowed.

"Not gonna answer that?" I ask, shifting my gaze between her and the road.

Wordlessly, she shakes her head. Once the phone stops ringing, she puts it back in her purse.

I sigh and shift in my seat. "Emily... Why aren't you speaking with your ma?"

She tenses and swallows audibly. "I can't..." she whispers.

"Why?"

Linking her lips, she dips her chin and plays with the hem of her shirt.

"Emily, talk to me. Why can't you talk to your ma?" I push.

She clears her throat, keeping her head down. "It hurts."

I sigh, unable to find the words to say. What can I say? If it hurts, I'm not going to force her to speak with her ma. I'm already pushing her to be sober, to eat. Feck, just to even go outside.

The rest of the drive to the estate is silent. Emily keeps her eyes trained out the window.

CHAPTER 44
Emily

I sit in my window watching Rhys and Liam instruct the rest of the men and give out orders. Declan and Paige left for Ireland this morning to officially introduce her to my ma after he proposed a few days. They had asked if I wanted to go with but just the thought of being in Ireland again terrifies me.

My ma lives too close to where they have the Farmers' Market and there is no possible way I could be anywhere near that place. I don't know when I'll be able to visit Ireland again.

My phone vibrates on the nightstand. It's ma again. She hasn't stopped sending me messages after I acknowledged one about Paige.

Ma

> I wish you were coming with them.

My vision blurs the moment I read the words. "Fuck," I mutter, tossing the phone onto the bed.

I run my fingers through my hair and grip tightly at the root.

I know I can't keep ignoring her but hearing her voice sends me back to when I was taken. Back to the last conversation I had on the phone with her.

When she was here after I was first rescued, I was okay. Granted I was probably in more shock than anything. But... I was still okay with being around her at the time.

Now? Now just hearing her voice sends me spiraling.

It's killing me slowly. My ma has been my best friend. I've always been able to confide in her and it's breaking me that I can't do that now.

I pick up my phone and start typing out my reply.

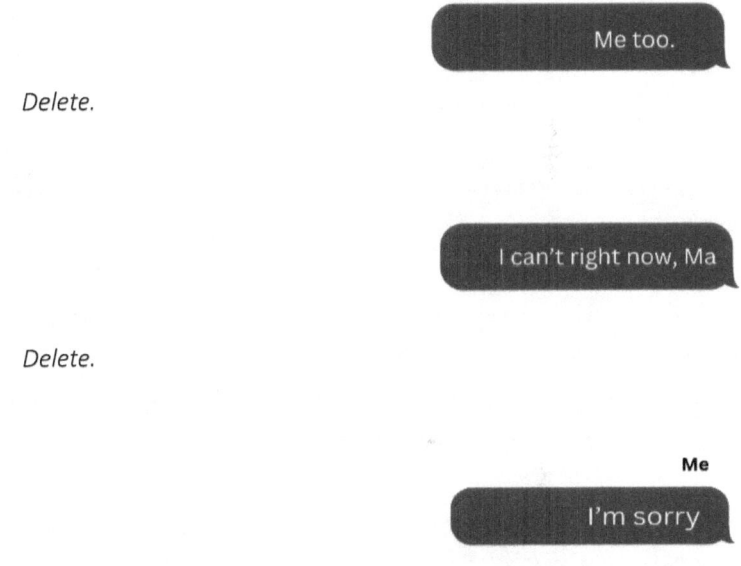

Me too.

Delete.

I can't right now, Ma

Delete.

Me

I'm sorry

Delete.

"Fuck!" I scream and throw the phone across the room. It shatters against the wall.

Liam steps before it lands on the ground.

"What's going on?" he asks, voice full of concern. His head whips around, landing on my phone.

His eyes come to mine, which burn as the tears begin to flow. He strides over and wraps me in his arms. He strokes my back, pressing his cheek against my head.

Liam doesn't ask for an explanation. He doesn't push for me to talk. He simply holds me tightly and continues to stroke my back.

"Tell me what you need." He whispers.

"I don't know..." I mumble. "I don't know what I need Liam."

His heart thumps against my ear in a steady rhythm. It's comforting. His chest rises and falls with each of his breaths.

We sit in comfortable silence for what seems like hours. His presence warms me. My tears stain his shirt, but he doesn't seem to mind. His arms never let go.

"I feel so lost sometimes," I whisper.

"I know, baby... I know."

After a while of sitting wrapped in each other, Liam shifts so we lie down. I settle against his chest, positioned right about his heart. At some point his breaths slow and I know he's fallen asleep.

I stare blankly at the photo on my nightstand. It's of me, Ma, and Declan in Ireland. I was about ten years old. My smile and eyes are bright. I look happy.

Slowly, I untangle myself from Liam's arms and climb out of bed. I look down at his sleeping face. The stress that he holds is gone, softening his features. His mouth is slightly ajar, faint snores fall from his lips.

Standing, I head to the ensuite and search my drawer for the razor I hid.

Once I find it, I bring my eyes to the mirror and startle. Liam is standing in the doorway watching me. Wordlessly, he removes his shirt and strides closer.

His hands wrap around my waist, and he turns me to face him.

He keeps his eyes on mine as he wraps his fingers around my wrist. His tender gaze remains on mine as he presses the razor against his chest.

My heart is beating erratically, my breaths are shallow.

His lips lift and a gentle smile forms on his face. He gives me a subtle nod and my eyes drop from him to our hands. I close my eyes for a moment.

Opening them, I release a breath and then press the blade into his skin.

I watch as the blood pools before flowing down his chest. It travels down the mountains and valleys of his muscled body.

Tears well in my eyes. The emotional turmoil in my body slowly releases its grasp on me. My gaze lifts to Liam once more. He's still staring at me through tender eyes. The first tear falls, and he watches as it slides down my face.

"I love you, *Féileacán.*" His voice is soft and sincere. My lip quivers and I release the blade. It clatters to the floor. I bring my trembling hand up to his chest and gently touch the wound I've created.

He doesn't flinch or remove his stare from my face.

"I will always bleed for you, Emily. I will always take your pain."

My face contorts and release a choked sob. I press myself into his chest, his arms wrap tightly around me, and he kisses the top of my head.

"I don't want to hurt anymore, Liam. I – I just want to be happy again."

"You will be. It might take some time, but you will be."

The following morning, Liam and I lie on a throw blanket in the garden. It's warmer today than it has been in a few days, so I'm wearing a pale blue sundress with white flowers.

Liam is wearing his usual, only this time, it's a black tee and not a white one. It still molds over his broad chest and muscular arms like it was made to his exact measurements.

And those cargo pants? Oof.

Liam traces circles on the exposed skin on my upper back. His calluses cause goosebumps to rise over my skin and he hums.

I'm not sure how long we've been out here but I don't want to leave. This space is becoming ours again and I don't want to lose that. I won't survive it.

"Em?" turning, I set my cheek on my crossed arms and face Liam.

"Hm?"

"Are you ready to talk about last night?" His eyes slowly roam over my face.

I turn over onto my back and let out a long sigh. I silently watch the clouds float by as I try to think of the right words. The gentle breeze causes a loose strand of my hair to cross over my cheek. Liam reaches over and uses his fingers to move it away.

"I can't talk with ma." I whisper. My brows pinch.

Liam remains silent, allowing me to continue at my own pace.

"Hearing her voice…" I clear my throat and lick my lips. "Hearing her voice sends me back to when Vladimir's men took me."

I see him nod in my peripheral.

"My ma was the last person I spoke to before they pushed me into the van and drove away." Liam scoots closer, his hand brushes mine before he curls his pinky with mine.

"You don't need to explain anymore, *mo ghrá*." He kisses my shoulder.

"I know. I just feel guilty about avoiding her. I feel guilty that the voice that once gave me so much comfort now brings me so much pain." I turn over to my side to face Liam, tucking my arm under my head. Our noses are nearly touching.

"She's my ma, Liam," I say in a shaky voice.

His eyes are warm and understanding. "There is nothing wrong with distancing yourself from someone or something that hurts you. Emily. Just give yourself time. She'll understand."

I know she will... and that's one of the reasons why it hurts. Because she'll understand my reasoning and she'll forgive me without a second thought. I know it doesn't make any sense. A lot of things in my life don't seem to make much sense right now.

But having her understand why I need to separate myself from her hurts almost as much as her not understanding.

My ma is still grieving from the loss of my da, and now she has to deal with me pushing her away so *I* can heal.

We continue to lie facing each other, nose to nose. Our breaths are intertwined. Liam brushes the tip of my nose with his before angling his head and gently pressing his lips to mine.

CHAPTER 45
Liam

The past few weeks have been a blur of missions, spending time with Emily, and barking orders at the other men. Declan and Paige are set to return sometime next week, and he wants to throw an engagement party for Paige.

So, now we're working to make sure all the preparations are set for that. Declan wants it to be a surprise, so we've been ordered to keep it from both Emily and Sarah.

Clearly, Declan overestimates my and Rhys's will to keep secrets from them. Even something that is supposed to be a surprise.

Sarah is already suspicious. She's like a damn bloodhound. She figured something was up before we even started to prep. Emily also knows something is going on but she doesn't seem inclined to figured it out.

I walk up to Rhys who stands outside by one of the SUVs.

"Where you headed?" I ask, slapping him on the back in greeting.

"I gotta check out the newest shipment from Ireland at the docks. Wanna come?"

"I need to head to Manhattan for a second to head lead the unloading of the shipment that was hauled there this morning."

He nods. "Oh right." He slaps my back and moves to open the driver-side door of the SUV. "I'll see you when I get back, yeah?"

"Aye." I agree.

He climbs in and closes the door. I watch as he drives down the driveway and out of sight.

I spin on my heel and walk up the steps to head inside and find Emily.

Emily sits at her window, watching the men do what they were assigned. She's wrapped in a fluffy blue blanket.

Sensing my presence, she peeks over her shoulder. Offering me a warm smile, she turns all the way around.

"Hi," she whispers.

I grin and walk over to her. She tips her head up and meets my lips without hesitation.

"How are you feeling?" I ask, pulling away.

She shrugs. "I'll be okay."

My hand cups the side of her face and she leans into my touch, eyes fluttering closed.

"Anything you need or want to talk about?" my thumb gently caresses her soft skin.

Her turquoise blue eyes open and meet mine. For a moment I get lost in them. Each day, they seem to brighten more and more. It brings a sort of peace in my heart that I've missed.

"Just be with me?" she says, standing.

I wrap my arms around her and she circles hers around my middle. I set my head atop her head and breathe her scent in.

I smile when the scent of wildflowers and berries flows through my nose.

Feck, I've missed this smell.

"Are you smelling me?" She asks, voice full of humor.

"Aye," I say, taking another deep breath.

She chuckles and pulls away. "Why?"

I kiss her forehead, refusing to release her from my arms. "You smell like wildflowers and berries. It's a smell that I will never tire of. It's a smell that soothes my soul in ways I can't explain."

She hums and smiles up at me.

"I need to go to Manhattan. I'll be gone for a few hours. Will you be alright?" My eyes roam over her face, studying every beautiful freckle.

"I think so. I want to hang out in the garden again today."

My heart expands every time she says she wants to go out in the garden. I'm getting my Emily back.

I plant a kiss on her cheek. "I'll be back as soon as I can, okay?"

She nods, stroking my jaw with her fingers.

"Be careful." She whispers and then stands on her toes and kisses my lips.

I step away and exit the room.

Me and a couple of other men pull up to our Manhattan warehouse. It's in the heart of one of the lower industrial areas so it's easy to keep our dealings discreet.

"Liam, how goes it?" James, the one overseeing the operations while we're gone, asks.

"Grand. How goes it here?" I ask, taking his offered hand in mine and shaking it.

"The weapons we received this morning all appear great. No damages were noted, and the ammunition is all accounted for."

I nod as we make our way inside.

"Good. We have an MC in Arizona that needs a shipment in the next two weeks or so." I scan the warehouse. Boxes are loaded and unloaded in different vans and trucks.

"Right. Right. I'll have everything ready to go in a few days."

I bring my attention back to him. He's a stout man with a bald head. He smells of cigarettes and gunpowder.

"Show me the books," I say, turning on my heel and striding toward the office at the back of the building.

James's strides are quick as he tries to keep up with mine. I'm not as tall as Declan or Rhys but he still has to make an effort to match my steps.

"Payments to Cormac were made for the next two months. The men have received their payments for the month, and we are stocked on all shipping supplies." He says, huffing and puffing.

I step into the office and round the desk, taking a seat. James pulls the folders that hold our documents — we don't want to risk the Feds or rivals hacking into our system, so we document with pen and paper.

For the next few hours, James and I go over the books. It's tedious but it's safer than getting caught. Everything is stored in a fireproof safe that only Declan, Rhys, James, and I know the code to.

Once we finish going through everything, we exit the office and I assess the weapons and ammunition. We have a small, private shooting range in the warehouse where I personally test the weapons.

After ensuring the gun isn't loaded and flicking the safety on, I set the rifle down on the table in front of me.

"Excellent." I nod in approval.

James steps next to me and picks up the weapon, handing it off the one of the men who accompanied me. He leaves the room to clean it and load it into one of the many boxes we have here.

I slap James on the back, and he tenses. Despite working with us and being around us regularly, Declan, Rhys, and I make him uneasy.

"I'll be back in a few days to check on everything. Good job, James."

He nods quickly. "Thank you, sir. I'll see you then."

I leave and make my way toward the SUV. Climbing in, I order the driver to take me back to the estate and return for the other two men who will be staying here.

I need my woman.

CHAPTER 46
Emily

"How are your symptoms?" Dr. Morrison asks from the other line.

Over the last two months, I've been slowly reducing all of my medications until I'm completely off them.

The withdrawals have been manageable and not too overwhelming for the most part. I owe a lot to both Dr. Morrison and Liam for that.

I haven't told Liam about the supply I keep in a hole that I made behind my dresser. I don't plan to use any of it. But it's nice to have the security there.

It's stupid, I know but it helps me.

"They've been good. I don't have many panic attacks. My nightmares are also few and far between. It's been really good."

"That's wonderful. You haven't mentioned if you ended up getting a second opinion regarding your eyes. Do you still plan to do that?"

I need to. I know I'll need glasses; I just don't want to face another reality of what's been done to me that's irreversible.

"Emily?" Dr. Morrison says and I startle.

"Sorry! I got lost in my thoughts for a second." I chuckle nervously. "I haven't gone in to see anyone. I don't know if I am ready to face their recommendations."

"That's understandable. However, I think it would be smart to speak to someone, Emily. You're putting strain on your eyes that will likely worsen your vision."

My fingers gently stroke the petals of the sunflower in front of me.

"I know," I say with a sigh. "It's just... I want to pretend. Just a little longer."

I feel Liam before I see him. Spinning around, I see him making his way toward me.

"I gotta go Dr. Morrison."

"Of course. I'll talk to you soon."

I hang up without saying goodbye and then stand from my throw blanket. I slide my hands down my yellow sundress to smooth out the wrinkles.

The smile Liam gives me sends my stomach into orbit. I can't believe life is giving me a chance to be with him again. Only this time, he loves me.

Stepping up to me, Liam grips my chin lightly and tips my head back. He brushes the tip of his nose against mine before bringing his lips to mine.

Our kiss is sweet, gentle, and full of love. It's everything.

"How are you, *Féileacán*?" he whispers against my lips.

"Better now that you're here," I reply with a smile.

"Good. I missed you." He pulls away. His hazel eyes are bright with adoration.

"I missed you too. How was everything?"

Normally, I don't care about the ins and outs of my family's illegal operations, but I'm interested in Liam and how his day went.

He purses his lips and then smirks. "I don't want to talk about work with you, Emily." His voice is low and husky.

"Then what do you want to talk about?" I whisper, biting on my lower lip.

"Why don't we go inside?" his hands wrap around my waist and he pulls me into him. My hands press against his chest and his erection presses against my pelvis.

He lets out a low groan that goes straight to my core. Dipping his head, he pushes against the side of my jaw with his nose. I tip my head to the side, giving him access to my neck.

His nose caresses my skin, and his hot breath sends chills down my spine.

I let out a small moan and Liam moves so fast, I yelp. Next thing I know, I'm tossed over his shoulder and he's striding toward the mansion.

"What are you doing?" I laugh.

His fingers that are wrapped around my thighs tighten. "I'm going inside to fuck my woman."

My pussy squeezed, looking for something to wrap around.

"Mm. I can smell your arousal, baby."

One hand releases me and slides up the back of my thigh. My breathing becomes shallow as I wait for him to touch me where my body needs him to.

When he doesn't, I whine, and he chuckles darkly under his breath.

"Patience, *Féileacán*."

I bounce as he takes the steps two at a time. He kicks the door closed and then takes the indoor steps two at a time. He hurriedly walks down the hallway toward my bedroom.

He quickly opens and shuts the door. Within seconds I'm tossed onto my bed. I push my hair out of my face and prop myself onto my elbows.

Liam towers over me. Chest heaving, eyes dark, his gaze travels down my body hungrily.

I squeeze my thighs, trying to relieve the building pressure but it's no use. I need him inside me, *now*.

He grips into the collar of his shirt and pulls it over his head. The cuts I've placed on his skin are on display and my heart drums against my chest at the sight.

He's taken my pain and continues to do so without hesitation or complaint.

Liam is my rock. He keeps me grounded.

He looks down at his chest when he sees my stare. Returning his eyes to mine, he smiles softly.

"I love you," I whisper, and he freezes.

"Say it again," he says, his voice a mixture of different emotions.

"I love you, Liam."

His hands wrap around my ankles, and I yelp when he pulls me to the end of the bed. He climbs over me and cages my head between his forearms. My legs wrap around his waist, and he presses himself against my pussy.

"I've loved you since I was nineteen, Emily. And I'll love you until the heavens no longer exist."

Tears well in my eyes and slide down my cheeks and into my hair. Liam's eyes roam over my face before stopping on my lips. We meet each other halfway.

Our lips open for each other, our tongues caress one another in a slow dance.

Slowly, Liam presses the straps of my dress down my arms, exposing my breasts. He kisses the center of my chest then the mounds of each breast before finally taking a hardened nipple into his mouth.

I arch into him. My hand slides into his hair and I grip onto the short strands.

He groans, nipping and sucking on my breast. His hands slide up and down my thighs, pushing the hem of the dress upward. He rolls his hips, grinding into me, and I whimper.

"Please," I say breathlessly.

He brings his lips to the crook of my neck and nips lightly. The different sensations he's sending through my body are overwhelming and my pussy is a sopping mess.

Liam slides his hand up my dress and wraps his fingers around my panties. They slide down my legs slowly and I whimper impatiently.

Tossing them aside, Liam pushes my knees open, fully exposing me to him. He wastes no time in bringing his fingers to my core. I gasp and lift my hips.

He sucks on my neck as he uses two fingers to spread my lips and push another into my pussy.

"Feck, Emily." He groans against my skin.

CHAPTER 47
Liam

Her wet cunt squeezes my finger and I feel like I'm going to explode in my fecking pants. I keep my strokes slow as I move my finger in and out of her. She rolls her hips with me, chasing me.

When I pull out, she whimpers in protest.

"Don't worry, baby. I'll give you what you want." I say, standing from the bed. I kick off my boots and slide my pants and boxer briefs down my legs.

My cock is hard as stone and demands the warmth and wetness of Emily's delicious pussy.

"Take off the dress," I grunt, pumping my cock.

She bites down on her bottom lip as she reaches up and pulls the dress over her body.

Over the last few months, Emily has gained weight and her amazing curves have returned. Her breasts are fuller, and her hips are wider.

"Feck, Emily. You're excruciatingly beautiful."

Kneeling on the bed, I nudge her legs open. I slide my hands up and down her skin. My fingers lightly brush against the large scar on the outer side of

I trail kisses up her thigh until I reach her glistening pussy. My eyes flick to hers. They're hooded, her pupils are blown. Her chest rises and falls rapidly with each of her breaths.

Keeping my eyes on hers, I dip and run my tongue slowly up her folds.

"Oh fuck," she moans, falling back against the mattress.

I sink my tongue into her pussy, fucking her slowly. She lifts her hips and I slide my hands under her, gripping her ass.

My tongue moves from her core, and I circle her clit. Her moans get louder, egging me on. I plunge two fingers into her and curl them to stroke that sweet spot that drives her mad.

"I'm gonna come, Liam. Oh fuck, I'm gonna come." She gasps, her fingers grip tighter on my hair, my scalp tingles from the force.

"Come for me, *Féileacán*," I say, finger fucking her faster until she detonates.

"Liam!" she screams, back arching. I continue to plunge my fingers in and out until she comes down from her high.

She has a thin sheen of sweat coating her flushed skin. I climb over her. Grabbing onto my cock, I slide the tip up and down her wet folds, coating myself.

Lining myself with her, I press into her pussy. She widens her legs, giving me room to sink further and further into her.

We simultaneously let out a low, satisfied moan when I'm fully seated. Pulling out to the tip, thrust back in with a slow, controlled roll of my hips.

Her arms wrap around my shoulders and her nails dig into my back. I welcome the pain. It heightens the sensations that overwhelm my system.

Her moans are music to my ears. She holds my gaze, meets me thrust for slow thrust, our lips are so close that our breaths become one.

My eyes close tightly when the base of my spine begins to tingle. Leaning onto one forearm, I lift my free hand and circle her clit with my thumb. I apply just enough pressure for her breaths to become short gasps.

I clench my teeth when her walls tighten around me.

"Come on baby. Come for me." I grunt and she does.

She clenches around my cock and I have no control over my orgasm crashing into me. She screams my name, nails cutting into my flesh, pussy tightening.

I bite down onto her neck, and push my cock harder into her pussy, filling her with all of my cum.

Bodies intertwined, skin coated in sweat, Emily and I lie together absorbing our high. My head lies against her chest, listening to the beating of her heart, feeling the rise and fall of her breaths. Her fingers trace a figure-eight on my back.

Everything about this moment is soothing.

Pushing myself up, I hold out my hand and pull Emily to stand. She follows me to the ensuite and leans against the counter, watching as I turn on the shower.

I turn toward her and hold out my hand once more for her. She takes it and steps into the water.

Stepping in, I pull her into me. She curls into my chest, and we stand silently feeling the water cascade down our bodies.

After a while, we go through the motions of cleaning ourselves up. I wrap a towel around her body once we're finished and we walk to the room.

We slide into bed without dressing. Emily presses her back to my front. Draping an arm around her waist, I pull her tightly into me and press my nose against her neck.

I take a deep breath in, the scent of berries fills my nose, calmness spreads over every part of my body and it's not long before I fall asleep with Emily wrapped in my arms.

Over the next few days, Emily and I are either wrapped in each other or spending time in the garden. The final preparations for Declan and Paige's engagement party were finished today, and the warehouses have been checked. Everything is perfect.

Declan and Paige are supposed to arrive tonight, and the party is set to take place tomorrow. Caetlin is also set to arrive sometime tomorrow morning.

I haven't spoken to Emily about Caetlin's arrival, and I admit I'm feeling a little uneasy about it.

She mentioned being unable to speak with her, but I couldn't *not* have her here when Declan invited her.

I only hope Emily won't be too angry with me when she finds out.

CHAPTER 48
Emily

For the first time in I don't know how long, I feel happy. Well, I guess as happy as someone in my situation can be. Every day it becomes easier to breathe. It's easier to ignore the voices in my head that mock me. It's easier to decipher what is real and what is not.

I'm not haunted by the women and children as often. Nikolai doesn't come around anymore.

It's just... calm. My mind is calm and I'm grateful beyond words.

"Emily!" Ingrid shouts from the front of the mansion. I turn around from where I am sitting in the garden, and she gestures for me to go to her.

I close my journal and stand. I dust off my sundress — today I chose yellow — and straighten any wrinkles that formed from how long I've been sitting.

"Your brother and Paige will be here within the next two hours. Niall is preparing a large dinner to welcome them home." Ingrid says when I stand at the end of the steps.

She looks up at the sky which has begun to darken with the sudden arrival of a summer storm. "Shite. I better go tell him to plan to have the dinner inside." She turns on a heel and walks inside without another word.

I open the door to my room right as Liam steps out of the closet. He is pulling a black Henley over his head. Muscles, and tattoos on full display.

Closing the door, I lean against it and cross my arms. Once he's pulled the shirt over his abs, he smiles at me.

"What?" he says, walking toward me.

He crowds my space and cups my jaw. He kisses me hungrily before pressing his forehead against mine.

"We never talked about you moving in here," I whisper.

"Emily," he says, and I look into his eyes. "Can I move in your room with you?"

My lip tips upward and I chuckle. I stare into his eyes that are full of humor and shrug.

"I mean, I guess you can," I say sarcastically.

He presses a kiss to my neck. "Are you getting sassy with me?" he asks, nipping my collarbone.

He kicks at my feet, so my legs spread further apart. I shift my weight, and he presses me against the door. My eyes close and I soak up the feel of his breath traveling up my neck.

"I need to get ready," I mutter, not making an effort to move away from him.

"Not yet," he whispers, peppering my skin with gentle kisses.

Heat spreads throughout my body and arousal pools at my core.

"Liam," I moan.

The *ping* of his phone breaks our bubble, and he growls under his breath. He shoves his hands into his pocket and pulls out his phone.

"I gotta head to the airport with Rhys." He says, rolling his neck in annoyance. He brings his face closer to mine. "We'll finish this when I get back." I nod and he kisses my lips with a quick peck before reaching for the doorknob. I step aside. Sending me a wink, he leaves, and the door shuts behind him.

June 3

He makes me feel alive in ways I thought were no longer possible.

CHAPTER 49
Liam

Paige and Declan climb into the back seat of the SUV. The airport staff load their luggage into the trunk.

"I haven't told Emily about Caetlin coming to the US," I say the moment the door is shut. My uneasiness grows the closer it gets to the party and to Caetlin's arrival. I don't know how Emily is going to react, but my gut is telling me it's not going to be good.

"How has she been?" Paige asks, settling against Declan's side.

The trunk slams shut, and Rhys quickly shifts into drive and pulls away from the private jet.

"She's been doing great. She hasn't had any issues with weaning off her medications, and Dr. Morrison is hopeful for her future." I can feel Declan's eyes burning through the seat and into my back.

"That's amazing!" Paige exclaims with a clap of her hands. "Isn't that great, Declan?"

"Yeah, I'm really happy she's doing so well." He says, his voice calm.

The tension in my spine seems to completely disappear. I'm glad I don't need to defend myself against Declan again. Everything with Emily has been heaven and I won't let anyone take that from us.

"Great. Now the traffic is going to be shit. I swear, every time it rains people forget how to drive." Rhys mutters angrily.

Not five minutes later are we sitting in traffic. Horns are honking and people are shouting at each other.

Pulling my phone from my pocket, I send a message to Emily

> It's looking like I'm going to be a little while longer than I thought. The traffic is shit.

> <frowning emoji>

> I'll make it up to you.

"When she doesn't reply, I pocket my phone and get comfortable in my seat.

"Do you think it would be better to tell her that your mom is coming?" Paige asks Declan.

I catch Declan's eyes in the side mirror.

"Er, I don't know if that's a good idea," I say, turning to face Paige.

Her brows are pulled inward, and she tilts her head to the side.

"How come?"

I scrub my hand down my mouth, the scruff scratches my palm.

"She hasn't been really speakin' to her ma." I say and I feel the burn of Declan's stare against the side of my face.

"What do you mean?' he asks, leaning forward and resting his forearms against his knees.

242

"You'll need to ask her about that," I answer before turning back around to face the windshield.

Declan's hand wraps around my seat and he leans in. "What aren't you telling us, Liam?" he says through clenched teeth.

"If Emily wants you to know, she'll tell you herself."

"Let's see what she says when we get back home, yeah?" Paige whispers to Declan. He releases the seat and settles back, pulling Paige into his arms.

The rest of the drive is silent.

Some of the men get to work unloading Declan and Paige's luggage as soon as Rhys parks the SUV in front of the mansion. Paige and Declan are huddled in each other's arms in the field.

Before their flight home, Paige had asked Declan to make a detour to her ma's home and I guess the whole ordeal finally got her. She bolted from the vehicle and ran through the grass before she fell. Declan chased her and they sat in the rain.

Rhys had decided it was best to leave them be and we drove the rest of the way to the mansion. When they're ready, we'll have someone pick them up and bring them inside.

Emily swings the door open and steps onto the porch. She scans the driveway. Bringing her eyes to mine, she arches a brow.

"Where are Paige and Declan?" she asks.

A moment later, Sarah's car pulls up next to the SUV.

She steps out and Rhys walks over to where she stands.

"Are Declan and Paige supposed to be sitting in a field during a rainstorm?" Rhys kisses her lips and then drapes an arm over her shoulder, facing us.

I squint from the rain landing on my face and eyelashes.

"Aye. They are havin' a moment. Leave them be."

"Is everything okay?" Emily asks, stepping down the stairs. I meet her halfway and pull her into my arms.

Ingrid stomps onto the porch and flays her arms outward in annoyance. She starts to curse us in Irish before shouting in English for Sarah to understand.

"I had Niall prepare dinner in the dining room to avoid being in the rain, but you lot decided to say the Hell with it and stand outside anyway."

I peer down at Emily who smiles up at me. Raindrops land on her face causing her eyes to flutter.

"Dance with me?" I whisper, releasing her and holding out my hand.

"Now?" she asks, nibbling on her bottom lip.

"Aye," I answer, dipping my chin.

She places her palm in mine, and I twirl her around. Her head tips back and she lets out a laugh that could thaw even the coldest heart.

From my peripheral, Sarah and Rhys are dancing and laughing as well.

Ingrid mutters angrily under her breath but when I meet her eyes, they're soft and warm. She shakes her head and smiles before going inside.

Clothes sticking to our bodies, hair drenched in rainwater, we walk into the mansion and make our way to the dining room. Ingrid stands with her hands on her hips and a scowl.

"And who do you reckon is going to clean that mess?" she asks, gesturing to the trail of puddles behind us.

The front door slams shut, and we all turn our heads to see Declan and Paige walk into the dining room.

Her make-up streams down her face leaving a stream of black, but her eyes are clear, and she seems at peace.

Looking down, he chuckles at the pooling of rainwater at his feet and then down the hallway to the foyer.

"We'll clean it up, Ingrid. Don't worry about it." Paige says, placing her hand against Declan's chest.

She raises a skeptical brow at Paige.

"Promise," Paige says tracing an x over her heart, giving Ingrid a big toothy grin.

Ingrid huffs before leaving the dining room and walking down the hall.

The six of us exchange glances before bursting out in laughter.

CHAPTER 50
Emily

After dinner, everyone separates to change into dry clothes. Liam and I are in my – *our* – closet, changing after a warm shower. He sits on my bed as I dress in a gray oversized tee and a pair of black sweatpants. I pile my hair in a messy bun on top of my head.

Liam's eyes leisurely travel down my body and he smirks when he spots the blush that has spread over my neck and face.

"Comfy?" he says with a grin.

"Mhm." I nod.

He pats the mattress and I saunter over and sit next to him. His arms wrap around me, and he falls back onto his back, pulling me with him.

I giggle when he nuzzles his face into my neck.

"Liam, what are you doing?" I squeal.

He relaxes and splays his arms above his head. "Just loving you."

I cuddle against his side and set my head on his chest. The heart beats against my ear and I swear I can feel mine syncing to it.

We both look up when there's a knock at the door.

"Come in!" I yell before settling back against Liam.

Paige pops her head in and smile sheepishly. "Can I talk with you for a minute, Emily?" she asks, looking over at Liam before meeting my eyes again.

"Of course," I say, moving to climb out of bed.

Liam wraps his hand around my wrist, and I fall back against his chest. His hand wraps around the back of my neck and he pulls me in for a kiss.

"Hurry back," he whispers with a wink.

I chuckle and follow Paige out of the room.

Sarah and Paige sit across from me in Paige's room. Declan left to keep Rhys and Liam occupied. For what reason? Welp, apparently, I'm getting interrogated.

"How long have you been avoiding your mom?" Paige asks quietly. There is no judgement in her eyes, only curiosity.

Sarah's stare is curious, as well as calculating.

"It's not that I've been ignoring her," I say with a sigh. My fingers fiddle with the string on my sweatpants. "I just can't hear her voice without feeling like my heart is going to burst from my chest."

Tears begin to well in my eyes and I struggle to keep my lips from quivering.

Sarah moves to sit next to me, and she wraps an arm around me. I lean my head against her shoulder.

"Why are you guys asking me this anyway? How do you know?" I meet Paige's eyes before they flick up to Sarah's.

"She's coming here."

I jolt upward and stare at Paige, wide-eyed.

"What are you talking about?" I sputter.

247

Sarah starts to rub her hand up and down my arm to try and comfort me, but it doesn't help. My blood is a rapid river that's flowing through my blood stream with unimaginable force.

Paige grimaces slightly. "We invited her to come back to the US with us. She originally said no, which is why she wasn't on our flight. But after Declan and I reached the airport, she changed her mind."

My ma is coming here. I'm going to see her in person. I won't have a way to avoid her. I take a deep breath in through my nose and release it through my mouth.

My nerves are shot, and I feel anxious.

"Hey, it's going to be okay," Sarah whispers in my ear and kisses my temple.

I bite down on my lower lip until I taste blood. The pain helps distract me from the threat of a panic attack. I shouldn't feel this. I shouldn't feel the dread of being in my ma's presence.

She's my ma. She loves me unconditionally. She has always been a pillar of strength in my life.

Fuck. Fuck. Fuck.

Paige reaches over and lightly squeezes my knee. Her eyes are warm and understanding.

I guess if anyone can understand a strained relationship with their mother, it's Paige. She was the subject of unimaginable pain and agony her entire life before she was taken by Vladimir.

I don't have that though. My relationship with my ma is different. It's my fault our relationship is not what it used to be.

"When will she be here?" I mumble.

"Tomorrow morning."

My eyes flutter closed, and I clench my hands into fists. I swallow tightly before opening my eyes and looking between Paige and Sarah.

"Okay," I say, lifting my chin to feign the confidence that I don't feel.

I didn't sleep a single minute last night. My anxiety of seeing my ma in person was too much to ignore. I sat in the chair in front of my window staring at nothing. My thoughts were a jumbled mess. It was a disaster.

Liam sat with me for a while and tried to offer me some comfort, but I had him go to sleep. He has been working so hard alongside Rhys and needed to rest more than I did.

The sun rose a few hours ago and I'm still sitting at the window. Declan left to pick up ma, and I'm uneasy with each second that passes and their SUV doesn't come driving up the road.

"It's going to be okay, *Féileacán*," Liam says as he dresses. His hair is still mussed from sleep and sticks up in different directions. Waking up with him at my side is a dream. His scent is embedded in my sheets. It's crazy to see how different my life is now despite what has happened to me.

"I know," I mutter. "It's silly for me to be feeling the way I am. I know that. I'm just filled with this fear that something bad is going to happen."

Liam steps up behind me and sets his hands on my shoulder.

"There are no rules that say how you should feel in situations, Emily. You went through a lot and your subconscious is trying to protect you."

I sigh and my shoulders slump. "Protect me from what though? She's my ma." My voice cracks from my throat tightening.

Liam's thumbs rub my shoulders. "From experiencing any trauma again. It might not seem rational, but it makes sense. The last person you spoke to before your life drastically changed was your ma."

The sound of tires on the dirt road causes my spine to become wrought iron straight. My stomach falls to the floor and my heart begins to gallop in my chest.

Ma is here.

CHAPTER 51
Liam

Emily didn't want to come downstairs to greet Caetlin. She wanted to breathe and gather the courage to see her. I offered to stay but she all but shoved me out of the bedroom.

I walk down the hallway and meet Paige at the top of the stairs. She peers over my shoulder before her shoulders slump.

"No Emily?"

I shake my head solemnly. "She's not quite ready to see Caetlin yet."

Paige frowns but nods in understanding.

"She'll come down when she's ready." She walks down the steps and I follow her lead.

The door opens just as we make it to the last step and Caetlin steps in with Declan right behind her. She smiles wide when she sees us.

"Liam, it's so good to see you," she opens her arms and pulls me in for a tight hug.

She greets Paige in the same way and then her smile drops when she notices that Emily is not with us.

Her eyes fall to the ground, and I watch her throat bob when she swallows the thump that has grown.

Do you think she'll be upset if I go up to her room?" She murmurs, peering up at Declan.

His eyes bounce between mine, Paige's, and Caetlin's. Whatever he sees on my and Paige's faces must make the decision for him.

"Let's get you settled and then we'll talk about Emily."

He places his hand on the small of Caetlin's back and leads her down the hallway.

We sit on the back patio that overlooks the denser part of the surrounding forest. Paige and Declan are cuddled on the outdoor loveseat. Caetlin is curled in a hammock chair with a cup of tea in her hands. I lean against the banister.

As much as I didn't want to, I told Caetlin about Emily's reasoning for avoiding her. Seeing the two of them in pain is gutting me. They *need* each other.

Caetlin is peering down at her tea; tears have stained her cheeks.

Way to fuck up her first day in America, Liam. Fecking eejit.

She swipes away a tear that slides down her cheek and then releases a sigh. "I'm going to go speak with her," she says, setting the cup on the outdoor table next to her.

We watch as she pushes herself off the seat and enters the house.

I rub the back of my neck and roll my shoulders. I hadn't realized how much tension I was holding in them until she walked out of sight.

"Do you think one of us should go with her?" Paige asks, placing her hand on Declan's chest.

"No. They need to see each other in private. This isn't something any of us can truly help with." Declan replies.

Pursing my lips, I nod.

Paige's phone *pings,* and she pulls it from her pocket.

"Sarah and Rhys won't be on their way until later tonight." I meet Declan's eyes for a second before he replies.

"That works. Let's head to the room. I want to talk with you about something." He stands and holds out his hand.

Paige intertwines her fingers with his, and together they leave me on the patio.

I lean my forearms on the banister and stare out at the vast property. I shake my head as my thoughts run ramped.

The uneasiness I've been feeling is growing. There is a pressure in my chest that is building as I rub it in hopes it'll improve.

I need to find a way to relieve this tension.

Pushing off the banister, I head toward the shooting range.

I'm not sure how many guns I've shot or how many targets I've destroyed but the pressure in my chest has lightened enough for me to be able to breathe.

"Feeling better?" Declan asks, striding toward me.

"Ask me after I see how Emily is doing."

Standing before me, Declan turns his attention to the target I just finished shooting.

"I wasn't aware of her feelings toward our ma." He whispers, his voice breaking toward the end of his sentence.

I shove my hands into my pockets. "I know. I made the decision to keep it from everyone so she could get better at her own pace." Declan meets my eyes; his expression is unreadable.

"I want to be angry with you," he murmurs. "But I would have done the same if it was Paige."

I remain silent.

"You're good for her." He adds and my brows raise to my hairline. He chuckles and shakes his head in amusement.

"Don't pretend you don't know that already."

"I do, it's just shocking for you to say it."

He smiles. "I've seen enough of how she is with you to admit I was wrong about you."

"Wow. A compliment and an admission in less than thirty seconds." I tease and Declan punches me in the shoulder.

I grunt and grip the joint.

"I'll deny everything." He says playfully with a wink.

I smirk. "Well, I appreciate your words." I dip my chin. "They mean a lot."

"You might want to tell Emily about the party tonight. I told Paige and while she was happy and excited, she nearly kicked my ass because she didn't get to find a dress for tonight."

I chuckle. Paige is a spitfire and despite her small stature, she'd definitely kick his ass.

"I'll make sure she knows."

"Good." Declan slaps me on the back and turns toward the house. "Rhys and Sarah should be arriving soon, and we still need to drive to the venue."

CHAPTER 52
Emily

I stand frozen against the wall opposite my ma who stares at me with sad-filled eyes. I expected her to come and see me, and I thought I was prepared for it. But seeing her before me has me feeling a plethora of emotions.

She looks older. The place between her brows has two lines indicating how often she furrows her brows. Her once bright red hair is dimmer with more gray strands than the last time I saw her.

"A*irím uaim thú,*" she whispers. *I miss you.*

My chest constricts and my throat swells to the point of suffocation.

"*Is fada liom uaim thú freisin ma*" *I miss you too, ma.*

She moves toward me with her hands out, palms up. My lip quivers as the space between us shrinks. When her arms wrap around me, tears flood my eyes and I sob.

My knees give and we both fall to the ground. My arms circle her middle and I bury my face in her chest. Her hand strokes my hair lovingly.

"It's okay, *mo stór.*" She whispers, pressing her lips to the top of my head.

"I'm so sorry, ma. I'm so so sorry." I cry and my vision is even blurrier with the tears that fall.

"You don't need to apologize, Emily. You needed time."

Seeing my ma is nothing like simply hearing her voice on the phone. Instead of paralyzing fear, everything inside me needs the comfort only my mother's love can provide. Her floral scent calms my soul and feeds the peace I've been searching for.

She rocks our bodies back and forth and begins to hum the lullaby that soothed me in my prison and helped lull me to sleep. I sob until my body is vacant of tears.

She pulls me away from her chest, holding me at arm's length. Her eyes match mine, puffy and red-rimmed from crying.

"I understand if you need more time – "

"No. I don't need time away from you, ma." I cut her off. "I might need more time before I'm able to go back to Ireland though."

She sniffles while nodding. "Of course, Emily. Whatever you need."

There is a soft knock on the door before it's pushed open. Liam steps into the room and pauses when he sees my ma and me on the ground.

He clears his throat, shutting the door with a soft click. "Everythin' alright in here?" he asks, putting his hands in his pockets and rocking on his heels.

"Aye," my ma answers, pulling me with her to stand.

"Good," the corner of his mouth ticks upward. "Emily, we should probably start getting ready." He says and my ma looks at me with a grin.

"What for?" I ask, my brows pinching.

"Declan has a surprise for Paige, and we need to get ready if we're going to make it on time."

"Uh, okay," I say turning toward my ma. She pulls me in for a tight hug and then kisses my cheek.

"I'll see you in a little while."

She saunters toward the door and gives Liam a gentle pat on the chest before leaving the room. Liam turns to face me the moment the door clicks shut.

"Are you okay?" he asks softly.

I nod. "I think so."

He strides toward me and cups my face. His thumbs gently stroke my raw skin from the repeated rubbing I did while crying.

His eyes are warm and full of love and pride.

"I'm glad you were able to speak with your ma, Emily."

I press a kiss to the palm of one of his hands. "Seeing her was different than hearing her voice over the phone," I whisper, peering up at his hazel eyes.

"Do you think it has to do with the fact that when you were taken, your last conversation with her was over the phone?"

I shrug. "I think that makes the most sense. Seeing her and having her hug me felt like a huge weight lifted and I could breathe easier."

His face lights up with a smile and he presses a kiss to my forehead.

"That's amazing, baby."

"What is Declan surprising Paige with?" I ask, changing the subject.

"Well technically it's no longer a surprise because he told her, but he is throwing an engagement party for her."

Every muscle in my body stiffens.

"A-an engagement party?" I stutter.

Liam's eyes fill with concern and his brows furrow. "Is everythin' okay?"

Shit. Shit. Shit.

Why can't I just enjoy a celebration without feeling nervous? What the fuck is wrong with me?

My mind races with different scenarios of what chaos will ensue.

No. It'll be fine.

I chant that mantra until I start to believe it.

Clearing my throat, I plaster a smile on my face. "Yeah, this is okay. It'll be wonderful."

"Will it?" the small voice at the back of my mind asks.

Shut. UP.

"We're going to have a great time," Liam smiles and presses a kiss on my lips. His hand wraps around mine and he leads me toward the ensuite.

Driving toward the venue, I nervously rub my hands down the fabric of my dress. At this point, I don't care if my sweat stains the silk. I'm a mess of unease.

My dress is emerald green and made from Mulberry Silk. It rests just above the knee. I've paired it with champagne-colored pumps. Liam is dressed in a white button-up with a tie that matches my dress. His black slacks mold to his thick thighs, emphasizing their muscle.

Logically, I know that the chances of having the near-exact situation happen at another engagement party are slim to none. But my emotions are uncontrollable and override the logic.

Liam's hand reaches over, and he intertwines our fingers, giving my hand a gentle squeeze. Peering over at him, he gives me a reassuring smile.

"You okay?" he whispers.

I doubt he knows what's bothering me, but there's no doubt he knows something is up. He's always been able to read me without any issues.

Not wanting to cause him any stress, I shake my head and give him a small smile. "Yeah, I'm okay."

He studies my face for a moment before nodding and turning to look out of his window.

It'll be fine. It'll be okay.

I'm fine.

CHAPTER 53
Liam

Climbing out of the SUV, I turn and offer my hand to Emily. She tried to hide the fact that she was nervous and trembling during the entire drive over here, but I noticed. I notice everything about her. I hate that I can't figure out what is bothering her though.

Emily straightens her dress and takes a deep breath. Placing my hand on her lower back, we walk toward the entrance.

The ballroom is decorated with champagne and light green accents. Fairy lights hang from the ceiling and meet in the center where a crystal chandelier is suspended.

There is an open bar and I spot Sarah and Rhys sitting together on the stools. I gesture with my chin and Emily follows my line of sight. As we walk over, Rhys lifts his drink.

"Liam, looking sharp. Emily, you, as always, look beautiful." He says, smiling softly at her.

She smiles and places a kiss on his cheek. "Thank you, Rhys. You look great, too."

Sarah hops down and pulls Emily into a hug. "I love your dress!" she exclaims, holding Emily away from her so she can assess her.

"You look beautiful, Sarah. Red really suits you." Emily replies with a smile.

Sarah's dress is wine-red and made of the same material as Emily's. It hugs her figure like a glove and highlights her trim frame.

"Eat your heart out, baby." She says with a wink and flirty smirk.

I chuckle, which pulls her attention to me.

"You clean up nice, Liam."

I shrug and smirk. I lift my finger, catching the attention of the bartender, and order myself an Irish whiskey. Emily orders two shots of tequila and quickly knocks them back the moment the bartender sets them in front of her.

I lean into her ear. "Are you okay?" I whisper.

She orders two more shots before turning toward me. "Yep." She smiles widely.

"Do you want to go home?" I ask, my eyes pivot between hers. I feel Rhys and Sarah watching our exchange but don't move my eyes from Emily's.

So many different emotions are swimming in her ocean-blues before she masks them.

"I'm okay. Everything is fine." Her voice is calm, but it sets me on edge.

"We can leave whenever you want to. Just say the word."

She nods then knocks back the additional shots she ordered.

I spine her to face me, "Do you think it might be best to slow down?" I ask.

"Everything is fine." She repeats, turning to face Sarah.

I meet Rhys's eyes and he raises his brow. I subtly shake my head and purse my lips.

Emily's posture is stiff, and I hate that I don't know what is going through her head. I hate that I don't know how to help her feel at ease.

Sarah's phone pings and she quickly moves to capture everyone's attention.

"They're here!" she shouts.

Everyone quiets down and waits for Paige and Declan to step into the ballroom.

We're the only ones who know Paige is aware of the party, everyone else still thinks it's a surprise so the moment

Paige startles but quickly shakes it off and begins laughing with excitement. Sarah and Emily rush to greet her, pulling each other into tight embraces.

Rhys and I step up to Declan and shake hands with him and slap him on the back.

"Congratulations, Paige," Rhys says, pulling her into a hug.

"Thank you so much for doing all of this, you guys. It looks beautiful." She tips her head and slowly spins, taking in all the decorations.

Despite the smile on her face, Emily is clearly very uncomfortable. When she catches my gaze, she gives me a tight smile.

I pull her into my arms and kiss her temple. "I love you," I whisper into her ear.

She peers up at me, her eyes are sad but also filled with love. "I love you, too."

She quickly steps away and heads back toward the bar. I am at her heels the entire way and when she tries to order another set of shots, I tell the bartender to bring her water instead.

"What are you doing?" she frowns.

"You haven't eaten yet and have already taken four shots," I reply with a hard stare.

Her chin lifts defiantly. "I told you that I'm fine, Liam."

I cup the back of her nape and bring her face closer to mine. "Your mouth says one thing, but your actions and body say another."

She tries to move away from me, but I tighten my grip.

"Talk to me, Emily."

"There is nothing to talk about. I'm fine." She hisses but her eyes hold no aggression.

Emily flicks her gaze over my shoulder and her blood drains from her face. I turn and spot Caetlin making her way over. She smiles at Emily, but Emily doesn't return a smile. In fact, she's barely breathing.

"What is wrong, Emily?"

She finally meets my eyes and doesn't mask the panic in hers.

"I-I can't be here." She stutters.

"Why?"

Caetlin steps next to me and sets her hand on Emily's shoulder.

"What's wrong, *leanbh?*"

Tears begin to well in Emily's eyes and fall down her cheeks.

"It's going to happen again."

Caetlin and I glance at each other and then it hits me. She's remembering the night Conor was murdered. She's remembering another traumatic event in her life and she's spiraling.

"I need to leave." She says and then takes off toward the doors.

Paige sees Emily running and blocks me from going after her.

"Is she okay?"

Ignoring Paige, I run after Emily.

CHAPTER 54
Emily

I can't breathe. I can't fucking breathe! This is too much. I shouldn't have ignored everything telling me that I wasn't okay. That being here wasn't okay.

"Give me the keys!" I scream at the valet. He frantically searches for the SUV keys before tossing them into my palm.

"Emily!" Liam calls my name, but I can't face him. Not now. I need to get away from here. I need something – anything to make this panic stop.

I'm in the vehicle and driving away right as Liam reaches me. He runs next to the SUV, slamming his hand on the window and screaming for me to stop.

My foot slams on the gas and I speed down the road.

As I drive back toward the estate, I have flashes of that night. The bullets flying, the sounds of screaming and cutlery crashing on the ground. The feeling of blood splattering on my skin.

It's all too much. My vision is blurring more with each passing second. The tears are making it nearly impossible to drive. Horns honk and curses are thrown my way as I rush through traffic.

"Move!" I shriek, swiping my arm back and forth, trying to get people out of my way. I nearly crash multiple times in my attempts to put distance between me and the party.

When I finally start driving up the private road to the estate, my breathing becomes a little easier. My mind continues to flash with the memory of driving up this road, of Liam holding my body, of throwing myself into Declan's arms.

Skidding to a stop and shifting into *park*, I throw open the door — not bothering to turn off the SUV — and sprint inside and up the stairs to my room.

I'm desperately moving my clothes and my dresser to get to the hole where I know my escape hides. Where I know I'll find the numbness I need right now.

My hands are trembling uncontrollably when I pull the box containing the stash of medications I kept away from Liam. I open the lid with enough force to send the capsules and tablets flying around me.

I blindly pick up a tablet and dry swallow it.

The sound of the front door bursting open and hitting the wall startles me.

"Emily!" Liam yells but I don't respond.

As quickly as possible, I collect as much medication as possible and throw it into the box.

The sounds of Liam's steps draw closer. I'm not going to have enough time to hide this.

Fuck. Fuck. Fuck.

I search for a shelf to set the box on and then push the dresser as close to its original spot as possible.

"Emily, where are you?"

I swallow another pill before exiting my closet and facing Liam.

His face is flushed, eyes are wide with worry. When he sees me and rushes toward me and cups my face.

"Are you okay?" He gasps.

My knees give out and I crumpled to the floor. Liam's arms wrap tightly around me, and I sob into his shirt. My hearts continue to gallop in my chest and the sound reverberates in my ears.

"No... I'm not okay." I cry.

The alcohol I consumed finally hits me, sending tingles through my fingers and lips. Liam rocks us back and forth and mutters comforting words under his breath.

We sit on the floor long enough for the medication to flow through me. My mind and body begin to relax, and Liam immediately takes notice.

My eyelids droop and my head lulls to the side.

I feel weightless.

Liam's body pulls away from mine and I mourn its loss.

He grips my shoulders and holds me at arm's length.

"What did you do?" he whispers.

The weight of my tongue seems to triple. I mumble incoherently and Liam gently shakes me.

"Emily, what did you do? What did you take?" he demands, panic seeping from his voice.

Thump... Thump... Thump...

The beat of my heart slowly as seconds pass.

"What did you take, *Féileacán?*"

Liam's voice becomes distant and faint.

Thump... Thump...

Thump...

Thump...

Then everything goes black.

The muffled sound of steady beeping emerges from the fog of my subconscious. My eyes flutter but refuse to open. The heaviness of my body feels as though the entire force of Earth's gravity is lying on it.

I try to move my lips, but nothing happens.

I'm acutely aware of someone's presence. But Who?

Darkness overtakes me with the whisper of someone calling my name.

Fingers gently caress the skin of my cheek. The scent of musk and spice fills my nose. Warmth flows through my blood and I know it's him.

"Wake up, *Féileacán*. Please, wake up."

I try to force my eyes to open with no luck. My body doesn't feel like my own. It's sitting on the edge of reality and whatever limbo my soul has gone.

"You were close. So close." A voice says.

Blood rushes toward my heart, sending it into a race.

"You're weak. Pathetic."

I fight with my body, trying to gain some semblance of control to wake up.

"You thought you'd escape us? Ha! You'll never be free of us."

My eyes flutter harder, and my muscles finally begin to give in to my influence.

A deep and dark chuckle dissipates when my eyes open. Black dots fill my vision before color starts to take form. The hospital room comes into focus.

"Thank God," my ma cries and then quickly stands at my bedside. She takes my hand into her and peppers it with kisses. Tears stream down her face and the guilt of what I've done comes rushing.

Liam stands at the end of my bed with pain etches over his beautiful face. His eyes glisten with unshed tears before he blinks them away and swallows tightly.

My ma continues to pepper me with kisses and her hands roam over my face and arms, assessing for any visible damage.

When she finally steps away, Liam slowly walks toward me. His brows are pinched with concern, and he studies me as if he's confirming I'm truly awake. Truly here.

My ma steps out of the room, the door shuts with a soft *click*.

"What were you thinking?" Liam whispers in a shaky voice.

My brain still feels foggy, and I struggle to form words. My head feels heavy, so I remain pressed against the pillows.

Liam lowers his chin to his chest and traces circles on the blanket with his fingers.

"I thought you were going to die, Emily. His voice is full of sadness and pain.

Tears flow down my cheeks and Liam leans over, swiping them away with his thumb.

"I'm so sorry," I rasp.

CHAPTER 55
Liam

Declan, Caetlin, and I sit in the office of the hospital psychiatrist. My leg hasn't stopped bouncing since I left Emily with Sarah and Paige. We've been discussing the best course of action regarding Emily's lapse and how to prevent it from happening again.

I refuse to believe she intentionally tried to overdose.

When she lost consciousness and started seizing, I felt my heart completely shatter. I thought she was dying before my eyes, and I fucking froze. I didn't know what to do or who to call until one of the guards came running in.

I had apparently been screaming her name and for help, but I don't remember doing it. I don't remember anything but the emotional turmoil that was attacking my body and watching Emily convulse in my arms.

The guard had called Dr. Robbins who administered Narcan before an ambulance arrived and rushed her to the hospital.

I lost my mind and threatened to blow the brains out of every person in the vicinity when they denied me being able to ride with Emily in the ambulance. It wasn't until Caetlin arrived and cooled me down that I was okay following them to the hospital.

"Does that sound like an acceptable plan for everyone?" Dr. Nelson asks, glancing at the three of us.

Caetlin and Declan both turn to me, and I realize they're asking me for confirmation.

The plan is for Emily and I to live on our own, and identify any and all her triggers. Declan had mentioned moving off the property completely, but I don't want to take Emily away from her garden. Dr. Nelson agreed.

So, we will be moving to one of the guest houses on the property that is close enough to the mansion that we won't be completely alone but also far away enough to allow Emily some privacy.

Declan has removed me from any missions until further notice so I can focus on helping Emily.

She will have a team that will work with her along with Dr. Morrison to ensure she has round-the-clock care but with the stipulation of not being suffocating for her.

I made sure they understood what would happen if Emily felt any negativity with their presence.

I turn toward Dr. Nelson and nod. "Aye."

Declan and Caetlin both nod and settle into their seats.

"Excellent. I have no doubts that Emily will make vast improvement with the plan we've discussed. She has a large support system and that makes a huge difference."

He stands and holds out his hand. The three of us take turns shaking his hand and saying goodbye.

Caetlin's small hand presses against my back and she sets her head against my shoulder. "Thank you, Liam. Thank you for much for being here for Emily."

I wrap my arm around her, and we continue down the hallway. "Of course, Caetlin. Emily is my life."

She smiles warmly, squeezing me closer to her body.

Reaching Emily's room, Declan clasps a hand on my shoulder and gives it a gentle squeeze.

"I'm going to take Paige and head home."

I nod and we enter the room.

Sarah and Paige are sitting in the couch next to the window adjacent to Emily's bed. Their eyes are puffy and red-rimmed. Paige sniffles and Sarah daps her eyes with a tissue.

Declan is at Paige's side within three strides and pulling her into his arms.

"I'm okay Declan," she says, swiping at the tears that flow down her face.

His using his forefinger to lift her chin and kisses her lips gently.

I walk over to Emily's side and push back the strands that have fallen over her forehead.

"Hi," she whispers, looking up at me with warm, soft eyes.

"Hi," I smile and lean down, pressing a kiss to her skin.

Declan and Paige say goodbye to Emily before leaving with Sarah in tow.

Caetlin hugs her tightly and whispers in her ear before kissing her and stepping out.

The next half hour is spent discussing what we planned with Dr. Nelson. Emily doesn't say much during the entire conversation, but she doesn't have to.

Her body language and facial expressions reveal her emotions. Shame, sadness, grief, and frustration flash across her face quickly and repeatedly.

She dips her chin causing her hair to fall from behind her ear.

"What are you thinkin'?" I ask, moving to sit on the bed. She shifts, making room for me.

She shrugs but keeps her eyes trained on her fingers that she fiddles on her lap.

"My mind is thinking too much for me to really pinpoint something specific."

I nod in understanding and place my hand on her thigh and rub my thumb up and down the fabric of the hospital blanket.

"Do I need to stay here?" she whispers.

"Dr. Nelson would like you to stay for a few days while you're recovering." She raises her head, her eyes pivot between mine. "Still feeling groggy?" I ask, pushing her hair behind her ear.

"A little."

"You need your rest." I smile softly.

She releases a deep breath and turns to face the window. The natural light casts a glow across her eyes, causing them to appear translucent.

I pull one of her hands from her lap, intertwining my fingers with hers. Her gaze moves to our hands and her brows pinch.

"Are you leaving?"

I shake my head despite her not looking at me. "Never."

CHAPTER 56
Emily

Just as he said, Liam hasn't left my side since I was brought to the hospital. The doctors have kept me on fluids and the groggy, fuzzy feeling I was experiencing has since gone away.

When they questioned me about my motives, the only person who didn't look at me with pity was Liam. There was nothing but understanding and love in his eyes.

During the time that I've been here, Declan has had my and Liam's belongings moved to our new home. Everything I felt when I was informed of what they planned for me was negative.

I know they're doing what they think is best for me, but my mind and heart are at war with what I believe should be happening.

I didn't mean to take the amount of medication I did. I just wanted all the noise to stop. I wanted the peace that they bring because I truly believed that was my only option.

My stash was found during the moving process and Liam, Declan, and Rhys were livid. Declan yelled of course, Rhys was angry but didn't speak to me, and Liam... He was more hurt than anything.

That broke me more than anything.

I failed him.

I failed myself.

I failed everyone.

But what did they expect me to do?

Everything inside me was screaming for an escape and I found it.

The pain I saw in his eyes was too much that I couldn't look at him for the rest of the day.

A knock comes from the door and Dr. Nelson steps into the room. "Good morning, Emily. How are you feeling today?" he says with a grin.

Liam stands from the couch and steps to my side, setting his hand on my shoulder.

"I'm okay."

"Are you ready to go home?" he asks, studying my chart.

"I think so," I reply while picking at my cuticles.

He glances at my hands for a moment before meeting Liam's eyes. When his gaze finally lands on mine, he smiles warmly with a tilt of his head.

"My colleague is going to be coming in to check your vital signs and your physical health. When that's finished and she's cleared you, we'll get you set up to get out of here. How does that sound?"

"Good. That sounds good. Thank you."

With a final smile, Dr. Nelson leaves the room.

"I'm going to head down to the cafeteria for some coffee. Do you want me to bring you anything?" Liam asks. I turn toward him and silently shake my head.

He kisses the top of my head and then leaves the room.

The weight of the room becomes heavy, and I struggle to breathe as the air thickens.

What is happening?

The atmosphere fills with sadness and tears well in my eyes. My heart begins to race, and my palms become sweaty. I don't know what is happening to me.

It feels as though these feelings aren't my own. Like my body is no longer mine.

Suddenly images of a woman flash through my mind. She's beautiful with long dark curly hair, smooth ebony skin, and deep chocolate-brown eyes. Her full lips lift into a sad smile.

Oh my God. She's one of them... One of the women I saw when I was with Vladimir.

I can't hold back the sob that breaks through my lips. The woman doesn't say anything, she simply watches as I break down.

"I'm so sorry," I cry.

Her head tips to the side, questions running through her eyes.

"I'm so sorry for what happened to you." I sputter.

Her brows slightly pinch. Shaking her head, she sets a hand on her chest and her smile widens.

"I'm at peace."

The softness in her voice flows into my ears. My heart hurts at the fact that she is no longer here but it's also appreciative that she's no longer suffering.

She disappears and flashes of other women come and go. They show me that they've found the tranquility they searched for. They show me the peace they've found after the suffering they experienced.

Their spirits are untainted, unblemished.

The door opens and Liam rushes to my side, pulling me into his arms. He doesn't say a word as I shatter in his embrace, clutching onto his shirt.

June 23

Something good that happened today...

I woke up without feeling like I shouldn't have.

CHAPTER 57
Liam

The days' following Emily's release from the hospital have had an odd sense of calmness. I panicked when I stepped into her room and saw her sobbing uncontrollably in her bed. She ended up falling asleep in my arms from exhaustion and I sat for hours stroking her hair until the doctor came in and said she was cleared to go home.

On the drive home, she shared that she was visited by multiple women she had seen during her time in captivity.

My emotions were all over the place when she explained how they shared the peace they found and the encouragement her spirit felt to keep going. To keep fighting.

She still has such a long road ahead of her and her addiction will always be something to work at, but I have all the faith in the world that she will make it through this.

It's late in the evening when Emily and I finally come home. We had spent the entire day in the garden. We fell asleep under the shade of the trees after we had lunch, and it was absolutely amazing.

Emily steps out of the ensuite with a towel wrapped around her. Her red hair sits on the top of her head in a large messy bun.

lie in bed and watch her go through her nightly ritual. We've settled into a comfortable routine. Declan has made it a point to have her things checked periodically for any hidden drugs. I don't entirely approve of this method, but I understand his reasoning so, for now, I'm allowing it.

Once she's finished, Emily comes to bed and lays her head on my chest. My fingers lightly caress the skin on her arm and goosebumps rise. Over the last few nights, we've been working on her fear of having the lights off when she sleeps.

Reaching over, I switch off the lamp on my nightstand. Emily tenses but remains in my arms. I softly play with the ends of her damp hair.

"You alright?" I whisper into the dark room.

Her head dips in a small nod but she remains silent. Her body shivers with tension and I wrap my arm tightly around her, pressing her against my body.

I keep my breaths even and feel her mimic them. Her body steadily begins to relax.

"Are you ready to turn your light off?" I ask and she tenses again. "I'm right here, *Féileacán*. You're not alone." I whisper, pressing a kiss on her head and stroking her hair.

Tentatively, she pulls away and leans over to shut her light off. When the room is cast into darkness with only the soft glow of the moon shining through the window, Emily burrows herself into my side.

Her shivers become trembles and her breathing shallows. Rubbing my hand up and down her arm, I whisper soothing and encouraging words until I feel the stiffness in her muscles dwindle.

"Talk to me, *mo ghrá*."

"About what?" she asks softly.

I shrug. "Anything. Everything. It will help clear your mind and help distract you."

We move into a comfortable conversation until sleep eventually takes Emily. Her soft snores fill the silence in the room and a content sigh escapes my lips.

Her scent billows around me and I breathe as much of it in as humanly possible.

I'm not sure how long I lay staring up at the darkened ceiling soaking in the warmth of Emily's presence until I finally drift off to sleep.

I wake up to Emily's soft whimpers. Peering down, her face is twisted in pain, and she kicks her feet as though she's running.

"Em?" I whisper, pulling my body away from her.

A thin layer of sweat coats her forehead and a few strands of her hair stick to her skin, and small pants burst through her slightly ajar lips.

I push the sweaty strands away from her face and she begins to wake. Her eyes flutter open and gradually focus on my face.

"Everythin' okay?"

I know it's a stupid fecking question because, clearly, it's not but I don't know what else to say at this hour of the night.

She blinks her fatigue away and then rises onto her elbow.

"Do you think we can go for a walk?" she whispers.

"We can do anything you want, Emily."

The two of us quickly put on our shoes and Emily grabs a mustard-colored cardigan.

We walk hand-in-hand along one of the many paths that cut through the property. The moonlight silhouettes the many guards that patrol the estate. I dip my chin and Emily smiles at each one we pass.

"I still hear them." She whispers, keeping her eyes trained forward.

"Who?"

She slows to a stop, and I turn to face her. She studies my face with slightly pinched brows and gives me a forced smile.

"Their cries." She scoffs humorlessly. "Despite seeing them and knowing they're at peace, their cries echo in my head like a broken record."

My eyes soften and I softly caress her cheek with the back of my fingers. She leans into my touch and smiles sadly.

"Do you think they'll ever go away?" her voice is so quiet; I nearly miss her question.

I gently shake my head. "I don't know, Em. I really don't."

She nods and nibbles on her bottom lip. Lifting my hand, I use my thumb to pull it from her teeth.

"What if they never stop?"

"We'll figure it out. Together." I stare into her eyes so she can see the sincerity in those words.

She starts to shake her head, but I grip the back of her neck and pull her forehead to mine.

"Look at me, Em," I say when she closes her eyes.

They pinch tighter and I give her neck a reassuring squeeze.

"Look at me." I demand softly and she finally opens her eyes. The blue in them is so deep from the tears that have started to fill her eyes but she keeps her gaze on mine.

"I'm not going anywhere, Emily. Not this time. Not ever."

"What if it becomes too much? What if you realize that I'm no longer worth the trouble?" Her lip quivers.

I wrap my fingers around her hand and bring it to my chest, right above my heart.

"You feel that?" I whisper, caressing her skin with my thumb. She nods, staring at our hands. "I belong to you, *Féileacán*. There is no force strong enough that will ever make me walk away."

The moonlight dances across her face when she peers at me through her lashes. The glow casts a halo around her, causing my heart to thump rapidly in my chest.

Her fingers twitch when she feels the change in my heartbeat.

"I love you, *Féileacán.*"

She swallows and clears her throat. "I love you too, Liam."

CHAPTER 58
Emily

It's been three days since Liam and I walked through the grounds in the middle of the night. The truth in his eyes was unmistakable. I'm trying not to let my fear of his walking away get to me. I'm trying to trust that we're going to get through this. That *I* am going to get through this.

I walk into the mansion and make my way toward the kitchen. Yes, Liam and I have a kitchen and Niall has offered to come cook for us there when he's not here, but I like the comfort of eating here.

When I step into the room, it's empty. My brows furrow as I scan the kitchen and pantry.

"Is anyone here?" I ask loudly.

A few moments later, Declan walks in with his hands in his pockets. "I had everyone leave for a little while."

"What's going on?" my mind starts to race with negative thoughts. "Is everything okay?"

Declan holds his hands up to keep me from going into a panic. "Everything is fine. Paige has just been having a rough day and wants to be alone."

My brows pinch with worry. "Is she okay?"

Bowing his head, he rubs the back of his neck. "She had a nightmare and it really hit her hard."

Paige had the worst of the violence in comparison to me. She was beaten, tortured, and raped every day. The brutality she faced is unlike anything I'd ever heard of before. While I internalize my trauma and keep quiet. Paige has released the anger and resentment that was trapped in her body.

She tortured and murdered some of the men that Declan captured during our rescue.

"Do you think it's because she hasn't let out any of her emotions?"

The last few months have been uneventful as far as any altercations with anyone in the underground. Paige used violence to battle the violence she had inside, and I wonder if not having that is causing her to have nightmares again.

Declan rubs the scruff on his jaw and stares distantly at the ground. "It's more than likely. We haven't needed to kill anyone in a while, so she hasn't had anything to keep her distracted from whatever goes through her head."

"Maybe she could find something else to help her? Has she tried writing in a journal?" I ask.

He nods. "She started after you suggested it." He sighs and then stuffs his hands back into his pockets. "I think writing it all out is making her truly face what happened to her and actually deal with all her emotions instead of the ones she wants."

I walk over to my brother and wrap my arms around his middle. His arms wrap around me, and he rests his chin on my head. "I'm here if you or Paige need me."

His lips press against my hair. "How are you feeling?" he whispers.

I pull away and releases me from his embrace. "I'm taking one day at a time," I answer honestly.

He gives me a tight smile and nods. "And Liam?"

My brow raises and I tilt my head. "What about him?"

"Is he still treating you right?"

I smirk at him and cross my arms over my chest. "*Now* you ask how he's treating me?"

Smirking, Declan rolls his eyes and gently pushes my shoulder with his fist. "Got a reputation of an overbearing protective older brother to maintain."

Shaking my head, I chuckle and push him. He stumbles and barks out a laugh.

He sobers and smiles warmly at me. I return the gesture. "I love you, Em."

"I love you too, Declan."

The sound of footsteps coming down the hallways pulls our attention. Rhys steps into the kitchen and pauses when he sees me and Declan.

"What's up?" Declan asks, turning to fully face him.

Rhys hikes his thumb over his shoulder. "I was heading out to the docks to check the newest shipment."

"I'll come with you." He says before turning toward me. "Do you mind checking in on Paige in a little while? She's sleeping right now."

"Of course," I say with a nod.

They both kiss my forehead and leave.

I knock and then step into Paige and Declan's room. Paige is sitting on the bed with her knees drawn to her chest and her chin resting on her knees. She glances at me as I enter the room. Her hair is a mess, and she has dark bags under her eyes.

"Hey," I whisper, giving her a small smile.

"Hi," she mumbles.

"Doing okay?"

She shakes her head then shoves her face into her knees. Her shoulders shake when she begins to sob.

I sit on the mattress and pull her into my arms. She buries her face into my chest and clutches my shirt.

"I don't want to be sad or cry, Emily." She croaks.

And that's all I seem to feel and do.

"How have you been so positive?" she asks, swiping at the tears that stain her face.

"I'm not."

Her face rises from my chest, and she furrows her brows in question. "What do you mean?"

I sigh and lie back on the pillows. "When we were first rescued, I know that I seemed so okay and that I was doing great." I huff a humorless laugh "At least until I was sent to the hospital."

I turn to face Paige. "I haven't been okay in a long time. But I'm getting better." She nods and then lowers her eyes to the blanket.

"I've been so mad at the world and what happened to me, I didn't want to feel anything else."

My eyes trail over the scars that cover her body and the small one on her cheek. The scar on my thigh begins to heat.

"Declan said you've been writing?" I ask, pulling her attention away from the blanket.

"I have. And honestly, it's been surprisingly liberating to get those feelings out."

A grin spreads over my face, and I lean forward, setting my hand on her thigh. "That's awesome, Paige. I think we both deserve to be liberated."

I spend the rest of the afternoon with Paige until Declan returns from the docks.

"Liam is looking for you. He's outside."

I nod and leave after giving Paige a hug and a kiss on the cheek.

CHAPTER 59
Liam

Emily steps out of the front doors and smiles widely when she sees me standing at the bottom. I wink at her and her cheeks flush.

I pull her into my arms and press my lips to her the moment her feet hit the final step. She opens up to me without hesitation.

Blood rushes to my cock when she whimpers and presses her breasts harder against my chest. Her fingers slide into the hair at my nape. I groan into her mouth when she grips the strands tightly and tugs at them.

"Get a room!" Rhys shouts, breaking our kiss.

Emily's face and neck are bright red, and her pupils are dilated.

Chuckling, I give her a soft kiss then release her.

"Fuck you, Rhys," I shout back with a laugh.

He flips me off before walking away.

"Come with me," I hold out my hand and Emily places her palm against mine.

Emily's mouth falls open the moment we step into our home. Fairy lights hang from the ceiling, giving the space a soft glow. Wildflower petals are scattered all over the room. A white runner creates a path for Emily to follow.

She spins around to face me; her eyes are wide, and her chest rises and falls rapidly. "What is this?" she whispers.

I gesture for her to continue forward. "Keeping going to find out."

She swallows tightly and then steps onto the white carpet. It continues through the foyer before stopping in the living room.

Slowly she steps into the room. With her back to me, I remove the velvet box from my pocket and kneel. She slowly spins and gasps when she's me on my knee.

Opening the box, she raises a hand to her mouth. A sob escapes her lips and tears begin to flow down her face.

"Emily – *Féileacán* – The moment I laid eyes on you, I knew you were destined to be mine. When your scent of wildflowers and berries hit me, I knew it was a scent I'd never be able to live without." I swallow the nerves that build. "You're my best friend. The love of my life. My everything. You take my breath away only to breathe it back into my lungs. When you're not with me, I count the seconds until I can be with you again.

"There is no future where you're not mine and I'm not yours. The only future that we have is with each other. The only future I'll accept is a future in which you let me love you the way you deserve to be loved. I love you with every cell in my body. I don't want to live without you. Will you marry me?"

Emily throws herself into my arms and we tumble to the ground.

"Yes! Yes! Of course, I'll marry you Liam!" she cries, peppering kisses all over my face and neck.

I bury my face into the crook of her neck and breathe deeply.

She leans back and I remove the ring with trembling hands and slide it onto her finger.

The pear-shaped diamond seems to brighten against her complexion. The intertwining rose gold band is encrusted with smaller diamonds. It's perfect for her.

"Oh, Liam. It's beautiful." She whispers in awe. Her hands press against either side of my face and she smashes her lips against mine.

She adjusts her body to straddle me. Her pussy grinds against the fabric of my pants and I groan. She kisses me with such untamed hunger that I feed off it.

My body is on fire, my cock is painfully hard and I can't stop myself from lifting to grind harder against her.

"Please," she whimpers, trailing kisses down my neck and nipping at my skin.

"Tell me what you want, baby."

She feverously rips at my clothes until I'm left in my boxer briefs. Her palms my cock through the fabric and she moans when she feels its stiffness.

She pulls my cock from its confines. Licking her lips, her ocean-blue eyes rise to mine and the lust I see fuels mine.

"What are you going to do, *Féileacán?*" I ask in a husky voice.

She hums and then wraps her hands around my cock. She slowly pumps me with her eyes still on mine.

"Let me see you," I demand, gesturing at her with my chin.

She leans back on her heels and begins to slowly strip her clothes from her body. Her movements are unhurried and seductive. Precum leaks from my cock, and I move to grip the base to help relieve the pressure that's building.

Her perfect teardrop-shaped breasts fall beautifully from her bra and my mouth waters with the need to suck on her delicious pink nipples.

Once she's completely naked, she bends forward and returns her grip to my cock. I cup her face with my hand and thumb her bottom lip.

"You gonna suck on my cock, baby? You gonna choke on it?"

Her eyes flutter and she nods with a moan.

"Go on then, choke on it. I want to see you cry for me."

She licks her lips again then wraps her lush lips around the head and sucks. My eyes close and I jerk my hips. She widens her mouth then swallow me down until I hit the back of her throat.

She gags then slides back up my shaft before gliding down again.

"That's it, baby." I encourage.

She shifts and presses the heel of her foot against her pussy.

"You like sucking my cock, Emily?" she moans and rocks on her heel.

The wet sounds of her mouth gliding up and down my cock and her gags fill the room.

My spine begins to tingle, and I grip onto Emily's hair.

"I'm going to come in your mouth but you're not going to swallow, got it?" She nods and hollows out her cheeks, creating a vacuum.

I hold her head in place and fuck her face until my cum explodes from my cock and into her mouth. An animalistic groan escapes me, and I continue to pump into her until she's sucked every last drop of my cum.

She releases my cock.

"Show me," I demand.

She tips her head back and opens, sticking out her tongue.

"Good girl. Now, swallow all of it." She does as she's told and fuck if it doesn't make me hard again.

I crash my lips against hers and taste the slight saltiness of myself in her mouth.

"Lie on your back and spread your legs. I want to see how wet your cunt is from sucking my cock."

CHAPTER 60
Emily

I swipe my forefinger along my bottom lip and suck the cum that collects. Falling onto my back, I spread my legs as far as they'll go. Liam kneels and his eyes fall to my pussy, and I burn from their heat.

"You have such a pretty pussy, Emily." He groans.

His fingers leisurely coast up my leg until he reaches the apex of my thighs. His touch is so close to where I need it that I whimper when he moves away.

Before I get a chance to open my mouth to complain, his tongue is swiping through my folds. My back arches off the floor and I moan loudly.

Liam's arms wrap around my waist, forcing me to stay still as he feasts on my pussy. His tongue laps at my clit sending pleasure rippling up my spine. He sucks on my lips and nips at my thighs.

My body is already in sensory overload so when he pushes two fingers into my core, my orgasm erupts through me like a volcano, and I scream his name.

I lie limply on the floor when I finally climb down from my high.

Liam trails kisses up my body before reaching my face. His eyes are filled with so much love and happiness that I can't help the smile that spreads over my face.

"I love you." I pant.

He gently kisses my nose. "I love you."

Lifting off me, Liam scoops me into his arms and heads down the hall. Stepping into the ensuite, he sets me on the counter then moves to fill the bathtub.

I climb down and Liam quirks his brow. "I need to pee," I explain, and he nods before pulling a bottle of essential oil from the cabinet. He adds a few drops then climbs in.

Once I finish, I step into the tub and settle against his chest.

He cleans us both and then we lie there until the water turns cold.

I'm so relaxed that I am weightless when Liam lifts me from the bath and dries me off. He carries me to the room and places me under the blankets.

"Are you okay if I turn off the lights?" he asks. With a small smile, I nod.

For the first time, I don't tense when the room is engulfed in darkness. Liam's body slide in next to mine and he pulls me into his warmth.

Setting my head against his chest, I'm lulled to sleep by the steady beat of his heart.

The following morning, I am digging through one of the boxes that was left in the closet. It is packed with an array of different things that seem not to have a proper place.

I have several piles from what will be tossed out to what will be donated when I spot my old journal at the bottom.

I pause and stare at the leather binding.

Hesitantly, I pull the journal from the box and set it on my lap. Inside this journal are the writings of young Emily who was not yet marred by the evils of the world. Who was naively in love and happy beyond recognition.

My fingers tremble when I open the cover. Tears gather in my eyes and spill onto the pages as I read what I've written.

Liam,
There are no words to articulate the happiness you bring me. You're my best friend and I am beyond grateful for the love we share.
We haven't said the words but I hope you can understand that I love you more than I could ever say.
You are everything to me and I know despite the issue of my father demanding me to marry Ryan.
You are mine and I am yours.
I will fight along side you for the love we have and the life we are going to create together.

You are my home.

Forever yours,
Emily

CHAPTER 61
Liam

"What time?"

"They will be releasing them at noon." The woman on the other end of the phone replies.

"Okay, perfect. Thank you." I end the call and smile.

"What are you smiling about?" Declan asks.

I pocket my phone and turn to him.

"I'm taking Emily to Central Park today for a surprise."

"Another one?" he asks with a raised brow.

"Aye," I say with a nod and a cheesy grin on my face.

He chuckles when he sees my expression and slaps me on the back. "Alright, you lovestruck puppy."

I check my watch and see I have just under two hours to get Emily ready and to Central Park for the event.

"Shite. I gotta go." I wave goodbye and head to our home.

I step into our room and halt when I see Emily on the ground surrounded by random items. She's hunched forward with a journal open on her lap.

When I hear her sniffle, I quickly stride over and kneel beside her. She raises her head and I frown at the tears that stain her cheeks.

"What's wrong?" I ask.

She smiles and shakes her head. "Nothing."

I peer down at the journal, and she moves to hand it to me. "Read it." She says.

I take the journal from her hands and turn it toward me. "What is it?"

My eyes roam over the words and my heart expands in my chest while also cracking. I swallow the emotions that squeeze my throat and blink away the burn in my eyes.

Settling the book aside, I cup Emily's face with my hands.

"You are my home too, *Féileacán*."

She buries herself into my chest and I wrap my arms around her.

"I have a surprise I want to show you. I think you'll love it." I say when she pulls away. "Get ready, baby. We're going to Central Park."

I swipe away the tears on her face and kiss her gently. When she stands and heads toward the ensuite, I ready myself to go.

We walk through Central Park until we reach the conservatory.

"What are we doing here?" Emily asks, tugging lightly at my hand.

I check the time and smile when there are only five minutes left until her surprise will be revealed.

"Come on," I pull her with me as we move toward the open garden where a crowd has gathered.

Emily furrows her brow and glances around. She pauses when she sees a group with some covered cages.

"Liam?" she whispers.

I smile at her reassuringly and squeeze her fingers. "Just watch. You'll love it."

A young woman steps in front of the group and clasps her hands.

"Thank you so much for coming to our butterfly release."

Emily sucks in a breath and her head whips to me before she returns her attention back to the woman. She goes on to talk about the importance of butterflies and their contribution to the ecosystems they reside in.

She gestures for the other men and women in her group to step forward. They lift the cages and move to her side. Emily's hand tightens around mine when they unveil the butterflies under the cover.

The crowd loudly counts down from ten. When they reach one, the cages are opened from the top and hundreds of butterflies escape into the sky.

CHAPTER 62

Emily

I have no words.

Releasing Liam, I step forward as butterflies surround us. Tears spring into my eyes and my lip trembles as they fly up and up.

Everything and everyone fades into the background. It's just me and these marvelous creatures. Their variety of colors are a kaleidoscope in the sky sending my heart into absolute bliss.

I still when one flies close. Slowly, I lift my hand and it lands on my forefinger. A shaky smile spreads over my face and I feel the warmth of my tears sliding down my cheeks.

After a while, the butterfly gently lifts from my finger and flies away.

I hold my arms out to the sides and slowly spin with my head tipped back. A laugh climbs up my throat and I let it flow out of me.

My chest feels light. My heart sings with happiness and awe.

Closing my eyes, I allow the feeling to drift through me.

I feel Liam's arms wrap around my waist. Lowering my arms and head, I smile widely at him.

"Thank you so much for this."

"Anything for you, *Féileacán*. Anything."

June 30

Today is the first day I've truly felt... free.

Free from numbness.
Free from the need to medicate.
Free from wanting to end it all.
Free to love and be loved in return.

Just... free.

EPILOGUE
Emily

"Absolutely not," Rhys grunts with his arms crossed over his chest.

Sarah's laughter fills my ears, and I can't help but chuckle alongside her. "It's funny that you think you get a say, Rhys."

I lean my head on Liam's shoulder, his hand slides up and down my arm.

"You're going to get yourself killed on that thing," Rhys growls, stepping toward Sarah and her new blacked-out motorcycle.

She pats the seat with a flirty smile. "Oh, come on, baby. You know you're ready to be my backpack."

They're bickering rises in volume and Liam, Declan, Paige, and I step away.

Paige shakes her head and laughs under her breath. "I wasn't expecting a motorcycle when Sarah said she had something to show us."

Declan laughs and pulls her into his side. "I wasn't sure what to expect but considering how impulsive Sarah is, I think a motorcycle isn't as crazy as she could have gone."

We laugh in our agreement and stop in front of the SUV.

"We better head out if we're going to catch our flight." Liam says opening the door for me.

Paige pulls me into a tight hug. "I love you, Em." She whispers and I swallow the lump in my throat.

"I love you too, Paige."

She wipes the tear that falls from the corner of her eye and smiles.

Declan wraps his arms around me and kisses my temple. "I'm so proud of you, Em. So fucking proud of you." His voice is thick with emotion.

I nod, my lip quivering. "Thank you," I whisper.

Releasing me, Declan hugs Liam. "Thank you for taking care of her."

Liam doesn't say anything, but his eyes and smile are warm.

Sliding into the car, we wave our goodbye then head to the private airstrip.

"Please buckle your seatbelts as we prepare to land in Ireland." The pilot says over the intercom.

My fingers clench onto the arms of the seat so tightly that my nails dig into the tan-colored leather.

Liam's finger curl around my hand and he pulls it into his lap. I peer up into his eyes. The swirls of amber and green soften and he smiles warmly.

"Everything is going to be okay." He pats the top of my hand with his then lifts it to his lips.

I release a deep breath and try to lower my shoulders from my ears.

I slightly jostle when the wheels of the landing gear meet the tarmac. My stomach twists with anxiousness and my heart threatens to burst from my chest.

When we slow to a stop, I feel seconds away from throwing up my lunch.

Liam reaches over, unbuckles me, and helps me stand. With shaky legs, I walk behind him to the exit. The flight attendant smiles and dips her chin.

"Welcome back to Ireland, Miss Emily."

I give her a tight smile and take Liam's hand when he offers it.

"Ready?" he asks, peering down at me.

I close my eyes briefly before looking at him. "I don't know."

"*Tá sé seo agat.*" *You've got this.* He whispers, squeezing my hand.

I blow out a breath then square my shoulders. "Okay."

We step through the door and for the first time in so long, I take in the place that I feared returning to.

The door to the SUV opens and my ma steps out.

"Ma!" I cry and run down the steps, practically shoving Liam out of my way. He chuckles as I sprint into her arms.

I plow into her embrace and breathe in her floral scent.

"I missed you, *mo stór.*" She whispers, kissing my head.

And for the first time in so long... I can breathe.

ACKNOWLEDGEMENTS

Thank you so much for reading Freeing Emily! I hope you loved Liam and Emily as much as I have. This story has been a rollercoaster of different emotions. I'm truly going to miss writing their love but I am so happy to share it with you! I've had so much support from so many people and I am so grateful for each and every one of them.

To my alpha/beta readers, Keri and Erin, I love you both so much and I don't think I would have been able to write this story anywhere near as good as it is without your help and support. Thank you for listening to my rambling when I had too many ideas bouncing around in my head and couldn't figure out how to get them on paper. I am forever grateful for the friendships we have.

To Maggie, thank you for editing Freeing Emily for me! I am so blessed to have you. You not only are a great editor and person, but you're also a great friend! I started my journey with you for my first book and I am excited that we continue to work together!

To my ARC readers, without you, I wouldn't have been able to get the word out about my books. Being an indie author is hard and it is with your support that we are able to spread the word about our stories. I appreciate you all more than I can put into words and I hope some of you will continue to support me and my journey as a writer.

ABOUT THE AUTHOR

Kaite M. has always had a love for reading. When she discovered the bookish community, she created a bookstagram and purchased a Kindle. Since then, she has read hundreds of books from indie authors, and fell in love with so many different characters.

It wasn't until early 2024, during an episode of insomnia, that she decided to start writing.

After writing and publishing her first book *Saving Paige*, Kaite has found a whole new passion for creating worlds that others can escape to.

Kaite loves interacting with readers so be sure to check out her social media!

https://www.instagram.com/kaitemauthor/

COMING SOON

Are you ready for Sarah's story?

Chasing Sarah: A Dark Irish Mafia Romance is coming early 2025

MORE FROM KAITE M.

www.ingramcontent.com/pod-product-compliance
Lightning Source LLC
Chambersburg PA
CBHW030646260626
47157CB00007B/2516